Blue Pete Works Alone

By

'Luke Allan'

W. Lacey Amy (1877-1962)

First Published by Herbert Jenkins in 1948

Stillwoods Edition 2017

Stillwoods.Blogspot.Ca

The Story:

In this exhilarating, fast-moving yarn, Blue Pete, against the express wish of Inspector Barker of the Royal Mounted Police, sets out to avenge the brutal murder of a rancher and his wife. Once again, relying on his ready wit and the lightning draw of his heavy six-shooter, he justifies his action and beats the murderers—but only after he has found himself in the most desperate situation of his chequered career.

"Blue Pete," the critics agree, "is the most famous cowboy in fiction." His reckless, snap-shooting exploits have proved immensely popular in a score of thrilling novels. This new one is the equal of any.

Catalogue Information:
Title: Blue Pete Works Alone
Author: W. Lacey Amy (1877-1962) aka 'Luke Allan'
First published by Herbert Jenkins Ltd. 1948.
This Edition by Stillwoods, 2017.
ISBN Canada: 978-1-988304-34-2
Storefront: http://www.lulu.com/spotlight/lulubook22
Blog: Stillwoods.Blogspot.Ca

Keywords: Blue Pete, Mounties, 1910 Alberta, Western, Cypress Hills. Fiction.

Cover art is by Mike Collins, 2017. Blue Pete and Whiskers.

Publisher Introduction: The Stillwoods series of books are a hobby; reading rather rare books is a pleasure, and it takes little extra time to reproduce the work, to make them available to all. The product is not perfect but considering time…

As time goes on maybe the products, the books, are getting a little more professional in appearance as the processes and the error pitfalls are made apparent.

Doug Frizzle

Contents:

Blue Pete Series in order:

Blue Pete: Half Breed
The Return of Blue Pete
Blue Pete: Detective
Blue Pete: Horse Thief
The Vengeance of Blue Pete
Blue Pete Rebel
Blue Pete Pays a Debt
Blue Pete Breaks the Rules
Blue Pete: Outlaw
Blue Pete's Dilemma
Blue Pete's Vendetta
Blue Pete to the Rescue
Blue Pete and the Pinto
Blue Pete Works Alone
Blue Pete, Unofficially
Blue Pete: Indian Scout
Blue Pete at Bay
Blue Pete and the Kid
Blue Pete Rides the Foothills
Blue Pete in the Badlands

Regular characters in the Blue Pete Series: Blue Pete, Mira Stanton, Sergeant Mahon, Inspector Parker.

W. Lacey Amy is known to have produced at least 45 novels. His second alias is unknown today, 55 years after his death.

Stillwoods.Blogspot.Ca

THE chubby little fellow with the two missing front teeth and a flock of freckles on either cheekbone braced his sturdy legs and raised the loop of the rope over his head. "Look out! Slicker Sim of the 7-Up, an' the V-Bar-V, an' the Flyin' R, an' the—"

His playmate raised a weary hand. "Aw, shut up, Tub. A real puncher ain't workin' for more'n one ranch. Choose yer brand an' let 'er go." He dropped to hands and knees, his body turned away but his head twisted to watch the throw.

Tubby snorted. "Slicker Sim's no ordina'y puncher. They all want him. Just now I'm from the Cross TU, an' I'm lettin' her go."

Once more his companion raised himself to protest. "Aw, shucks, Tubby. You're tryin' to throw left-handed. Anyway you can't get no swing on the rope with yer arm stiff like that. Bend yer elbow. Now let 'er go."

Tubby changed hands and once more the loop commenced to circle, the circle widening as its speed increased. It shot out—to land harmlessly on his companion's back and slide to the roadway. "Durn!" he exploded, with all the intensity of a tremendous oath.

The kneeling lad rose slowly, wearily, scornfully. "Aw, shucks!" he growled.

Tubby pouted. "Well, 'twasn't my fault, Mud. You ain't no cow with horns to catch the rope. 'Sides, cows don't dodge like you did. They jus' keep goin' till the rope—"

He stopped. His eyes were fixed on the slope of the cutbank beyond his companion and an eager light crept into them. Up at the crest of the slope, beyond which the prairie stretched to the horizon, a mounted cowboy had come into view, ambling down towards the town.

Mud turned and looked. "Gee, it's Blue Pete!" Kicking the rope aside, he set off towards the oncoming rider. Behind lumbered his rotund friend, trailing the rope behind him.

Blue Pete pulled in as they neared him. He grinned down on them, his crooked eyes seeming to rest on nothing in particular. He was a big fellow, larger in appearance because of the small pinto he rode. His Indian face spread into one broad twinkle. Then he sobered and frowned. "Tsch! Tsch! Tsch! I seen yuh throw that rope, Tubby, an' yuh wasn' doin' so bad neither on'y—"

"He held his arm too stiff," Mud interrupted breathlessly.

"But he ducked," protested Tubby, "jus' when I threw. Cows

can't do that, can they?"

"No, o' course they can't." The half-breed appeared to be considering a weighty problem. "One thing—yuh didn' hold it level 'nuff, Tubby. Yuh can't throw a loop hangin' up 'n' down. Not easy, I mean. Might's well do it the easy way. Le's see yer rope."

He leaned over with extended hand and took the rope, as the two boys crowded breathlessly nearer. "Hm-m! Durn good top-hand ef yuh kin use a loop like this. The knot's too loose. Yuh can't keep the loop right 'th a knot that slides too easy, an' when it drops over the horns it don't hold tight 'nuff so the cow can't throw it off if it fights. Gotta be loose 'nuff to slide, o' course, but it's gotta be tight 'nuff to keep the shape o' the loop an' to hang on when it gits hold when yuh're pullin' from the saddle."

He released the knot and retied it and commenced lazily to whirl the loop over his head. "See how it stays right shape now no matter how fast I go? Yuh go jes' fast 'nuff to keep the loop round."

The two lads watched every movement with bulging eyes. Many a time Blue Pete had furnished the youngsters of Medicine Hat thrilling entertainment with rope and six-shooter, and they had woven about him stories of hair-raising escapades, blood-curdling danger, devil-may-care courage, and superman skill—most of which was colourless version of the truth, had they known it, of experiences known only to himself, or in part to the Mounted Police for whom he sometimes worked, unknown to the public. The result of the stories was that whenever he came to town he was apt to move at the head of a procession of small lads appealing for a display of his prowess.

Now and then he yielded, not boastfully but because he liked children and liked them to like him. They at least, though not their parents, could forget that he was a half-breed. More than once these informal exhibitions led to sudden flight from town to escape the local police, but it was never remembered officially against him, for Blue Pete had long since become a "Character."

One trick that had been known to send women into a faint he had dropped at the request of Mira, his white wife. Inspector Barker, too, of the Mounted Police, had stormed against it, and those who knew of it were afraid now to ask for it. In it he would place the muzzle of a loaded .45 in his mouth and rapidly press the trigger to the exact point where the cylinder revolved without exploding the cartridge. A hair's breadth too far and the top of his head would go. Mira called it sheer lunacy, and when that failed to stop the act, she reminded him that he had a wife. That did it. Only she knew how to handle him.

"Throw it, Pete," pleaded Tubby. "Show us how to do it. Aw, come, on, Pete."

The half-breed grinned. "Thar ain't nothin' to throw at. I kin tell yuh how to do it 'thout that."

He examined the rope more closely and discarded it with shaking head. His own rope he released from the strap beside the horn, adjusted the loop, and held it out. "Yuh see yuh let it hang free fust so's to make shure 'twon't tangle. Then yuh throw it forward an' up . . . not too fast at fust but jes' 'nuff to keep the rope free . . . an' yuh raise it over yer head 'th the loop swellin' out near level. See?"

The loop sailed about over his head, lying at last almost horizontally. It moved easily, with no apparent effort, as he grinned down on the lads.

The pinto had shifted position a little, so that when he raised his eyes they ranged up the slope he had descended a few minutes before. Two riders were on the way down, and his eyes focussed on them. As he approached the town he had seen them in the distance, moving along a trail to the east, and had recognized them as strangers. In general appearance they were cowboys like himself, except that their chaps were hairy and very new, the sign of the tenderfoot, and they sat their saddles too stiffly and formally. In a vague way he had wondered who they were.

The rope continued to whirl as he watched them. They had broken into a gentle lope on the grade and in a few seconds were near. The one in the lead pulled his mount in to a walk, as if about to speak. His face was twisted into a smile of such unmistakable contempt that the half-breed's teeth clamped together.

"Showing off to the natives, eh?" jeered the man. He tugged at the rein to pass around the half-breed, forgetting that the Western bronco is guided by pressure on its neck. The result was that the bronco almost collided with the pinto.

His companion saw it and laughed, and was scowled at as the other remedied the mistake.

The movement ended abruptly as the loop Blue Pete had been whirling settled over his head and slid down to his elbows before he could brace himself to throw it off.

"Say!" exploded his companion angrily. The man inside the loop swore viciously and commenced to struggle. His mount edged away.

"Bes' say a kind word to yer bronc, mister," advised Blue Pete, "er he's apt to go on 'thout yuh . . . an' the roads in town are durn hard to git piled on."

The helpless rider spoke to his mount and it stood still.

He turned to the half-breed, his face purple with anger. "Get this rope off me, you damned Indian."

The more or less friendly grin that had returned to Blue Pete's face vanished. A slight tug at the rope so unbalanced the angry man that he was almost unseated. His bronco, uninterested now, stood with drooping head. It yawned.

The two boys noticed it and burst into loud laughter. The man, his arms held tightly against his sides, commenced to struggle, but he quickly saw how dangerous it was and desisted.

Tubby and Mud danced with gleeful excitement. "Pile him, Pete, pile him. Throw him an' hogtie him. Dirty them new chaps. Pile him hard, 'cause he threw our ball in the river the other day. Pay him back for us, Pete. Aw, do."

The man scowled at them. "They knocked the ball into my back. Does this hick town permit kids to play ball on the streets?"

"Pile him, Pete, an' hogtie him. Go on. He's a tenderfoot an' he's got to be broke in some time."

Blue Pete shook his head. He had begun to feel ashamed of himself. He leaned towards the boys and whispered loudly, still keeping the rope tight: "I jes' dassent, not here in town. 'Tain't right to rope a tenderfoot, even ef he's got on hairy chaps an' do' know how to ride. Ef 'twas out on the prairie now. Sorta got my goat—that grin o' his." He turned his face to the second rider, who had sent his bronco nearer, as if to try to do something for his friend. "Bes' stay whar yuh are, stranger, ef yuh don' wanta git into a mess yerself. Sorry. I was jes' showin' the kids how to throw a rope. Thar wasn' nothin' to throw at till you come 'long. Yuh see, all the lads wanta be punchers when they grow up. Nobody ain't hurt none—not yit—'ceptin' yer feelin's. I clean fergot 'bout them. Tubby, you go an' loosen the rope, will yuh?"

The lad did as he was told, but with no enthusiasm. Blue Pete released the strain and the knot loosened easily. The man jerked the loop over his head. But he did not release it. Instead his free hand made a swift movement towards his pocket, as if to draw a knife.

Blue Pete made no attempt to jerk the rope free. Instead he sent a swift loop flying along it and the stiff hemp jerked itself free and upward, striking the man on the chin so hard that he was forced to clutch at the horn of the saddle to keep his seat. It must have hurt.

"Say!" The other man forced his mount between them.

Blue Pete smiled at him. But there was more than a smile: a six-shooter was in his hand. "I sorta like that rope, yuh know. Made it muhself, an' I'd hate to see anybody hurt it. Mebbe funny that way, but that's how 'tis. Hope yuh ain't thinkin' none o' gittin' nasty, 'cause we're in town, an' the p'lice don' like gunplay." The tone was gentle, almost pleading, but the .45 gave it all the point it required.

The two lads were almost beside themselves with excitement. This was where Blue Pete was showing his stuff, the real stuff they would be able to talk about later, something to make their small friends envious—something they were playing an important part in. "Shoot his ears off, Pete. Shoot all their ears off, two for each of us. Ring their hats with holes so we can get the tops. Shoot em bald-headed. Yoo-hoo, mister! Curtains for you. Guess you didn know this is Blue Pete. He shoots a man for breakfast every morning."

There was no need to shoot; the little black hole of the .45 was enough. With an oath the one who had been roped spat contemptuously. Plainly he had thought at first to spit towards the half-breed but had thought better of it. The contempt in it, however, brought more colour to Blue Pete's face.

The stranger snarled: "If this were the East I'd know what to do with you, you damned Indian. I'm finding out things about this Godforsaken hole, and I can wait. You'll hear more of Biff Collins."

Blue Pete recoiled the rope and fastened it to the saddle. "I ain't much at readin' an' writin', so yuh bes' say it, stranger. Reckon yuh mus' come from Chicago way, the way yuh talk so big. Offen wanted to meet somebody like that, 'cause things sometimes git mighty slow 'bout the Hat."

He smoothed the rope out where it hung beside the horn. "Out this way yuh'll larn one thing—we ain't useta much talkin'. We *do* things, an' then all the talkin' we do is tryin' to talk ourselves outa it ef we shudn' 'a' did it. Yuh'll larn we do things 'th guns an' ropes. We do' needta go to Chicago to use a gun."

The fat boy stalked boldly up to the one who had called himself Biff Collins and shook his little fist at him. "Blue Pete ain't no Injun;

he's a half-breed."

A nasty laugh broke from the man's lips. "I should have known that. It accounts for anything crazy. A breed's a damn sight worse than an Indian."

Blue Pete nodded. "Some of 'em's a sight wuss to git sassy with, too. Bes' take that 'long 'th yuh an' chaw on it 'th yer chuck to-night."

Something in it warned Collins that he had gone as far as he dare, and he gathered up the reins. "Even a breed's soft stuff for a bullet," he snarled. "One shouldn't think twice before proving it."

Mud jeered: "Blue Pete eats bullets for dinner. He's been shot so offen the bullets flatten again' each other. If you—"

Blue Pete silenced him with a frown. "Shet up, you kids. Thar ain't nothin' wrong 'th talkin' like he done. I'd 'a' felt the same, on'y," with a wry smile, "reckon I'd 'a' bin shootin' fust. I never larned to threaten." He shook his head reprovingly. "Yuh gotta 'member, boys, he must hev a mighty sore chin. That's why he guv us so much of it. Shuda caught his nose in that curl I threw . . . Jes' the same I done wrong, an' you boys is to blame. See wot yuh got me into now: 'Yuh'll hear more from Biff Collins.' I shud otta 'member a tenderfoot ain't like other folks we know out this way. They jes' don't unnerstand our fun."

"They gotta learn," said Tubby.

"Shure . . . shure. But some's durn hard to larn. Yuh gotta kick 'em in the teeth to larn 'em . . . an' they don't like a breed doin' the kickin'." He frowned again. "I shudn' 'a' did wot yuh ast me to do. Ropin' strangers ain't nice till tha're useta it." He smiled and winked at the lads. "An' donchu go tellin' wot I done. Folks'll shure think I'm shure loco. 'Sides the cops wudn' like it. S'long!"

He tightened the reins and the pinto ambled off down the street towards the heart of the town. In a few seconds he had forgotten strangers and boys.

II   A WARNING

THE frown had returned to his face, and as he rode down Main Street it deepened. His crooked eyes saw nothing yet missed nothing—nothing that mattered. The pinto continued without urging or direction. She knew where she was going.

Blue Pete was plainly worried, for he scowled unseeingly over the pinto's ears, and mutterings broke from his lips: "Reckon Mira was right. It shure ain't no nice job I've took on, ole gal, an' I didn' needta. That's wot she said, an' I shud know by this time she's purty near alius right . . . I never see it till it's too late. That's me."

In token of understanding and sympathy the pinto nickered, and a slight ripple ran along her mottled flanks to her rider's knees.

"Ef I hadn' told her—I mean ef she hadn' made me tell her— mebbe I'd a went straight to Sam Dunlop's an' got it over 'th, 'stead o' skulkin' off to town, jes' puttin' it off. She got me sorta skeered. That's me. . . . But it does gimme a chance to think over wot I'm goin' to say to Sam, an' I shure needta do lots o' thinkin' 'bout that. . . I bin thinkin' a bit all the way to town, an' all I know is I gotta go through 'th it, now I started, durn it. But a hundred miles outa my way ain't makin' it no easier. I shuda went straight thar, I know I shud." He tightened his hold on the reins purposefully. "Wal, we're goin', ain't we, ole gal?"

He reached down and patted the pinto's neck. It arched beneath the touch, and he laughed. "Whiskers, ole gal, yuh shud otta be durn tired after eighty miles 'n' durn little rest, an' it's bin a durn hot day, too. Yuh knowned same's me we shuda went straight thar. Now we'll be two days late. . . . Late?" He raised his head suddenly and looked about. "Late fer wot? I dunno."

Whiskers showed that she understood every word and agreed: she capered a little and flicked her ragged tail. The eighty miles from the 3-bar-Y ranch was an old story to her, though they had seldom before covered so much of it through the heat of the day. It was so much more comfortable to start in the evening and miss the heated hours.

They had set out in the darkness of early morning, with no thought of Medicine Hat. Over to the homestead of Sam Dunlop, the new settler, was a mere thirty miles, but long before it was half covered Blue Pete's courage had failed and he had turned aside towards town. A day or two would make no difference, he told himself, for what he had in mind; and in the delay he would have time to forget Mira's warning and to decide how he would pass on to Dunlop the warning he had in mind. Both would be difficult.

For Mira had warned him without mincing words—and Mira was usually right. It was no business of his what happened to Sam Dunlop. A tenderfoot in the Canadian West, especially a homesteader in that ranching country, should be left to look after himself—whether he could or couldn't. It was the way of the West, a way that had its virtues: it developed self-reliance and established one's fitness—or the opposite—for such a life. By the time the new settler had established himself—and that was more a matter of time than of fitness—he could count on the support and friendship of every oldtimer. It was a subtle change in condition that made the initial period of ostracism seem like nothing more than a necessary and wise novitiate. Even the most disreputable oldtimer in the West attains a position, a local acceptance, beyond that accorded the most friendly and accomplished newcomer.

Blue Pete had been troubled for some time about Sam Dunlop. As a tenderfoot Sam was certain to have his troubles. As a would-be farmer in the heart of a ranching country where the ranges were free those troubles increased a thousand fold. Such an interloper, a breaker-up of feeding ranges, was anathema to the ranchers, something beyond any claim to the milk of human kindness. He was a robber of sorts—less to be accepted because he was backed by laws that had no authority in reason.

For weeks it had troubled the half-breed. He thought he had concealed it from Mira, his white wife. He should have known better, since she reacted to his every mood. She knew, too, how to open his lips.

He had brought his creaky saddle into the ranch house at the 3-Bar-Y and was seated beside it near the stove, rubbing warm oil into the leather. To him a saddle that would betray him by squeaking was a real danger; that it should not creak was as necessary as his .45 and for the same reason. A creaking saddle might be audible a half mile on the prairie. Even in the open that was dangerous for him at times. In the Cypress Hills it was foolhardy. Every rustler and rogue in the district had a bullet for him, even the rustlers across the Border in the Montana Badlands, all of whom knew him only too well. And a bullet in the fastnesses and isolation of the Hills was little likely to be traced.

With the oil can on the damper of the stove to keep it warm, and the saddle across two chairs before the open oven door, he set to work. About him Mira bustled at her daily chores. There was a long silence. He had almost forgotten her, though he was never unaware of her. In time the extended silence beat through his thoughts and he raised his face, suddenly uneasy, to find her standing at his side, looking chidingly down on him. He grinned uneasily up at her, as if she had caught him at something naughty.

"What's the matter, Pete?"

He bent over the saddle and commenced to rub more vigorously. "I—I was jes' wonderin' why we don' carry two ropes 'stead o' one, one on each side o' the horn. Ef a puncher had a pair of 'em—"

"He'd hang himself the first day," she broke in scornfully. "Pete, you never were a good liar."

He stopped to run the back of an oily hand across his chin. "I ain't had much reason to lie to you, Mira—ner much chance," he added with another grin. "But I'm alius hopin' I kin manage it some time. . . . Yuh see, I hate yuh worryin', an' ef a lie's—"

"I see. So there's reason for me to worry—again." She heaved a sigh. "You might as well out with it, Pete. You know I'll get it sooner or later, and it'll only worry you more to keep trying to hide it from me. What's on your mind, dear, what are you worrying about?" She leaned over the back of one of the chairs, her face close to his.

He shrugged. "I'm not worryin' . . . not much, that is. Jes' thinkin'—thinkin' things out, that's all."

"Has the Inspector another dangerous job for you? Is that it?"

"I ain't seed th' Inspector fer weeks. Ain't had nothin' to do fer the Mounties fer so long I'm gittin' fidgetty."

"At last you're telling the truth," she told him dryly. "So we'll drop that. Now what is it? I'm staying right here till you tell me."

He drew a long, helpless breath and laid both hands on the warm, slippery leather. The odour of warm oil filled the room, though the door was wide open. " 'Tain't nothin' fer you to worry 'bout, but it's that new settler over north o' the Hills. He's in fer a peck o' trouble, I reckon."

"You mean the new farmer, Sam Dunlop? . . . Is it the ranchers— the punchers? I thought they'd learned their lesson about interfering with a farmer. At any rate they should have learned by this time that no farmer has remained long in this semi-arid country. They only need wait; he'll pull out in a year or so when he finds out this is no farming country."

"Shure," he agreed. "But in a year er so lots o' cows'll mebbe be dead 'cause they can't git to water. Thar's Big Slough on his section. Anyways this is ranchin' country, Mira. It's nachurl fer the ranchers to feel sore when a farmer comes in an' cuts up the ranges."

"But we have no claim on the ranges; they're free for anyone. If there's any way to raise anything on them but cows and horses—"

"Yuh said jes' now thar ain't no way. Jes' cows 'n' broncs an' badgers 'n' coyotes 'n' gophers. It's bin tried before."

Mira had walked away and stood staring through the window to the sunlit outdoors. "That's what they said many years ago about the land around Moose Jaw and all through Saskatchewan and Manitoba. It was then semi-arid like it is here, but when they got enough of it ploughed up the whole land changed. It's the wind always blowing over dry grass that dries the land, they say."

He shook his head in firm dissent. "Ef thar was anythin' else started it 'ud kill ranchin'. Jes' a bit o' cuttin' up fer farms 'ud spile the ranges fer cows."

"Are the ranchers threatening Sam Dunlop?" she inquired suddenly, facing him. "Are you going to side with them?"

"Wal-l,"—he rubbed his chin thoughtfully—"'tain't goin' to do the 3-Bar-Y no good to hev Big Slough fenced off."

"Is Dunlop doing that? . . . If he does it won't hurt us as far west as this. We feed very little that far east."

"But—but we shud be able to ef we wanted to. . . . In real dry weather we might run herds that way."

"Big Slough is on his land, isn't it?"

He nodded.

"And he's fencing it off?"

"Shure. An' the cows jes' nachully make that way when the streams dry up. Ain't many of 'em work this way to Elk Lake, an' the boys don' like runnin' 'em so near the Hills 'cause o' the rustlers."

She went to the stove and poked thoughtfully at it. "Then the ranchers are threatening trouble for him, is that it?"

"They can't see it's anythin' but meanness to fence off Big Slough. 'Tain't no use to him, an' the cows wudn' hurt him none. Thar's water thar all the year round."

"But if he farms the cows *would* hurt him, and the ranchers should see it. He probably doesn't want to have to fence off his whole section to keep the cows off; that would be too expensive. So to discourage the cows coming around— But you haven't answered my question: Are the ranchers threatening trouble?"

He nodded reluctantly. "I've heard so. They say it's jes' cussedness fencing the slough. . . . 'Sides, wot's he doin' settlin' down to farm so far from town an' everybody when thar's dozens o' better sections nearer town. He come straight from the East er he'd see that. Yuh'd think they wanta be alone."

"Perhaps they do," said Mira. "They may be in love, you know."

He grinned at her. "Shure, that's so. The 3-Bar-Y ain't near town."

Mira stood staring down at the stove. "I'm thinking of his poor wife. She seems to be a nice woman . . . and so lonely . . . and—and sort of frightened. I rode over there the other day when you were away. She would scarcely let me in. . . . She seemed to be afraid of something—or someone. . . . It's a comfortable little hut, if it is just built of sod and mud. She's done a lot to brighten it up inside—a few coloured pictures cut from magazines, a bed with a bright coverlet, a chest of drawers, a table, a home-made cupboard for hanging clothes. It all seemed kind of pathetic, because she didn't appear happy."

She moved about for a few moments absent-mindedly, while Blue Pete continued to work on the saddle. "I had a funny feeling about the place. There was something in the air, though that may be because they haven't tried to make friends. There's a dog. A coyote howled almost a mile away, but Mrs. Dunlop started and seemed to cower. The dog bolted outside, and it howled—such an awful howl, like a wolf. I saw her tremble, though she tried to laugh it off, and a wild look came into her eyes."

"Did you see Sam?"

"I didn't meet him. I saw him as I was riding down to the hut. He was off near Big Slough with the horses. . . . They won't be able to do more than break a few acres this year. I took it for granted they intended to go back East for the winter, or at least into town, but Mrs. Dunlop was vague about it. . . . She was vague about everything. Perhaps I imagined things, because it all seemed so unnatural."

Blue Pete said nothing. He liked to hear her talk—liked it more now because there were disturbing questions she might ask, and he did not wish to answer them.

"How does it concern you, Pete?" she inquired suddenly.

That was what he had dreaded. "Wal-l, thar's sartin to be trouble."

"How does that concern you?" She pointed a finger at him. "Look here, Pete, you stay out of it. Don't get mixed up in it, either to injure or protect the Dunlops. It's dangerous. If you try to help them you'll make the ranchers angry, more suspicious of you than they are now. If you do anything to harm the Dunlops there's the Mounties to reckon with. We don't want to have to run away again. You hear what I'm saying, Pete?"

He snuffled and slapped the leather loudly with both hands. "I'm not plannin' to do nothin'—not jes' yit . . . not fer shure . . . 'ceptin' I'd hate to see the woman hurt."

She nodded. "So that's it—you're thinking of protecting them, are you? Have you thought what that will do to you—among the ranchers? You'll only get into trouble."

"I was thinkin' . . . mebbe . . . mebbe Sam Dunlop doesn' see wot he's doin' fencin' off Big Slough. He doesn' see wot it'll do to the cows. Ef he knew—ef I told him—mebbe he wudn' fence it off. Ef somebody talked to him reasonable-like—"

"You aren't a good talker, Pete. Leave it to someone else."

"But thar ain't nobody else to do it—not that wudn' be mad."

"I see." She flung out her hands and sighed. "It's always the way—you take on troubles that don't belong to you. It has always got you into a mess. For this is sure to be a mess and a nasty one. . . . Don't forget some of the ranchers would like nothing better than to see you in real trouble. You know they don't know what to make of you—"

"Anyways they don' know I work fer the Mounties sometimes," he broke in.

"Perhaps not. But they never feel comfortable with you, because they don't understand you; and sometimes you have interfered with their crooked work in the round-ups. . . . Because you were once a rustler they think you've never changed at heart. No, the more I think of it the more I say keep out of this. Dunlop knows all you can tell him; it's been taken to him in a hundred ways, I'll warrant. He'll probably tell you to mind your own affairs. And don't forget Big Slough is his property."

Blue Pete shook his head doubtfully. "Jes' the same ef anythin' happened to him an' his missus an' I hadn' done nothin' I'd feel a dang sight wuss 'n bein' told to mind my own affairs. . . ."

He recalled every word of their talk as he rode along the trail towards town. He heard Mira's voice, her arguments so convincing, saw her troubled eyes, saw that pointing finger of warning.

All it did was to delay his plan. He knew that now as he turned in to the Royal Hotel stable-yard.

His preoccupation did not fail to attract attention. Small boys hailed him as he rode along Main Street, but he did not hear them, and one of them explained it to his own satisfaction: "He's gunnin' fer somebody. Blood will flow this day." He was a lad of wide reading of thrillers, and his friends were impressed. The shouted greeting of a man about to enter the Men's Club at the corner of Fourth Avenue and Main Street was ignored, and with shaking head the man watched him ride on down the street. Even adults have imagination.

Whiskers had been forced to slow down at the corner to permit a buckboard to pass on to the bridge, but the moment the way was clear she broke into a lope, though it was the busiest part of the town.

Blue Pete noticed it and drew her in. "Easy, ole gal. Yuh like the Royal too durn well. Yuh'd think yuh was a puncher with a month's thirst. . . . But 'tain't sech a bad place fer both of us . . . mostly." He let his crooked eyes range on down the street to a low, faded brown building across the railway tracks. "I shure hope th' Inspector ain't watchin'. I ain't got time to do nothin' fer him, not till I git to see Sam Dunlop."

In the stable-yard of the hotel he dismounted and opened the stable door, and the pinto hurried in. She passed several filled and empty stalls and stopped, looking back at him and baring her teeth in protest.

He had followed her in. He saw her protest and laughed. "Somebody got ahead o' yuh this time, eh, ole gal? Reckon yuh'll hev to take 'nother stall." He leaned forward and peered more closely at the occupant of the stall. "Hm-m! Looks like we're goin' to meet 'n ole friend ag'n. Git 'long, ole gal. Thar's an empty one next. Reckon thar ain't nothin' we kin do 'bout it."

He tied the pinto and started for the door. As he passed the stall Whiskers usually occupied he scowled at the bronco there now. "Yuh're too durn good a c'yuse for that ornery cuss." He slapped the animal's rump and passed on.

Outside he remembered that he had eaten nothing all day and he hurried through the back door of the hotel, casting a glance at the sun to read if he was in time.

As he hastened along the passage towards the front of the hotel someone hailed him from the bar: "Hi-ya, Pete? Have one on the house." Red, the bar-tender, winked at the cowboys about the bar, for everyone knew Blue Pete never drank. "All right," as the half-breed passed with a wave of his hand, "there's some chuck for you in the dining-room. I'll be there myself in a few minutes."

Blue Pete crossed the corner of the rotunda and entered the dining-room. He did not look about the room but made straight for a table near the kitchen door. He knew no one liked that table, that he would probably have it to himself. The odours from the kitchen and the constant creaking of the swing door there were discouraging to other diners. That was why it suited him.

He liked eating alone, except at the 3-Bar-Y. He had always lived a lonely life. Even as a child in the Indian encampment over in Montana, where he was raised by his Indian mother, he had been much alone. His father, a white man, he had never seen, and his mother had kept him to herself. When, following her death when he was but fourteen years of age, he had left the encampment he had lived an even lonelier existence. He could never remember when he did not prefer it. Only after coming to Canada, before the guns of angry ranchers and cowboys who resented his rivalry in rustling, had he made friends. Curiously enough, those friends were the Mounted Police.

It was more curious because he had never had anything in mind but to rustle, not for a living so much as for the excitement and danger it provided. For a time he had turned his knowledge of brands and rustling towards helping the Mounted Police. Then a thoughtless judge had refused to accept his evidence in court because of his earlier career, and the half-breed had, in disgust and fury, returned to rustling.

It was at this time that he met Mira, his white wife. Her brothers, prominent ranchers in the Medicine Hat district, had been cornered by the Mounted Police as rustlers and had shot themselves rather than surrender or fight the Police, and Mira, shocked and angry, had turned to rustling.

Later they had turned back to the 3-Bar-Y, her brothers' ranch, having earned forgiveness by once more coming to the aid of the Mounted Police.

Blue Pete was still the expert with brands, with rope and gun, and Inspector Barker knew better than anyone else how valuable he could be. But any chance of open usefulness since the judge's decision was out of the question, and so he had been forced for three years now to assist the Police secretly. In fact the Inspector quickly discovered that in that way the half-breed was able to do more for the law than if he were a member of the Force. None but the Mounted Police knew the role he played, and they were careful to conceal it.

It was a difficulty partnership, largely because Blue Pete's methods were not only different from those of the Mounted Police, but his greatest successes came from methods the Inspector could not openly condone. That sort of assistant could do what was denied the law, but the law profited from it. And Inspector Barker would groan and gnaw his finger-nails and curse—and hope the Superintendent at Lethbridge would never hear. All he could do was lecture—and accept.

The table was empty as usual, and Blue Pete dropped into a chair facing the room. It was an instinct that he never unnecessarily turned his back. But he did not raise his eyes; he knew the diners in the room were staring at him.

A waitress handed him a hand-written menu, then remembered that he read only with difficulty and withdrew it. "Soup?"

"Shure. Big bowl." He made a large circle with his hands and grinned at her.

When she was gone he leaned his forearms on the table and appeared to be inspecting the dishes before him. A heavy silence lay over the room. From a plate on the table he helped himself to a slice of bread and commenced to butter it on his hand. He was uneasy, feeling the silence—feeling the eyes on him.

The soup was placed before him and he fell eagerly to eating.

He had just finished the bowl when he became conscious of voices at one of the tables near a window. They had risen gradually, drowning out every other sound. The words rang over the room like the blows of a hammer on Steel:

"Damn it, I didn't think any reasonable hotel would permit Indians or breeds in the dining-room."

Someone at the speaker's table tried to hush him, but the whispered admonition only made the conversation more compelling! "Hold off, Biff. Don't make a scene not here. You're not at home now."

"What the hell difference does that make? Down where I come from they don't even let niggers go about like this, and they're better than breeds. Surely they draw the line somewhere, even in the

Canadian West."

The dining-room door had opened as he spoke, and a big red-haired man entered, still wearing the protecting apron he wore behind the bar. For a moment he paused, then he made straight for the speaker, his face dark with anger.

Blue Pete was before him. "Never mind, Red. I kin look after this." He lounged towards the table where the two men were seated. The one who had talked so loudly half rose, then as if rising was an unwarranted honour for a half-breed he dropped back in his chair. A nasty smile twisted his face.

"So they let you in, Joe, did they?" he sneered.

Blue Pete stopped beside him, his hands on his hips. "I don't 'member ever tellin' yuh no name."

"You didn't. I wouldn't talk to you more than I had to. I call all breeds Joe." He turned to the bar-tender. "Say, Red, isn't there any limit to the scum you allow in this hotel?"

Red had removed his apron and held it now clutched in one huge fist. He was struggling to restrain himself. "Sometimes we get scum we don't know's scum till they start shootin' off their gab. Then we mostly kick 'em out. Around this place we've known Blue Pete for donkey's years, and he's comin' an' goin' as much as he likes. Most of the scum we get comes fresh from the East, some from down in the States where you come from." He moved forward as if to start the kicking.

Blue Pete chuckled and shoved him back. "Let him shoot off some more gab, Red. He's a new sort, even from the East." He turned to Collins. "Go on, bo, shoot off some more. Wot's bitin' yuh?"

Collins' face went red with anger. "Where'd you get the 'bo'?"

"I call all skunks bo."

Collins surged to his feet, upsetting the chair, but before he could raise an arm Blue Pete had hold of him, pinning his arms to his sides and, raising him easily from the floor, was about to throw him into the aisle when the door opened.

It was a Mounted Policeman who entered. Sergeant Mahon had been passing the hotel and had seen something of the affair through the window. He had recognized Blue Pete, had scented trouble, and had hurried in to forestall it. Blue Pete was his special friend.

The half-breed saw him the moment the door opened, and he gently lowered his victim to the floor and released him—so gently that it was insult.

Mahon pushed through the tables to them. "What's going on here, Red?" he demanded.

The bar-tender made a gesture as if about to spit and jerked a thumb at Collins. "Oh, he's been shootin' off his gab a bit too much. Better get him to repeat it."

The Sergeant faced Collins. "Stand back, Pete. Now what is it?"

Collins pointed at Blue Pete. "Ask him. I thought I was eating my dinner in a respectable hotel, then I saw him."

"And you gave expression to that disgust. I see."

"Surely there's a limit even in the Canadian West," snarled Collins.

"There is, and you've about reached it. Bear that in mind." He turned to Blue Pete. "What were you thinking of doing about it?"

"Jes' breakin' him in—doin' it so it wudn' hurt too much."

"In other words you were getting into a fight." It was an uncomfortable position for the Sergeant. He knew Blue Pete well enough, and Red had told enough, to make it plain that the half-breed had ample reason to fight, but the Mounted Police dare not make allowances—in public. "Go back to your table," he ordered.

Without a word Blue Pete slouched back through the tables and seated himself at his own table.

Mahon remained. He glowered down on Collins who had reseated himself. "I'm not doing anything this time, stranger, but in case you've learned nothing yet I warn you that you were about to learn from the wrong man—for your own good. There are other ways to learn, easier ones and safer . . . though perhaps less speedy and thorough. The Mounted Police are indulgent with a tenderfoot at first, but, as you suggest, there's a limit."

He turned his back, winked at Blue Pete, and started for the door. There he turned. "You'll see there's no further trouble, Red. I'll hold you responsible. Take your own measures." He left the room.

Collins had the last word. "They have to get the police to help them out," he growled to his companion. "Well, the Mounted Police won't always be around, and Biff Collins has a long memory."

RED joined Blue Pete at his table. He was very angry, and for a time neither spoke. Collins and his companion had left the room, the former throwing a sneering smile towards the table near the kitchen door.

Red jerked a thumb after them. "We get 'em like that now and then. They always make trouble—till they learn."

"Sorta like somebody else to larn 'em, not me," said Blue Pete. "I'm apt to fly clean off an' let 'em hev it whar it hurts. Good the Sergeant come in when he did. Thar'd shure 'a' bin a mess fer the gals to clean up. I was gittin' plum mad. Don' know wot I'd 'a did. . . . Wust o' me when I git mad I don' know wot I do. I clean fergot thar was Mounties, let alone them city police."

Red chuckled. "I'd 'a' kinda liked to see you get real mad with that blister. I didn't like him first time I saw him, and there's been no reason to change my opinion." He winked across the table. "I don't know anyone could teach him manners quicker 'n' more certain than you, Pete. A little gun-play might work fast."

"Shucks, I ain't wastin' no lead on skunks like that." He shook his head solemnly. "Jes' the same it sarves me right."

"Serves you right? What do you mean? You weren't doing anythin'—"

"Not here. But he had it in fer me, an' I desarved it. I roped the skunk coupla hours ago on Main Street, jes' to show a coupla kids how to throw a rope. Throwed 'afore I stopped to think—like I alius do. He got that grin off at me an' he was so durn right I got mad, so I let him hev the rope." A slow smile twisted his dark face. "Gor-swizzle, wasn' he mad! . . . Made like he was goin' to cut the rope when I let him loose."

Red had been laughing as he listened. "The damn fool! I can see him gettin' away with that."

"I cudn't. It's a durn good rope . . . I slapped the loop into his chin, an' I reckon it hurt a bit." He shook his head in self-deprecation. "Mebbe it sorta stuck to me, an' I was lookin' fer trouble when he started talkin' 'bout breeds. I knowed he was here; I seen his cayuse in the stable. It didn't help none to see it in Whiskers' stall."

He looked up, and his forehead wrinkled. "Gor-swizzle, I shudn' be here at all, Red. Mira thinks I've gone somewhars else. I told her I was. Then I got cold feet an' come away to town instead. I bin a fool all day, that's wot."

Red reached across and touched his hand. "You ain't been a fool here, at any rate. Nobody could blame you, so shake out of it, Pete. Biff Collins is just what you called him, a skunk."

They ate for a time in silence.

"Wot's he doin' in the Hat?" Blue Pete asked.

"Tryin' to buy a ranch. Been making a coupla offers out around." An amused look crept into his face. "He'll be out to make you an offer at the 3-Bar-Y. I'd like to be around when he does."

"I wudn't. . . . An' I hope he don't git no ranch in these parts. I'd hate to hev to ride in a roundup 'th him. But I don't think he's got much chance to buy, not after the good year we all had last year." He wiped his mouth with the back of his hand and rose.

Red rose with him. "Stoppin' the night, ain't you, Pete?"

"I don't rightly know; I ain't made up my mind. . . . Ain't got nothing to do in town neither. Shudn' be here." As they made for the door Red noticed the trouble in his face. "You ain't lookin' for trouble, I hope, not here."

"Reckon I was runnin' 'way from it, Red. 'Least Mira said thar'd be trouble."

"Anythin' wrong out at the 3-Bar-Y—or in the Hills?"

"Sorta reckoned mebbe I'd be able to stop some trouble. I was goin' to try, anyways."

They had come out into the hall. Collins and his friend were seated in the corner before a low counter behind which was a display of tobacco and cigarettes. Collins was cleaning his fingernails with a large knife in an obtrusive way. As the door opened to let Blue Pete and Red out his eyes flickered towards them and dropped back to his work. The smile that had so infuriated the half-breed reappeared. Neither Blue Pete nor Red gave any sign of seeing the pair but continued down the passage towards the bar-room and the back door. Red turned into the bar.

The half-breed continued on to the stable-yard. He had forgotten Collins. He was arguing with himself. Should he delay further by remaining for the night? After such a long ride a rest was due him and the pinto. He could start back to Dunlop's homestead in the morning. He would be more rested then, more himself, more able to face the promised interview.

No argument for further delay impressed him. He knew that if he lingered Mira's warning might be sufficient to interfere with his plan. And he knew equally well that he had delayed already too long. The semi-surrender disgusted him.

As he stood in the yard debating with himself the door opened and Red came out. "Better hurry and make up your mind, Pete. We're going to be full to-night. Coupla punchers have come for rooms—the last one, if you don't want it."

It made the decision for him. "I'm not stayin', Red. Here's fer me 'n' Whiskers." He drew some change from his pocket and handed it to the bar-tender.

Red watched him set off towards the stable. Friend and admirer as he was, he was glad to see him go. There might have been trouble if he had remained, and that would be bad for the hotel. It had trouble enough with its patrons. At the same time he would like nothing better than to be on hand to see Biff Collins receive a much-needed lesson. It was always thrilling to witness the shock of old-timer and tenderfoot—and if it came to gun-play no one had a chance with the half-breed.

Red was still there when Blue Pete emerged from the stable, the pinto close behind.

"S'long, Red!" He seemed to step into the saddle, so small was the pinto. He read disappointment on the bartender's face and laughed. "I'm not runnin' 'way from trouble, Red. Mira says I'm runnin' my neck into it—and she's most alius right."

He cantered through the gate and rode south along Main Street.

The sun still blazed over the cutbank, though it was almost nine o'clock. For an hour yet it would be visible up on the prairie. Three hours' ride would take him to the Mounted Police hut at Turner's Crossing. He might stop there for a little sleep. Corporal Simmons was always glad of a guest in that lonely spot. . . . But that would mean more delay—and more and more he was convinced that already he had wasted too much time, important time. He had come to think of delay as disaster.

He discovered that he was urging Whiskers to a long lope and he pulled her in. "Gittin' narvy, ole gal, that's wot. Mebbe that Biff—Biff—what was it he called himself? Oh, yep, Biff Collins. Mebbe he sorta got me goin'. Durn glad the Sergeant come in. I dunno wot I mighta did. It'ud 'a' bin nasty no matter wot." He shook himself. "Oh, wal, like's not I won't see him no more ever. . . . Time fer a bit o' rest, ole gal."

On long rides he always stopped for a rest every two hours—a rest for the pinto, not for himself. He could sleep in the saddle—often did. This time he stopped for almost an hour, remembering the distance Whiskers had covered since early morning, with only a little more than an hour's rest in the Hat. With such rests Whiskers had proven that she could continue for days and for any distance.

It was long past dark when they reached the Police hut at Turner's Crossing. He turned from the trail and drew up before the hut. He had made up his mind to go on, but a short rest was wise. He would need to be rested when he faced Sam Dunlop, and he did not wish to arrive before the new settler was awake.

Simmons had been in bed, but he came to the door in his shirt and welcomed the half-breed with the eagerness of one left much alone: "Hello, Pete! Glad to see you. Turn the pinto loose and come in. She knows her way to the stable. There's hay in the extra stall."

"I'll fix her up fer the night, Corporal, then I'll come in fer a bit o' rest." The Corporal's welcome sent a tingle of pleasure through him. He had so few friends, and the friendliness of the Mounted Police always bewildered him. What he did for them was so much for himself, since it satisfied his longing for danger and excitement. Without it he might have returned to rustling.

In five minutes he was inside the small hut. Simmons lay on one of the two bunks. He had placed on the table some bread, butter and jam. "Help yourself, Pete. Butter's a bit soft this weather. Guess I'll have to dig that hole deeper to keep it cooler in the daytime, but it tastes mighty fine to a hungry man, even if you have to spoon it."

He watched his guest as a slice of bread was spread. "Anything on your mind, Pete?"

The half-breed started. "No-o. Jes' thinkin'."

The Corporal laughed. "If it's something you can tell me, out with it. Has the Inspector given you another job for us? Is that it?"

"I ain't seen th' Inspector fer weeks. . . . No, this is a job fer myself. And," he added, "I shudn' 'a' stopped here 'fore doin' it."

"Pressing as that, is it?"

Blue Pete shook his head. "Dunno, but it feels like I shuda did it long ago. Dunno why." He pushed his chair back and sat with outstretched legs, his hands folded over his stomach, staring at the floor. "It's that new settler out Big Slough way."

"You mean Dunlop? What's the matter out there?"

"Nothin'—I hope. . . . Not yit. But he ain't bin here long 'nuff to know the rules."

"What rules has he been breaking?"

"He's fencin' off Big Slough."

Simmons whistled. "That would certainly be hard on the herds."

"Wuss 'n that, a durn sight wuss. Some o' the cows that way, the Triangle T, an' the Diamon' K, an' the Double Bar-Y, they'd shure hev trouble these hot days."

Simmons considered it gravely and shook his head. "But it's on his homestead—Big Slough, I mean. I can't see that anything can be done about it."

"The ranchers'll see to that."

"You mean they'll make trouble for him."

Blue Pete was not telling more than he need, not to the Mounted Police. "He do' needta fence it. Thar's water thar fer everybody. 'Tain't no more use to him fenced off 'n lef' open."

"But I can see his point: it would play havoc with his crops to have cows wandering around all the time. He can't afford to fence the whole section."

Blue Pete nodded unhappily. "That's wot Mira says."

The Corporal raised himself and examined his guest's face anxiously. "Look here, Pete, do you know of any trouble actually threatening?"

"Wal,"—the half-breed rubbed his chin uneasily—"I know how Slim Manson 'n' Ford Welch 'n' Middleton'll feel. I'd feel the same ef it hurt me like it'll hurt them."

"And you know more than you're telling me, Pete. Is it time for the Mounted Police to intervene? . . . But I don't see what we can do to prevent building that fence—unless, of course, he uses barbed wire. Perhaps someone should warn him that that's against the law out here in a cow-country."

"I'm going to tell him," Blue Pete ventured. "That's wot I'm here fer: I'm goin' to tell him lots o' things fust thing to-morrow. Mebbe he'll listen. He can't be jes' a plain cuss."

The Corporal lay down again. "Well, let us know if we're needed. Blow out the lamp when you're in bed."

At half past two Blue Pete was up. He helped himself to what remained of the evening meal and tiptoed outside. It was cold, as it almost always was at night on the prairie. Even the butter that had been left on the table all night was hard.

Simmons wakened but did not get up. "You're certainly in a hurry this morning, Pete. And don't forget to let us know if there's trouble. Oh, and remember me to that ugly little pinto of yours."

"Th' ole gal sends her love 'n' kisses—an' a kick in the slats," returned the half-breed. "Wotchu mean—'ugly'?"

He struck towards the south-east, branching off from the main trail shortly after leaving the Police hut. He did not wish to meet anyone. He was conscious of pressing urgency, and he did not wish to be delayed. Besides, cutting across the prairie would save half a dozen miles, and he was uneasy and anxious. The pinto sensed the urgency and increased her pace.

"Coupla durn fools likely," he grumbled to Whiskers, "but I ain't fightin' it. Mira'll hev the laugh on me, 'cause she's shure to git it outa me. Come to think, wot am I goin' to say to Sam Dunlop? Like's not I'll make a mess of it, like Mira says I alius do. But someun's gotta try it, an' I dunno nobody else to do it. . . . Mebbe he's got sense 'nuff to see wot I mean an' leave the slough open. Mebbe he'll—"

He stopped. He had been riding for hours, and the early morning heat prophesied an abnormally hot day ahead. He was near the hollow where Sam Dunlop had started his new home, and he slowed down a little, unhappy as he thought of the coming interview. A wolfish howl had suddenly startled him, and he reached automatically for his rifle. Wolves had been playing havoc with the herds about the hills of late, and to hear one in broad daylight so far from the hills was even alarming. At the same time it would give him a chance to get at least one of them.

The howl was not repeated, and he realized that it had come from the depression before him where Dunlop had built his hut. He moved slowly forward and reached the crest. Before him there fell away a long slope to a wide depression. Far away to the south two ill-mated sloughs looked black in the morning light. Even in this dry month of July both contained water, though the nearer and smaller was encircled by a wide border of white, showing that it was alkali and useless for drinking. The border of the further one, Big Slough, was muddy but clear of alkali, a strange difference in two adjacent bodies of water.

He peered about for the wolf. A dim trail through the dead grass led down the slope, a mere double line of crushed grass that wound along, avoiding two large ancient buffalo wallows and several cactus bushes, to end before an adobe structure scarcely noticeable in the general picture.

Beyond was a second building of sod and mud. It was the stable, and beside it had been erected a roof on wooden supports, protecting from the weather a mower and a plough. Before the stable stood an old buckboard.

Not a sign of life was in sight. There was something eerie about it, and the half-breed shivered. A wolf down there so close to an inhabited hut! He could not believe it, but he remained with his rifle in his hand, ready to shoot.

Then he remembered. Mira had said Dunlop had a dog with a howl like that. He replaced the rifle in the saddle holster and looked about for the dog.

He saw it then as it moved. It was tied beside the mower, and it came to view now and stared up at him. And as they stared at each other it raised its nose and sent that dismal, startling howl through the silence.

But no sign of human life. He sat and waited, uncertain what to do. An almost overpowering distaste for the coming interview swept over him, so that his hand turned aside, as if to swing the pinto away. But Whiskers, for a wonder, did not respond.

"Do' make no sense nohow, ole gal," he muttered. "Don' seem to be nobody at home, an' that dog's durn lonesome. I'd feel the same in this place." He continued to stare at the animal, and as if frightened by the attention it slunk back out of sight beneath the mower.

"Shure, ole gal, yuh feel jes' like I do. Yuh wanta go back but yuh know we shudn't. Looks like we got to go on more'n ever. I don' like the looks of it. Thar's that dog . . . an' nothin' else. Mus' be part wolf, an' 'tain't howlin' no welcome. But why don't it—"

He stopped abruptly. Whiskers' head had jerked up towards the south and her ears had stiffened forward. Blue Pete turned swiftly, a tingle of excitement racing through him.

Far away to the south-east, towards the dark heights that were the Cypress Hills, two riders had swept into view from a coulee. They were moving away at top speed, making directly for the hills. In a moment they had vanished into another coulee.

The half-breed's rein hand swung sharply in that direction, and his feet jerked in and out. Even in his excitement he made certain that the two-inch spurs he wore did not touch the mottled sides of the pinto.

There was no need even for that, for Whiskers was already away, as if shot from a catapult. In four strides she was at full speed, her wiry little legs spurning the ground. So low she lay in her stride that the half-breed bent his knees as if to keep his feet from the cactus and sage and long dead grass through which they swept.

"Jes' gittin' into more trouble, mos' likely," he muttered, "but you 'n' me, ole gal, we ain't goin' to let nothin' like that go 'thout findin' out wot it's fer. Them lads ain't burnin' the grass fer fun, ner fer exercise, an' they ain't after c'yutes er wolves er antelopes . . . an' thar ain't no cows off that way. . . . Sorta wanta find out, an' the on'y way to find out is—to find out. So you 'n' me, ole gal," we gotta ast 'em, an' to ast 'em we gotta git to 'em. An' I'm bettin' yuh kin git us thar, ole gal. 'Sides yuh ain't had a real run fer weeks."

Whiskers required no urging. Skimming the ground at a tremendous pace, she made straight across the prairie towards the spot where the fast-riding pair had disappeared. Blue Pete bent low over the saddle, the wind whistling through the pinto's mane and tail and past the half-breed's ears. His rein-hand was held well out, leaving a loose rein. The rest was up to the pinto. There was no need to direct her. Between pinto and rider was a communion born of years of pursuit and flight, of danger that could be evaded only by speed. He talked to her as to no one else, not even to Mira; and none understood him better.

Up and down they sailed, straight towards that dark ridge that was the Cypress Hills, rising and falling with the rolls of the prairie that from the train windows further north looks so uninterestingly level. Only dangerous cactus, bushy sage, and a few badger holes turned the pinto from her course. As they topped the ridges Blue Pete could see for miles, then they would drop where his range was limited to the opposite slope. Eight or ten miles to the south and south-east lay the hills, that strange world of forested heights, of sylvan, watered ravines, that cuts across the southern part of Saskatchewan to the Alberta border, an inexplicable break in thousands of square miles of almost treeless prairie.

When the view was wide the half-breed's eyes missed nothing. His glance flew in all directions, for he wished to know if others were as curious as he. Not a movement of any kind was in sight. Even the pair he had momentarily glimpsed appeared to have vanished for good.

It worried him. Had his eyes deceived him at the moment when his fancies had run wild as he looked down into the seemingly deserted home of the new settler? Or had the pair he had seen taken measures to evade him? Were they, driven by a guilty conscience, lying in wait for him? He reached for his rifle and held it ready for action. There were many means of escape, for the ground became more uneven as it neared the slope that ran up to the hills. If they were hiding he would have little chance to find them.

He kept on. He had an idea that they were as yet unaware that they were being pursued. In the glimpse he had caught of them they seemed to think only of reaching the cover of the hills; he had not seen them look behind. Racing at such a speed they were unlikely to alter their plans, with the thousand hiding-places in the hills before them, even if they knew he was after them.

There was one possibility, if they knew the prairie as well as he, they might turn in either direction and keep to the coulees that ran towards the hills. Only by sheer luck could he hope to overtake them if they did that. He would not even be able to see them until they were forced into the open on the slope rising to the trees.

No matter what they did the one thing for him was to keep on. Besides, the chase had resolved itself into a race, a test of Whiskers, and the pinto had to win. Neither she nor her rider ever refused such a test.

The glance he had caught of the pair had been too fleeting to see more than movement. "Dunno who they are, ole gal, er wot tha're doin', er whar they are now, but we mus' be gittin' nearer. Ef tha're cute they'll keep right on. It's goin' to be some race to ketch 'em then. . . . Thar's suthin' funny 'bout it. Looks like tha're runnin' 'way from suthin'. Then they'll keep right on through the hills to the Badlan's . . . an' you 'n' me we've had all we want o' the Badlan's. Keep yer eyes an' yer ears open, ole gal, 'cause yuh see 'n' hear better'n I do."

The pinto ran with her eyes on the ground, for the way was rough. Long minutes passed. Blue Pete was anxious, undecided. He might ride past them if they hid. A mere fifty yards to right or left and he might not see them in some coulee.

He had almost decided to slow down and pick up their trail when they shot into view straight ahead. With a grin he saw that he had gained even more than he had thought possible; now they were less than a mile ahead. But they still raced along at full speed.

A low whistle broke through his teeth. "Gor-swizzle! Neches!" It was the term of contempt he used for Indians. Though half Indian himself, he knew too much of his mother's race to have anything but contempt for them in general. No one knew them better, no one had more reason to distrust them; and the hatred that existed between Indian and half-breed since the Riel Rebellion had not lessened. To him their natural cruelty, their dishonesty, their faithlessness, their unkempt indolence were disgusting when not infuriating. Many of them, too, he had brought to justice during his work for the Mounted Police, and the marks of their hatred he bore on his body. The Blackfeet in the encampment beneath the cutbanks to the east of Medicine Hat would have nothing to do with him, and for ample reason. In his reckless, defiant way he scorned them.

He had made real friends among the Crees far to the north-west, in the foothills of the Rockies, but that was another story.

Whiskers, too, had seen the pair, and with a low whinny she announced it.

Her rider's eyes danced. "Thar's shure suthin' thar fer us, ole gal. They ain't cuttin' the air to feel the wind in thur shirts, not them Neches ain't. An' you 'n' me we're goin' to run 'em down ef we have to foller 'em to Montany."

He raised his eyes. The hills seemed to leap at him, cutting off the southern sky. He was surprised and shocked to find how near they were. With the lead they had the Indians could outrun him that far . . . unless—unless he did something drastic.

He let his mind roam over the intervening prairie. Every coulee, every draw, every ridge and depression, almost every old buffalo wallow was familiar to him. The years he had been in Canada had been spent there near the hills. He could have found his way blindfolded. Day and night he had ridden, sleeping in the open, in good and bad weather, using every height and depression for his purpose. Soft beds and enclosing walls had no attraction for him; only Mira drew him back to the 3-Bar-Y, and even she could not keep him there.

He knew that the coulee into which the Indians had disappeared curved away in both directions, either leading towards the hills. To the right it turned sharply after a few hundred yards and led more directly south. If the Indians turned in either direction he might miss them, since he would be unable to see them except from the height immediately over them. If they rode straight on they would reach the hills before he could stop them, rapidly as he saw he was gaining on them. Unless—

On a chance he shifted direction slightly to the west. In that direction the coulee was deeper. If they knew he was after them that was where they would turn.

A sudden low whinny from Whiskers brought him about to look in the other direction. Behind a sage bush at the top of a slope something definitely moved. It was gone in an instant, but he had seen enough.

He knew then that they must have heard him; their quick ears had picked up the sound of the pinto's pounding hoofs.

He had lost some ground by taking the wrong direction, but the Indians had lost more by stopping to see who was after them, and he laughed softly as the pinto shot forward. He reached the top of the slope in time to see one of the Indians dash out of sight around a curve in the coulee. The fellow was looking back, and at sight of Blue Pete he lashed his mount to more frantic speed.

They rode desperately now, recklessly, careless of their ponies, their minds fixed only on escape to the forest so near them. Blue Pete knew those tough little ponies. To her profit Whiskers had some of their blood in her veins. For an incredible time they could maintain top speed, ignoring ups and downs. They would run without a falter until they dropped; they never gave up. Proud as their owners were of them, the Indians had no thought for them when it came to their own safety.

He cut through the ravine at an angle and raced up the opposite slope. Clinging to the crest then he tore along until he could look down into the coulee beyond the curve. The Indians were in plain view now, and in the harder, smoother bottom they were holding their own. In another few hundred yards they would reach the slope to the hills, while he would be forced to cross the coulee in which they rode.

They saw him the moment he appeared and they made straight for the trees. Nothing now was to be gained by trying to conceal themselves.

The half-breed's teeth clamped together. "Reckon we gotta do suthin' now, ole gal," he grated, "er we'll lose 'em. Ef they git to the trees they'll ambush us. . . . We gotta do suthin. . . . an' I hate to."

As he raised his rifle it occurred to him, coming like a blow, that he had no right whatever to stop them, at least no right of which he was aware. It did not make him hesitate. "They got some reason to wanta git away, ole gal, an' thar's on'y you 'n' me to find out wot 'tis. I gotta take a chance. . . . Anyways, th' Inspector wudn' believe anythin' they told him," he added, with a slight smile.

He sent a bullet beside and across the face of the leading Indian. It failed to do more than increase their pace. In another hundred yards they would reach the slope and climb, and he had still the coulee to cross. The rifle came up again. Four hundred yards separated them now, an easy shot for him, even from the saddle. But the forest was there before them, seeming to laugh at him. In a minute or two they would be safe.

He sent the second bullet between them. It would tell them that he meant business.

It did, and their reaction surprised him. The second Indian turned in the saddle and raised his rifle. The Indians, too, could shoot.

It was his undoing. As the rifle came up, Blue Pete fired again. The bullet struck the stock beneath the Indian's arm and knocked the rifle from his grasp. It ricocheted downward. It caught the tip of the pony's ear, and the animal leaped sideways. So sudden was it that the Indian, already unbalanced by the blow on the rifle, was thrown from the saddle, to lie stunned for a few moments. Another bullet passed so close to his companion that the latter ducked and, looking back and seeing what had happened, he pulled in, holding his hands up to show that he had not drawn his rifle from the holster.

Blue Pete loped down the slope. The instant he saw that he had accomplished his purpose he felt uneasy about it. Not only did he not know what to say, but even if it developed that he had reason to stop them what would he do with them?

The Indian on the ground raised himself and commenced to test arms and legs to convince himself that nothing was broken. Surprised to find himself still whole, he glowered at the half-breed. In Blackfeet he demanded: "What did you shoot me for?"

Blue Pete did not answer; he was too busy looking them over, making certain that they carried no other guns. The Indian who had surrendered had ridden back and now sat sullenly watching him. Blue Pete knew he had seen them before, probably in the Blackfeet encampment in town, but he had had no earlier trouble with them.

The Indian on the ground repeated his question, this time more angrily.

That they recognized him the half-breed knew, and it made it no easier for him, since he could not withdraw now. "You shot at me," he said in their own language. "What were you running away from?"

The mounted Indian sat with his hands folded on the saddle-horn, a scowl growing on his coppery face. "We were going to the hills—to hunt wolves," he growled. "Why shouldn't we?"

"Huh! You were running *from* something. I want to know what it was. I've a right to know, because I run cows on these ranges. . . . Whar yuh come from?" he inquired suddenly in English.

The Indian on the ground pointed back the way they had come, and Blue Pete grinned.

"Shure, I knowed yuh cud talk. Wal, we bes' stick to talkin' that way. I don' like no Neche talk 'less I gotta. Whar'd yuh come from, I ast."

"From the camp at the Hat."

"Shure, I knowed that. But yuh didn' ride like that all the way from the Hat. Whar'd yuh come from jes' now?" When they did not reply he shrugged. "Awright, we're goin' back the way yuh come. I know yuh come from the new settler's back thar, an' I'm wonderin' wot's the hurry." He slid his rifle into the saddle holster and drew his .45. Riding up to the mounted Indian, he held out his hand. "I want that rifle, an' any other guns yuh got, an' durn quick."

His back had been partly turned to the other Indian, but a sudden flash of excitement in the eyes of the Indian he faced warned him and he whirled about, throwing himself from the saddle at the same time. Over the back of the pinto his .45 was ready for action.

He had moved just in time. The Indian behind him had recovered his rifle and had half raised it. He dropped it in the face of the .45 and raised his arms.

"Sly cuss, ainchu? Wal, I got eyes in the back o' my head—an' when I ain't lookin' Whiskers is." He collected the two rifles and fastened them to his own saddle with the rope. Indians seldom carried small arms, but he looked them over carefully to make sure. "Reckon yuh mus' be mighty skeered o' suthin' to risk that on Blue Pete. Yuh know me, an' yuh shud otta know I don' like nobody pointin' a gun at me, speshully Neches. Makes me curioser 'n ever. We gotta find out wot yuh're runnin' from."

He jerked his thumb towards the free bronco that had stopped only a few yards away to nibble at the grass. "Bes' git him, 'less yuh wanta walk, an' I ain' got time fer that. We're goin' to ast Sam Dunlop wot yuh're skeered of. The hull three of us'll go back

32

together."

One of the Indians growled: "Wot yu want with us? We don't know nobody back there."

"Then yuh bes' git 'quainted right now, 'cause Sam Dunlop's come to live here. Even a Neche's gotta know that soon." He saw the look that passed between them. "Shure yuh don' like goin' back. That's why yuh're goin.' Yuh're skeered, an' I'm wonderin' why. Whachu bin doin' at Dunlop's, eh?"

There was no reply, and the unmounted Indian walked to his pony and mounted.

"Now git goin'. Yuh come might straight from Dunlop's, an' yuh're goin' back the same way, on'y not so fast. I'll be right here behind yuh, an' yuh know my .45. It jes' itches to tickle Neches."

They set off towards the north-west, the Indians in the lead. They rode close together at first, though they did not converse. Now and then one or the other would turn as if to speak to their captor, but no words came.

"Reckon yuh bes' git apart a bit," ordered Blue Pete. "I ain't trustin' no Neches none. Ef yuh got anythin' to say I'm here an' listenin'."

So evident was their uneasiness that their captor felt the strain himself. And the longer the silence continued the more uncomfortable he became about the whole affair. Now that the chase was over he felt let down, more than a little ashamed of the excitement. He recalled that for much of the time his main interest in the chase was as a race in which he backed Whiskers against the Indian ponies. Beyond that at no time was more than curiosity. And anyone had a right to ride as fast as he wished on the ranges, provided he did not disturb the herds. He realized how he would resent anyone attempting to stop him, and he often rode fast.

Now that he had overtaken the Indians what should he do with them? The return to Sam Dunlop's was merely a postponement of the decision he must make. If Dunlop could furnish no reason for their flight, if they had been merely hastening toward the hills to hunt wolves—and that was a popular errand, with the ranchers so worried about the losses among the herds—he would feel foolish. And before the hated Neches there was nothing he would face with less complacency than that. On the other hand, if there was some guilty reason for their running away, the only thing to do would be to take them all the way to Medicine Hat, a journey of almost sixty miles. And sixty miles through the night with a pair of Indians as prisoners was a task that offered no attractions.

It was not that he feared them, but he knew that if they had done something to merit handing them over to the Mounted Police they would surely take measures to escape during the darkness. That in itself did not disturb him. What did was that if they tried it he had a good idea, of what he was apt to do to them, and that was where the Mounted Police—the law—would demand an accounting of him.

There was, too, the unpleasant picture of what the citizens of Medicine Hat would think if he acted as policeman. It was the last role they associated with him, the last both he and the Inspector wished made public. In the minds of the public he was still one whom the Mounted Police considered it wise to keep an eye on. To be sure there were times when he was known to have assisted the Mounted Police, but that was for the protection of the herds, a stand any rancher would take if he had the chance.

He even considered turning them loose immediately. They would jump at the chance to escape and no questions would be asked, but he was too curious for that, and he could not face the thought of the laugh when his back was turned. Besides, one of them had shot at him, had even attempted to shoot a second time when he thought he was not on guard. And their very uneasiness as they rode back decided him to hold them until he had some sort of explanation better than they had given.

He recalled Mira's warning that his visit to Sam Dunlop's was certain to get him into trouble. But this, he told himself, had nothing to do with that. . . . Or had it? The question popped into his head and startled him, since he could not see the connection.

The pair before him rode steadily along, now twenty yards apart. Their uneasiness increased, yet somehow it did not impress him as guilt so much as a desire to explain, a desire silenced by fear. Thinking that over, he saw that they had yielded much too readily to point to any deep sense of guilt. He had had too many encounters with Indians to be in any doubt about that. The momentary resistance they had offered was natural enough when pursued.

It made him no more comfortable to read fear into their manner, rather than guilt. The latter he knew how to handle, but fear might arise from so many conditions he could not picture. Never knowing fear himself, physical fear, he was unable to account for it in others.

The long and fast chase had tired their mounts, and they rode more slowly. About them was no sign of life, though in the coulees within range of their eyes must be several herds with their attendant punchers. The lifelessness, the silence, impressed the half-breed more and more. It seemed to prophecy some condition ahead that he would have to face alone, something that would justify Mira's warning.

It was more than an hour and a half before they reached the height that looked down into the depression where Dunlop had built his hut. The Indians, he noticed then, had veered off to the right, as if to keep to the heights, and he ordered them to turn towards the hut, angling down the slope. There was still no sign of life about the buildings. Even the dog was not to be seen.

But as they came nearer, the dog emerged slowly from beside the mower and lay watching their every move, wary and silent. The half-breed noticed then how different it was from the horde of curs that infest every Indian encampment, mangey, sneaking, starved creatures that had often made his work so difficult. It was a large black, short-haired animal, and the Indians eyed it nervously, though it was plain that it was tied. Once as he swerved towards it he fancied that its tail wagged faintly.

He pointed to the hut. "Git over thar. Thar's suthin' funny here." He knew it, felt it. Something was wrong.

Long before this either Dunlop or his wife would have appeared if either had been there, and from what he knew of them the woman had never left the hut since her husband had brought her to it. In the manner of the Indians, too, he read mystery and a growing nervousness.

They reached the hut. The door was wide open, but no one was in sight.

"Git down."

The Indians slowly dismounted. One of them turned to him. "Indians no do it," he pleaded. "Indians find it an' run. You see."

He pointed to the open door. "Git in thar." With drawn gun he drove them before him. "No trick er I shoot." He could feel tingles running through him.

The dog raised its nose and howled, and the Indians whirled towards the sound, then looked at their captor. Slowly they advanced to the open doorway and there they stopped.

"Git in, I said." He could not wait but pushed them roughly before him. They entered and slid along the wall, their eyes fixed on him.

For a few moments he could make out little in the shadowed room after the bright sunlight outside. Then his eyes focussed on something on the floor beside the stove. A sharp breath broke from him, and his teeth clamped together.

In a blaze of fury he turned on the Indians, gun pointing. "Git into that corner, an' yuh're durn lucky ef I don't shoot 'thout astin' wot this means."

VII MURDERS

HE forgot them then. In four long strides he hurried towards the stove and dropped to his knees, to bend over the lifeless form of a woman. She lay face down. A trickle of blood from a bullet wound behind the ear had congealed to a dark brown. With a finger he touched one small hand. It was stone cold. Without touching her again he examined the body more closely. He even lowered his head to the floor in an effort to see her face.

A blaze of anger darkened his own face. "Who done this?" It came through closed teeth.

"Indians not know," one declared falteringly. "Indians see and run."

He knew the crime had not been committed that day, and certainly the Indians, had they killed the woman earlier, would not have remained so long at the scene or returned so soon. Their headlong flight proved that they spoke the truth. He let his eyes roam about the room. He had no idea what he was looking for, but surely there would be something to lead to the murderer, something to explain the crime.

The room was small and crowded, but to one brought up in an Indian tepee, one who spent most of his life in the open or in the caves of the Cypress Hills, it told of a woman's care. A stove, two chairs, a table, a bed, a small chest of drawers, and a home-made clothes cupboard were all the room contained except what was on the walls.

There were bright pictures there, framed in cardboard, a few hanging garments—and a rifle resting on two wooden pegs driven into the hardened mud. His attention fixed itself on the rifle for a long time. He went to stand before it, his forehead wrinkled thoughtfully, puzzled, too. Then with a shake of the head he turned to the bed. The frame of it had been knocked together from poles, but over it was spread a brightly-coloured quilt, and, neatly turned back, two red Hudson's Bay five-point blankets were visible. The sunlight fell on the gaily-coloured spread, lighting up the room. The dead body only a few feet away was the more shocking for that spot of colour.

On the little chest of drawers was laid out an expensive toilet set of enamel and gold, an incongruous detail that caught his eye and drew him nearer to stare down on it. There was so much that was incongruous that he felt almost that it was all a dream.

He shook himself from it and, muttering, walked about the room. He was conscious now of the Indians, standing silent and watchful in the corner. He would have liked to fasten the crime on them, not so much because they were Indians as because it promised the solace of punishment. They cowered before his glances.

A low whinny from Whiskers outside the door sent him hurrying to see what it meant. Even before he reached the door the sound of approaching hoofs reached him, and he looked about the room with startled eyes. Up the trail he saw the brown working jacket and dark riding breeches of a Mounted Policeman, and a great breath of relief broke from him. It was Sergeant Mahon.

Mahon drew up before the door. "Hello, Pete! What in the world are you doing here? I didn't know you were a friend of Dunlop's."

He saw then that something was wrong and he dismounted hurriedly, leaving Jupiter, his big black, to nose familiarly at his old friend Whiskers.

"What's the matter?"

For answer Blue Pete pointed back towards the room. He stepped outside and let the Sergeant pass.

When the latter saw the Indians he stopped and turned. He had as yet noticed nothing else. "What in the world does this mean? What has happened? Where are—"

He had turned back to the room, and his roving eyes had alighted on the body. "For God's sake, what's this?"

He took a single step towards the body and stopped. "Stand in the door, Pete, and keep your eyes on them," he ordered. As he spoke he ripped off his gauntlets and dropped them on the floor. He sank to his knees besides the body. "It's—Mrs. Dunlop! My God!" He leaned back on his heels while he felt the woman's pulse. "Where's her husband?"

"I ain't seed him," replied Blue Pete. "Thar's on'y the dog."

Mahon stooped over the body and examined it more closely without moving it. "Shot!" he announced. Then he added, "murdered!" He looked at the Indians. "Had they anything to do with it?"

Blue Pete shrugged. "I dunno. I seen 'em runnin' towards the hills an' I stopped 'em an' brought 'em back."

"You mean—just now?"

"Jes' come in."

Mahon looked down on the body. "But this was not done to-day. That blood has been dried for hours, and rigor mortis is almost gone." He turned the face about. When he saw it he recoiled and let the body fall.

Blue Pete had seen, and his jaw set.

The face was scarcely recognizable. One side had been crushed in by a brutal blow with some heavy weapon, and a great black scar covered the other cheek and part of the nose and forehead. On that side eyebrows and lashes were burnt off.

Mahon stepped over the body and touched the stove. It was cold.

"It was hot when she was killed," he grated. "That fire's been out for a day. When she was shot she fell against the stove." He looked down on the congealed blood behind the ear. "She wasn't dead when that bullet was fired, but the blow was struck first."

He knelt again and examined the body more carefully. "The bullet is still there. That'll help. . . . If this was done in the heat of the day rigor mortis would set in quickly. There's no knowing how long it lasts, but the cold stove tells us something more. The murder was committed yesterday, probably early in the day."

He looked up at the Indians as if to speak but said nothing and returned to examining the body. "Yes, the blow came first. She fell against the stove, struggled a little while the hot stove burned her face, then she was shot to complete the job. What a brute!"

He rose and eyed the two Indians, now cowering into the shadowed corner. "What about these fellows?"

Blue Pete shook his head. "All I know I seen 'em ridin' hell fer leather away so I brought 'em back. I knowed they musta come from here. I didn' know nothin' 'bout this till we come back."

One of the Indians stepped forward. "Indians know nothin'. Indians come an' see this an' run away."

"At least they didn't do it to-day," said the Sergeant.

"But I don't see— Who are you? What are your names?"

"Me He Dog. He Wadoo. We live at the Hat—the camp."

"Yes," snapped the Sergeant, "and you can speak a lot better English if you want to. You say you came and found this. What were you doing here?"

"We come for drink of water—mebbe somethin' to eat."

"What were you doing out here so far from town?"

"Indians go to hills to hunt wolves. Wadoo and me good hunters.

Wolves killin' cows—"

"Yes, I know. . . . What else did you see while you were here?"

"Indians no wait to see more. Just run—fast."

"They shure done that," said Blue Pete.

"Did you see Dunlop?" inquired the Sergeant.

"No see nobody—only the dog out there. Indians go too fast."

The Sergeant considered. "It must—have been done—early yesterday. . . or the day before." He was muttering to himself. He shook himself then and turned to Blue Pete. "We must find her husband—if he's around. I see the buckboard out there. Where are the horses?"

"I ain't looked fer 'em. Thar's this." Blue Pete pointed to the body and shivered. "Thar's the dog out thar, that's all. It's skeered; yuh kin see it's skeered."

Mahon started for the door. "We'll look about. Come on, all of you." He had reached the door when he turned suddenly and frowned at Blue Pete. "How did you happen to be here?"

Blue Pete snuffled and twisted unhappily. One large hand rubbed across his lips. "I was jes'—jes' ridin'—"

He saw the Sergeant's eyes fill with sudden suspicion, and his own eyes dropped. "I was jes' comin' to do a durn fool thing. Leastwise that's wot Mira called it, an' I reckon she—" He turned abruptly and looked down on the form of the murdered woman. "Gorswizzle, ef I'd come straight here it—it—I mighta bin a time to stop it."

"What do you mean by that?"

"I was comin' to try to git Dunlop not to fence Big Slough. The cows'll need it in the dry months, an' ef he fenced it off thar'd shure be trouble, an'—" His lips closed; he stared at the Sergeant with frightened eyes. "But it cudn' bin trouble like this, not from the ranchers—not this bad."

"Never mind speculating what sort of trouble it might have been. Leave that to us and go on with your story. You say you didn't come straight. Of course you couldn't have, since I saw you in town."

The half-breed nodded miserably. "I slunk off to town; I run off. The nearer I come to it the nastier a job it looked, 'cause I ain't much good at talkin'. 'Twasn't none o' my business, 'cause the 3-Bar-Y cows don't run this far east."

"But you knew there was going to be trouble if he fenced Big

Slough. How did you know it? Had you heard any threats?"

"Wal-l . . . thar's bin lots o' talk, o' course. Punchers was sore, an' the ranchers. I cud see thar was bound to be trouble, an' so—"

"You *knew* there was going to be trouble," Mahon interrupted impatiently. "We'll find out more about that later. We've no time now." He looked down on the body and as if talking to himself muttered: "Surely—surely they wouldn't do a thing like this."

"Thar ain't no puncher er rancher I know 'ud do it," Blue Pete declared. A moment later he qualified it: "When it comes to cows thar ain't much else that counts in a cow-country. Sam Dunlop was cuttin' up the ranges. That's bad 'nuff. But when he was fencin' off the on'y water the cows kin find sometimes this side the hills he was shure lookin' fer trouble. . . . I dunno."

The Sergeant eyed him with a suggestion of scorn. "But you know how badly the ranchers would take it, and you know to what lengths they will go to retain this country for themselves."

He led the way outdoors. "Things have been shaping up like this for a long time. Farmers were certain to come, sooner or later, and the ranchers would go to any lengths to resist the movement. We've seen it coming . . . but we never pictured anything so horrible as this. Free ranges have laid the foundation for it. The ranchers have come to consider the open prairie their own, making easy fortunes for them. What Dunlop was doing was to them akin to rustling, and rustling has long been accepted as justifying bullets. I suppose it isn't a long step to—to this."

He set off towards the stable. "All the Mounted Police have to consider is that there's a law, and it protects the farmer. Dunlop has a right to homestead anywhere a homestead is available, and the law permits him to do anything he likes with it, so long as he performs the necessary work on the place. Of course out here he is not permitted to use barbed wire, on account of the cattle, but beyond that Big Slough is his to do as he likes with it. The ranchers are helpless—according to law. . . . But I'm not going to do any guessing; it's much too serious for that. Where's the dog you spoke off?"

The dog had retired to the shadow of the mower, and for a time he did not see it.

Blue Pete pointed. Bright eyes shone from the shadow. "Yuh see how skeered it is—an' that dog don' skeer easy. It seen suthin'. It knows."

"If only it could talk!" The Sergeant stood at a distance, frowning at the eyes that watched him in silence. Slowly he swung about, taking in the desolate scene bit by bit. "My God! What a place to bring a woman! What a life to ask her to live! Why in the world would he select such a God-forsaken locality? I can't imagine he was a real farmer or he'd have known this was no place to homestead. . . . And it doesn't look as if he had high hopes. Things look—temporary. A few hundred dollars would cover all he has spent on the place. Everything is home-made or second hand."

He went to the stable door and opened it. "What's in here?" He saw that it was empty. "Then where are the horses? He had a team. It isn't likely he'd take both horses if he has skipped out. The buckboard's still here."

Blue Pete stared at him with wide eyes. "Yuh mean he—he done it?"

"I mean nothing. I'm looking for that woman's husband."

The half-breed bent over the ground. "The broncs come off in this direction." He pointed towards Big Slough. "He was workin' over thar most o' the time, gittin' that fence up. . . . I kin see part o' the fence now from here."

He set off along the trail the horses had left. In a few yards he stopped and pointed to wide trails of scraped and flattened ground. "He hitched up to suthin' here."

Sergeant Mahon was close behind. "That's a stone-boat. He had one, I remember. Come on." He beckoned to the Indians.

Blue Pete had broken into a run that left them far behind. They saw him pass the smaller slough and stop. There he turned and beckoned excitedly, and the other three commenced to run towards him.

The depression narrowed as they advanced, tightening about the two sloughs. They skirted the white alkali of the smaller slough in which only a little water remained. In the spring, however, it must have been much larger.

Blue Pete waited for them, pointing to something they could not yet see around a curve in the sides of the coulee. Then the Sergeant heard horses whinny, and he understood. Instinctively he knew, too, that they had come to the end of the trail.

Big Slough lay before them. It was almost half a mile long and in spring flood must have been a couple of hundred yards wide, for there the depression widened. The ground was low and muddy for some distance about its edges before rising to a drier level. Forty yards away thickets of cottonwood trees dotted the space before the sides rose gradually to the upper prairie.

The Sergeant's eyes took it all in. Then he saw the horses. They were hitched to a roughly-made stone-boat that had caught between two stumps and held them fast. Beside the stone-boat lay two large rolls of barbed wire. The broncos whinnied hungrily and tugged to get free.

"Tha're near starved," said Blue Pete. "They bin thar more'n a day."

Mahon sent his eyes roving over the depression. "But where's Dunlop? This doesn't help much."

Blue Pete walked slowly about the broncos, examining the ground, while they tugged to free themselves. Then he moved off towards the slough, pointing to the ground before him.

"Suthin' happened here. Dunno wot—not yit. . . . 'Tain't the brocos bin here, but thar's suthin'.'"

Sergeant Mahon called to him: "Wait. I'll be back in a few minutes." He set off at a run towards the buildings. The half-breed moved about, examining the ground. The two Indians stood watching every move, their stolid faces betraying nothing.

In ten minutes the Sergeant was back. He had the dog on its rope. It came along without urging, its nose to the ground. Mahon led it to where the broncos stood and it ran about, sniffing the ground.

Blue Pete beckoned. "Bring it here."

At the half-breed's feet the dog caught the scent instantly and set off at a trot towards the slough, whimpering as it went.

Blue Pete was close behind, nodding approval. "Shure! Shure! That's whar they lugged him. He's got it."

Near the edge of the water where the ground was soft the dog commenced furiously to dig, sending the damp earth flying. Blue Pete ran back to the stone-boat and brought a spade he had seen there. He shoved the dog away and commenced to dig. Not more than six inches below the surface they came on the body of Sam Dunlop, the new settler. There were two bullet holes in it, one in the neck, the other in the chest.

THE moment the body came in sight the dog sank back on its haunches, raised its nose, and sent a long, wolfish howl over the prairie.

Mahon could not restrain a shudder. "If I heard that anywhere else I'd swear it was a wolf."

"Mus' be wolf blood in him," said Blue Pete. "That's wot I heerd fust. It made me shiver. I think it skeered the Neches 'most as much as—as the woman back thar."

They laid the body on the loose earth they had dug, and the Sergeant examined it. "Shot in the neck first, I should say. It didn't kill him; then the second bullet was shot from close range and went in there," pointing to the wound in the chest. "We'll find out more when we make a better examination. Take a look around, Pete; you may find something."

The half-breed raised the spade he had been using and shook his head at it. "Buried with his own spade, the dirty skunks." He held it between two fingers, as if it contaminated him. "They dragged him here. I seen that. Musta shot him back thar somewhars near the cayuses. . . . Thar was more'n one o' them to drag him like that over that ground."

Mahon turned to look back towards the buildings. "And to think he hadn't his gun to defend himself with! Strange, that . . . I never saw him without it close at hand, I even mentioned it. He said it was for coyotes and wolves. He said the wolves often howled about the place, perhaps after the dog."

He pointed towards the line of fence-posts about the slough. A single strand of wire was already strung along one side of the water, and most of the posts were in place about the other side. "That's barbed wire. Surely he knew he wouldn't be permitted to string that here!" He moved restlessly about. "There's so much of it I don't understand."

He tied the dog to a tree and set about examining the ground more carefully about the stone-boat but found nothing of importance. "I can see now they dragged the body," he said, "but that's about all."

The dog whined piteously, now and then raising its nose to send that shuddering wolf-howl into the air.

"If only it could talk!" muttered Mahon. "It knows what happened."

"Ef it cud talk," Blue Pete ventured, "it wudn' be left to do it. They killed everythin' but the broncs an' the dog."

They released the team and drove it to the stable, with the body on the stone-boat. The dog attached itself to Blue Pete's heels and would not leave him.

He shook his head at it. "Never knowed any use fer a dog in this cow-country . . . 'ceptin' them wolf hounds o' Jerry the Pole's, an' they ain't no use to nobody but Jerry. All a dog does 'bout a range is start a stampede . . . an' they ain't a durn bit o' use to stop one. Looks 'sif Sam Dunlop hadn't kep' it tied it mighta bin some use to him at the end."

"I must have another look in the hut before we go," said the Sergeant. "Are you coming? The Indians will look after the broncos."

Blue Pete shook his head. "I seen all I want to thar. I'll stick around an' keep an eye on the Neches. . . . Reckon yuh'll need the buckboard to take—things to town. I'll hitch it up."

"Yes, and I'll need you with me."

Blue Pete shook his head. "The Neches kin help yuh. I'll stick around here. Mebbe I kin find suthin' more."

"You're coming with me," ordered the Sergeant. "I'll need you. The Indians are coming, too, of course. The Inspector'll want to talk to you. You were the first to find the bodies—after the Indians. . . . I'm not entirely satisfied about them, but that'll be up to the Inspector." Without waiting for a reply he set off towards the house.

Blue Pete's teeth came together defiantly. He wasn't working for the Mounties—not now; he didn't want to be bothered with them. At times he had no patience with their methods. One thing he wished most of all was to get back to where they had found the body of Sam Dunlop—and alone. There were things there plain enough to his keen eyes, and he wished to know more of the story they told. In his defiance of the Sergeant's orders he even went so far as to climb into the saddle.

Then he noticed the Indians: They were watching with an interest amounting to excitement. And he knew that he dare not be responsible for teaching them that anyone might defy the orders of a Mounted Policeman.

And so he dismounted and commenced to hitch the team to the buckboard. Peremptorily he beckoned them to him "Git into this, you. Lend a hand. Do up them tugs an' be quick about it."

Meekly they did as they were ordered. At his orders they lifted the body of Sam Dunlop into the buckboard, and the antiquated vehicle was drawn to the hut door. The Sergeant came out as they stopped. He beckoned to Blue Pete and pointed back into the hut.

The half-breed shook his head. "Git the Neches to help yuh. I don' like it."

The Sergeant's eyes widened with something deeper than surprise. "Good lord, Pete, it's not the first dead body you've seen—or the hundredth."

"I ain't seen nothing like that in thar, never before. Makes me sorta sick."

A cold and unbelieving smile flitted into Mahon's face and was gone, but he beckoned the Indians to him and the three entered the hut. Blue Pete crept to the door and watched. Something drew him, something that he hated but could not resist. And when he saw the Indians fumbling at the woman's feet, while the Sergeant took the head, he hurried in and pushed them aside without a word.

As the body came through the door the dog set up a howl and slunk beneath the buckboard. There it crouched, watching through a wheel.

The Sergeant regarded it questioningly. "What in the world are we going to do with it? I suppose we'll have to take it along; we can't leave it here to starve . . . I suppose we might leave it at the Inverted T. Jerry the Pole might like another wolf-dog to add to his little band."

He returned to the hut and closed the door. For several moments he stood considering, then he stooped, fumbled at something at the base of the door, and turned away.

"Get up there and drive," he ordered, pointing to one of the Indians.

The Indian, He Dog, hesitated, standing beside his pony.

"Your bronco will follow, you know that—or Wadoo can lead it. Get up."

Wadoo started to obey, then stopped. "Indians go to hunt wolves. Mounties no need Indians; ranchers want wolves killed."

"It happens that this Mountie needs you. Get up when I tell you. Your wolf-hunt can wait—till the Inspector gives the word. Hurry up; it's going to be dark shortly.

The rifles the Indians had carried Blue Pete had pushed into the buckboard. The Sergeant noticed them and examined them. When he saw they had been emptied he nodded.

"Shure. I wudn' trust no Neche no time," said the half-breed. "Shure I know they didn't do this, but 'tain't 'cause they cudn't.'"

Sergeant Mahon smiled. "I see you think the same as I do. No one could have reason to do it but the ranchers.

It was almost dark when they reached the Inverted T. They had travelled more slowly than buckboards usually move over the prairie. Broncos hitched to a buckboard seldom trot, never walk; always they gallop. But speed, with such a cargo, was to the Sergeant akin to sacrilege; and the Indians were in no hurry.

The lights were lit in the ranch house of the Inverted T as they drove down the slope. Long before they reached the door Don Farren, tall, rugged, with the strong features of one who had suffered much and had fought through to success, stood in the doorway to welcome them, his gaunt frame on widely-braced legs outlined against the lighted room at his back. A huge calabash pipe hung from his lips, but he removed it when he recognized the Sergeant.

"Hello, Don!" Mahon did not dismount.

Farren came slowly out to him. He was plainly puzzled; he knew that something was amiss, and he looked inquiringly from the Sergeant to the Indians and off to Blue Pete. He did not speak.

"Sam Dunlop and his wife have been murdered!" The Sergeant seemed to hurl it at the rancher, almost an accusation. As he spoke he leaned forward to peer into Farren's eyes.

Farren recoiled a step. "Murdered?"

"We found them both shot to death. It must have happened the day before yesterday or early yesterday." He saw Farren's gaze turn to the Indians. "They found the bodies first, that's all," said the Sergeant. "Blue Pete came later; he was on his way to visit Dunlop. We're taking everything in to the Hat."

Farren seemed to gulp. "Is there—anything—I can do? I had no friendly feelings towards Dunlop. He was going to fence in Big Slough, and that meant death to many a cow of mine, but this is something else."

The dog came suddenly out from under the back wheels of the buckboard, raised its nose, and sent into the growing darkness the lonely, blood-curdling wolf-howl. Don Farren started back. "Hell, that's the Dunlop dog. Jerry has told me of that howl. I didn't hear it when I was there—" He stopped and laughed uneasily.

"When were you there?" Mahon demanded.

Farren shrugged. "Of course I was there, so were half-a-dozen other ranchers. We all tried to get him to leave the slough open."

"I asked when you were there."

"It must have been more than a week ago."

"Did you quarrel?"

Farren was embarrassed. "Well, when he refused, told me to mind my own business, I didn't kiss him, you may be sure of that. But neither did I kill him—if that's what you want to know."

"I want to know who did. I'm not accusing you or anyone else. But you did quarrel?"

"He was stubborn as a mule, even before he became angry. Talked about his rights with his own land and about the lazy ranchers who think the world belongs to them. Didn't want to see any of us about the place. I could have knocked his head off. I admit it. It would have been a fair fight, at any rate, not murder. . . . And his wife, you say. My God, who could do a thing like that?"

"I'm asking it. . . . The Mounted Police will ask it till they find out. Did you threaten him?"

"I suppose I did—if he fenced the slough. There isn't a rancher within a hundred miles who wouldn't. It was sheer meanness on his part. But—Mrs. Dunlop!" He shuddered.

The dog howled again, and Farren clapped his hands to his ears as answering howls came from over a ridge to the east. He jerked a thumb towards the sound. "Jerry's hounds think they're in for a wolf-hunt to-night. What the blazes would a farmer want with a dog like that? What are you going to do with it?"

"I'm leaving it with you."

"With me?" The rancher shook his head. "I've no use for it, no place for it."

"Give it to Jerry; he can look after it. It should be a good wolf-dog."

"Not with his hounds. They've formed a family compact; they fight with any other animal that comes near."

Someone appeared in the doorway, blocking the light. "Is that a coyote I hear or a wolf?" a voice demanded. Another had come to stand at his shoulder. "Sounds like the real West all right, Biff."

The Sergeant's face hardened as he faced the pair. The dog

48

snarled and retreated as the two men came out towards the group.

"Is that a tame wolf you have? Who's this, Farren?" He recognized the uniform then. "Oh, one of the celebrated Mounted Policemen who always get their man."

At the slight note of contempt the Sergeant stiffened. "You've been reading cheap Westerns, Collins. Now you're in the real West you may learn a few things. It's to be hoped for."

Biff Collins laughed. "Oh, if it isn't the worthy Sergeant! A more peaceful meeting this time, isn't it? I'm glad to get better acquainted. We'll need to be if one of these stubborn ranchers will only be reasonable and sell. The sound of a wolf howling sends a thrill through me. I want more than ever to settle here where there's game worth while. I love hunting."

The dog had crept slowly into the open, teeth bared, a low snarl breaking through.

Farren laughed. "You might start on a dog with wolf blood in it—that is, if it doesn't start on you first. It doesn't seem to like you, Collins. Perhaps it heard you threatening its half-brothers and doesn't like that. Even the wolves around here are apt to dislike a tenderfoot. . . . Or perhaps it thinks you're already a rancher, and anything that was Sam Dunlop's would bristle up at that."

Mahon had stolen a glance at Blue Pete. The half-breed sat with tight lips and set jaw.

"I'm not so easily scared as that," laughed Collins. "I've heard about the wolves, and I'm going to earn the gratitude of you ranchers by shooting a few of them. I hear they're thick in the Cypress Hills. It may be one way for a tenderfoot to get accepted around here." He moved nearer to the Sergeant. "What, no scarlet tunic? I thought the very success of the Mounted Police depended on scaring everyone with scarlet. All the pictures—"

"You saw scarlet in town," interrupted the Sergeant shortly. "When we're working we dress for it. You should widen your reading, Collins. It isn't the Mounted Police for the most part who write Westerns. By the way, you'd better keep an eye on that dog."

For the dog had edged out from behind the Sergeant's horse and was creeping nearer Collins from behind.

The latter turned quickly and kicked. The dog easily evaded the boot but did not retreat. Snarling more angrily than ever, it lay close to the ground, as if about to leap.

Collins read the threat and stepped quickly back. "Did I hear him say he was leaving that brute here, Farren? Surely you won't let him."

"I take it the Inverted T still belongs to Don Farren," said Mahon icily.

Collins smiled ruefully. "It's his until he accepts my offer—if he ever does. Just now he's joined the conspiracy to hold me off. Isn't there an anti-trust law in Canada? This is the fourth ranch I've offered to buy. I haven't had— Damn that brute!" He lashed out at the dog again. "It's too dangerous to have around."

"Nevertheless," said Farren, "if the Sergeant wishes it stays here till he finds another home for it." He added then, remembering Western hospitality: "Of course I'll keep it where it won't harm my guests . . . so long as they don't annoy it." He turned to the Sergeant. "Jerry the Pole will look after it till you find someone to take it." The dog rose and, still crouched, its eyes fixed on Collins, moved purposefully towards him. Collins recoiled, at the same time whipping out an automatic.

Before he could do so much as aim it Blue Pete had his own .45 out. "No, stranger, reckon yuh ain't shootin' it, not while I'm lookin'. 'Tain't the dog's fault it don' like yuh. I don't neither."

At the sound of the half-breed's voice the dog stopped, one paw raised, as if awaiting the order to attack.

Collins' face reddened with anger. "What are you butting in for, you damned—"

It was Mahon stopped him. The Sergeant had leaped from his horse and had caught the hand that held the gun, wrenching the weapon free.

"You're new around here, Collins, too new for your own good." The words came like the stacatto snap of a machine gun. "I've had occasion to remind you of that before, you and your friend. Most of us carry guns around here, but we don't like a tenderfoot to wave one about. We've reasons for going armed. You haven't—that I know of. I'll keep this gun of yours till you get some common sense. There can't be any legitimate reason for you to carry one."

"But—but—"

A coyote howled sardonically from far to the south, and it set the hounds going beyond the ridge. A whole pack of coyotes took up the clamour. At the first note Collins had started visibly, and he controlled himself with difficulty. He tried to laugh it off, but the sound was unconvincing. "Even the coyotes jeer at us," he said. "I confess it startled me. I was badly bitten by a dog when I was a kid, and I've never liked any of the breed since. That's one reason why I'm going to take it out on their cousins, the wolves, before I leave, whether I get a ranch or not. Even a coyote makes my hair stand on end."

He was striving to relieve the tension, and his companion came to his aid: "It's all new to us, Sergeant, you see—all these sounds, and the vast silences and all that."

Mahon had control of himself. "We're usually not so rough with newcomers, Collins, perhaps because they usually lie low until they learn more of the ways of the country. That's where you made a mistake. It happens that we have our ways, our habits—and the Mounted Police are here for good and sufficient reasons. That is something you'll learn—if you stay with us." He looked down on the gun in his hand, studying it thoughtfully. "By the way, you drew too swiftly for one unaccustomed to using a gun. How's that?"

Collins laughed. "Just a little knack of mine. I belong to a revolver club at home, and I practised the draw. We have a few accomplishments back there."

"I can see that—such as they are. Thanks for showing us so soon, we always like to know. . . . Since you appear no stranger to a gun I'll let you have it back. You may need it for that wolf-hunt. At any rate you're not likely to shoot yourself."

He returned it, and Collins flipped it out of sight with a dexterous movement. There was a touch of scorn in the laugh that went with it, a laugh that convinced the Sergeant that he had been too lenient.

"A bit of advice," he offered. "It would be better to carry the gun in plain sight. We all do, except in town. It means that we carry it for legitimate purposes. A cowboy carries a gun for many reasons, not the least of which is to shoot his mount if he should be thrown and left with a foot caught in the stirrup. You'll have to ride, of course." He started to mount, but with a foot in the stirrup he turned. "Another word: The dog is Farren's responsibility while it's here. He'll keep it where you needn't be rough with it." He glanced at the dog. It stood with one paw still raised. "I don't doubt that it could give a good account of itself against anything but a gun. . . . And a warning: Animals have many seconds of activity even after they're shot through the heart. That applies to wolves as well as to dogs."

Farren said: "You're not going on to-night, are you, Sergeant? You'll stop the night—"

"No, we're pushing on through to the Hat. This sort of thing can't wait. The bodies there," pointing to the buckboard, "must be examined as soon as possible." Collins took a single step towards the buckboard. "The—bodies? You mean—someone's—dead—there?"

"Two of them," Farren told him. "A new settler and his wife. Murdered!"

Collins looked dazed. "You mean—someone—killed them?" He laughed uneasily. "No wonder you all carry guns . . . or should you? Someone must have used one—for what he considered good reason. What do the Mounted Police think of that?"

"That it's murder," snapped the Sergeant. "And out here we find the murderer and punish him."

Collins turned to his friend. "Looks as if we'd better think again before we get a ranch and settle down here."

"Afraid of getting shot—or of being found out?" inquired Farren with a laugh.

"It's always wise to think twice about anything," said Mahon. "It saves trouble."

"And," he murmured to Blue Pete as they rode away, "if he dare shoot that dog he'll answer to Don Farren, then to me. . . . He's the sort of fellow we don't want in the West; he'd never make friends here. I don't like him."

"Ef he shoots that dog," Blue Pete promised grimly, "I won't wait fer Don Farren er fer you."

IX INSPECTOR BARKER ASKS

THE long night ride into Medicine Hat ordinarily would have been no unusual strain for any of the four who attended the buckboard with its tragic burden. Night-time was favoured for long prairie travel during the warm months, to escape the heat and the blinding rays of the sun. For weeks at a time the summer sky is cloudless over the prairie, an unbroken glare for sixteen to eighteen hours a day, an almost shocking radiance aggravated by the vast expanse of dead yellow grass.

To Blue Pete, so far as his activities were concerned, day and night had ever been little different, and the Mounted Police were on duty twenty-four hours a day. To the Indians, with no duties, no responsibilities, time meant nothing, and at any rate the pair the Sergeant was taking with him to the town were too frightened and anxious to protest.

The only delay occurred at Turner's Crossing, where the Sergeant stopped long enough to telephone the Inspector at his home in town.

The strain on them was not from the long ride but from other causes. Blue Pete was worried. The discovery of the bodies had impressed him deeply, and only vaguely did he understand why. The picture of the dead woman's face haunted him through the dark hours of the night, try as he might to keep his mind from it. Something else troubled him as well. He could think of so many things he might have done to prevent the crimes, things he had considered and rejected as promising unnecessary trouble. And the day's delay in riding to town accused him.

Sergeant Mahon was tense and silent, the brutal nature of the crimes, and the thought that suspicion could be directed only to the ranchers with whom he lived, whom he met every day and most of whom he liked, bearing down heavily on him. He knew they were none too particular about ownership of cattle, but he could in his mind connect none of them with such cruel murders. He saw, too, something of the difficulties the Mounted Police faced in running down the murderer. Everyone, however shocked and innocent, would be ranged against him. Dunlop had been about to do an unforgivable thing, an act that was to them akin to murder. Now everyone would be close-mouthed, guarded, antagonistic where search was made for the guilty one. It was so easy for them to think of the man's death as justified. The woman? He did not know where they would stand in that in the long run.

The Indians, one slouched over the reins in the buck-board, the other riding beside him and leading the free pony, kept glancing at the dim figure of the Sergeant throughout the long ride. There was fear and apology in their eyes. It might mean that, innocent, they still did not blame him for suspecting them. Or it might mean that, guilty, they hoped to earn some consideration by their docility. Their association with the Mounted Police was always an uneasy one, even though the red-coats did so much to make life freer and more secure for them.

At intervals Blue Pete managed to shake himself free from his sombre reflections. More than once Mahon heard him chuckle, and in some impatience he inquired the reason.

"It's Whiskers," the half-breed explained. "Th' ole gal's sorta lonesome sence we left the dog back thar. She sorta took to him, an' she's astin' why we left him. I bin tryin' to tell her but she ain't satisfied."

The Sergeant laughed. He knew the pinto only less well than did her owner, knew the almost human relationship that existed between the pair, the uncanny intelligence of the little spotted creature. "Then why don't you get a dog for her, Pete?"

The half-breed considered it. "Reckon it wudn' do. Thar's too many times a dog'd be in the way—things I do an' the ridin' I do. . . . It's hard 'nuff keepin' Whiskers 'n' me hid when we do' wanta be seen, 'thout hevin' to think of a dog I ain't got control of like a bronc."

"Perhaps if you had a dog you'd find some reason to remain settled."

"Why shud I? Thar ain't nothin' needs me at the 3-Bar-Y . . . 'ceptin' Mira o' course. An' she'd git tired o' me. . . . When I settle it'll be in a long box—ef they kin find whar I got to."

"Reading your own future, eh?"

"Shure I know I'm goin' to git it—a bullet. Some day all the shootin' ain't goin' to be from my .45."

"Stop talking like that. When you settle down the Inspector'll be sorry. You're useful to us the way you are, free to come and go—and liking the going."

They rode for a long time in silence. Far away on both sides of them coyotes howled, and their howls were like a dirge to the two white men, as if the brutes knew—as they certainly did—what was

54

passing along the trail. The starlight made the night clear in the few hours of sunless sky. The brown dust from the double ruts of the trail, modern adaptation of an ancient buffalo trail, raised by the wheels of the buckboard and the hoofs of the horses settled thickly over them.

At Turner's Crossing the Sergeant stopped long enough to telephone the Inspector at his home.

During one of their short rests the Sergeant said: "I'm betting the Inspector'll want you to work on this case, Pete, It'll be a tough nut for us to crack alone. Whoever killed those poor people will keep quiet about it. They'll know we're out to run them down, and the only clue we can hope for is someone's loose talk. There'll be no loose talk, because the ranchers and the cowboys will all be backing the murderer in the crisis, however the affair may shock them. You can go among them and listen to what they say. We can't. They won't talk within our hearing."

Blue Pete was uncomfortable. "Yuh seem dead sartin it was ranchers done it." He would have given much to hear the Sergeant deny it, though he could not see how that was possible.

The Sergeant felt the same: "Who else could have done it? . . . It might not be the ranchers themselves, but it must be someone connected with the cows."

"I ain't doin' nothin' in this fer the Mounties," Blue Pete grunted.

"What do you mean?" To Sergeant Mahon it was akin to treason. They had dismounted to rest and stood some distance from the Indians, so that they could not be heard. "Surely you want to know who did such a horrible thing! Don't tell me you'd protect the murderer, even if he is a fellow-rancher."

"I ain't doin' nothin' in this fer the Mounties," the half-breed repeated stubbornly.

With a shrug Mahon gave the order to move on. After all it was not his business to decide what his half-breed friend should do; that was for the Inspector. But he was hurt and worried about it, and he rode to the head of the little procession and remained there until they reached the outskirts of the town in the early morning.

With orders to the Indians to drive directly down Main Street to the Mounted Police barracks he dropped back to ride beside the half-breed. It was almost seven o'clock, and few were on the streets as yet, but the procession, headed by the Indians, one driving the buck-board that had something suggestive stretched beneath a brightly-coloured blanket in the rickety frame, brought everyone who passed to a halt to watch and wonder. Blue Pete, too, and a Mounted Policeman beside him! There was something in it for the imagination to develop into the wildest kind of gossip.

Mahon had considered dropping Blue Pete outside the town, since their companionship was certain to arouse suspicion, but word of the part he had played in the discovery of the crimes would quickly spread, and to let him go now would be even more suggestive to some sort of understanding.

They followed Main Street through the shops and passed over the railway tracks to the gate of the corral behind the barracks. The gate was open for them, with Priest and Langley waiting excitedly inside.

The Inspector had been there an hour, waiting for them. Outwardly calm, the fact that he had left his office door open showed how anxious and impatient he was. He was nervous, too, and apprehensive. Not infrequently he had been forced to take stern measures with some of the ranchers, even the most important in the district. So long had they had the prairie to themselves that they had come to think they owned it. So long had the position of the oldtimer been recognized that there were occasions when they were inclined to think themselves above the law. Few had any confining compunctions against a modified form of rustling—picking up calves whose mothers had permitted them to wander, rebranding cows whose true brands had become indistinct—yet they were the backbone of the country, most of them well educated and in general law-abiding, all wealthy and important. With almost all of them, he was on the friendliest of terms, though it was understood that he never permitted that to interfere with his enforcement of the law—with such allowances as conditions warranted. But murder was different, murder of the vilest kind. He could see himself driven to action repugnant to him, and some friend was certain to suffer.

He heard the pair advancing along the hall and he called to them to enter.

Mahon pushed Blue Pete before him and took his stand inside the door.

The Inspector looked around. "Where are the Indians?"

"I left them, sir, with Constable Priest."

"And the bodies?"

"They're still in the buckboard, sir. Langley is looking after them."

The Inspector jabbed thoughtfully at the blotter pad on his desk with a paper-knife. "You've sure spoiled my sleep for many a night, Mahon. I got up right away after you called up. The doctor will be here any minute, though I don't see what he can do for us. . . . Better get the bodies into the back room where he can examine them. Did you find anything more than you mentioned over the phone—anything in the form of a clue?"

"Not a thing, sir. I looked about in the time I had, but I wanted to get the bodies in as quickly as possible. Besides, I had the Indians. There was nothing whatever I could connect with the crimes. . . . For one thing, there was no sign of robbery."

"What did you expect?" demanded the Inspector scornfully. "Ranchers aren't robbers, not that sort of robbers." He laughed bitterly. "And so it has reached the point where I qualify robbery! They might be rustlers but not robbers, in the ordinary meaning of the word. They might even descend to murder but they wouldn't rob. Oh, no! Ridiculous thought . . . ridiculous distinction. Even a Mounted Policeman can find something to laugh at in that." He cleared his throat noisily. "I'm not saying it was ranchers did it—not yet. It's just one of the possibilities. . . . What in hell the others are I can't imagine."

He turned to Blue Pete. "You found the bodies, the Sergeant told me. How did you come to be there?"

It was a question for which the half-breed should have been prepared, and he thought he was until the Inspector put it. Instead he snuffled and wiped the back of his hand across his lips. "I was—jes' ridin'—"

Inspector Barker interrupted with a muttered curse. "Stop it, Pete. You've more to tell me than that. You were in town day before yesterday. You must have gone straight out there. Corporal Simmons tells me you were at Turner's Crossing for the night and did a bit of talking.

"Now do some talking to me. If the murders were committed the day before yesterday it lets you out." He saw Blue Pete's lips fall apart in utter amazement. "Oh, don't misunderstand. I'm not even hinting you could have played any part in it, but we have to examine every angle, every possibility. Everyone around here thinks you capable of almost anything; it would ruin your reputation if they thought otherwise. An alibi will be useful to you, and I can give it.

"Now you weren't just riding when you visited Dunlop's place and came on the bodies. Don't waste my time telling me that. Come on, Pete, what happened—and why?" He straightened violently, and the old swivel chair shook and rattled dangerously. "Good God, Pete, this is murder. Don't beat about the bush. What were you doing at Sam Dunlop's place."

The dirty grey Stetson in the half-breed's hands fumbled over and over. "I—I went to see Sam."

"What about?"

"I—I was affeerd."

"For him, you mean. You never were afraid for yourself. Why were you afraid for him? "

"Wal, he was fencin' off Big Slough, an' that 'ud be mighty nasty fer the cows."

"Yes, yes. Go on. It wouldn't hurt your cows; you're too far west. Are you telling me you went to threaten him?" The Inspector had darted his lean body forward and sat glaring at the half-breed.

"I wasn' doin' no threatenin'. I thought mebbe I cud show him wot it 'ud mean to the cows, an' how he needn' do it, not fer his own good."

"It wouldn't be for his own good, you mean. Why, that's a threat."

Blue Pete frowned. "I didn' mean that. I meant it wudn' do him no good to fence the slough off; it 'ud be jes' as useful left 'thout a fence . . . I thought mebbe I cud talk him out of it."

Inspector Barker snorted. "Good lord, I'll wager every rancher within fifty miles has tried to talk him out of it—and they all failed." Again he jerked himself forward; it was a habit that was apt to upset the calm of anyone he interviewed. "You went with more than that in mind."

"Wal, I heerd say thar was apt to be trouble. The cowmen wasn' goin' to stand fer it."

"Who wasn't going to stand for it?"

"Everybody."

"You're trying to protect someone, Pete. You knew there was going to be trouble, that someone had threatened it if Dunlop fenced Big Slough. Who was it?"

Blue Pete shifted from foot to foot. "Everybody," he repeated.

58

"Damn you, Pete, this is too serious to keep anything back."

"I ain't keepin' nothin' back, nothin' I knowed fer shure. I heerd thar'd be trouble, so I went to warn him."

The Inspector was silent for several uncomfortable moments. "You were in town two days ago. What brought you here? Is there any sense in anyone hinting that it might have been to establish an alibi?"

Blue Pete drew a sharp breath, as if a sudden pain had darted through him. It showed in his face. "Shure I was here. An' ef I hadn' bin sech a durn coward thar mebbe wudna' 'a' bin no murders. I started out to warn him, an' I hadn' the guts to do it right off. Mebbe . . . mebbe 'cause Mira warned me I'd git into trouble over it. I put it off; I come to town. I got cold feet. . . . Musta bin then they was killed."

The Inspector's manner softened. "Nobody could blame you for that, Pete. It wasn't a pleasant job to take on—particularly for you."

"Mebbe nobody else wud blame me but I blame myself. I knowed all the time I shuda gone straight thar."

"But you can't be certain when it happened," the Inspector soothed. "If it had already happened before you arrived you'd have been under a dreadful suspicion. Yes, even if it had happened soon afterwards. And you know how prone this part of the West would be to blame you." He straightened, seeming to shake himself back to another line of thought. "The point now is that we must lose no time in getting to work. We can take it that the murderer or murderers left no adequate clues; they'd have all the time in the world to destroy them, since no one was apt to visit the place. We're up against intelligent murderers who had the whole thing carefully planned. Ranchers wouldn't go into a thing like that without every move planned."

He sank back in the old chair and thought for a time, then he turned to the Sergeant. "Mahon, you're going right back. You didn't have time to make a thorough examination. This time don't miss a nook or cranny. I haven't much hope but we mustn't neglect a thing. Take the day to rest and start this evening. You can stop at Turner's Crossing for the night. I don't think anyone would dare visit the place for a few days. . . . There never was a crime that left no clue."

Mahon nodded. "I'll start this evening, sir. I'm not very tired. . . . I—I was wondering if Blue Pete couldn't help us."

The Inspector regarded the half-breed reflectively. "No," he said at last. "Pete, you'd better stay out of this, strictly out of it, at least until we have to call to you for help—which I hope we never have to do. I don't want you to make yourself more unpopular with the ranchers. We need you too much for that. We'll try to do this ourselves. So keep out of it."

"I seen that woman," Blue Pete growled.

"Yes, yes." The Inspector scowled at him. "It must have been a shock, but we'll finish this thing ourselves."

"I shuda went straight thar."

The Inspector struck the desk with his fist. "I mean what I say: Stay out of this."

Blue Pete's teeth clamped together, but he said nothing. The Inspector's mind was elsewhere the next moment. "There'd be several ranchers more interested than others in that fence. We must tackle them first." He spoke as if to himself. "Some of them we might convince ourselves are capable of it . . . and others we couldn't think would do it. But nothing is impossible in a cow-country where the lives of the cows are concerned. Check me on these, Mahon: There's Don Farren, of the Inverted T. He—"

"But, sir, we stopped at the Inverted T to leave the dog. I watched Don. I'm convinced it was news to him."

The Inspector nodded. "Yes, Farren seems to be one of the least likely. He's still too English to stand for such lawlessness. But we can't afford to neglect anyone. He's quick-tempered and stubborn. . . . Then there's Slim Manson, of the Diamond K. He was in that nasty affair we had before with a would be farmer.[1] But one would think that the narrow escape he had that time would make him more careful. . . Cooney Featherstone? I can't believe the Double Bar-Y owner's sense of humour would permit such a thing . . . Ford Welch, of the Double X? He might be capable of anything for profit. Then there's Jim Allen of the T-Inverted R. . . . That about covers the more intimately interested, doesn't it? Of course there's Scotty Runyan, of the Lazy M. Might be something there. And Ross Middleton, of the Triangle H. . . . That covers the lot, I think."

Mahon said: "I was wondering, sir, if we mightn't go a little further. What about the cowboys? To them the fencing of Big Slough would be a personal affront. They might act on the spur of the

---

[1] *The Vengeance of Blue Pete.*

moment, goaded by something Dunlop might say. He was defiant and stubborn, you know. Some of these outfits might take it more seriously even than their masters."

Inspector Barker nodded. "That's right . . . and it makes our task that much more difficult." He sighed. "I still feel the ranchers themselves must be mixed up in it somewhere, if not the actual murderers."

There was silence in the room before he spoke again:

"In the meantime we must try to find out something about Sam Dunlop and his wife. Where did they come from? You know, Mahon, we've found out nothing about them. Dunlop brought cash and put it in the bank, or we might trace them back from there. . . . There's something odd about that, too. Besides, why did he settle away out there?"

Someone passed before the window. "Oh, there's the doctor now. If there's a bullet in either of the bodies we'll find it. You have the Indians' rifles, of course?"

"Yes, sir."

"We'll take a look at the bodies now, with the doctor. Then we'll have a talk with the Indians. You, Mahon, get your rest and be off."

He started for the door but turned and frowned at Blue Pete. "Remember what I said, Pete: I want you to stay out of this. You wouldn't be much use to us if the ranchers got really down on you, if they got the idea you were helping us." He left the room.

Mahon and Blue Pete followed. Mahon eyed his companion doubtfully.

"You heard what the Inspector said, Pete?"

The half-breed nodded, but his teeth were tight together. Suddenly they parted. "But I cuda stopped it ef I hadn' bin sech a durn coward. . . . An' I seen that woman!"

ALL through the day Blue Pete hung about the Royal Hotel, uneasy and unsettled. Now and then he went out into South Railway Street where Inspector Barker was bound to see that he was still in town. Red, the bartender, noticed it but for a time said nothing. Finally, when the half-breed was seated at his usual table in the dining-room for the evening meal, he handed over the bar duties to J.J., his assistant, and went to have his own meal. Seating himself, he proceeded to butter a slice of bread.

Finally he said: "Rather nasty bit of work out your way, Pete. That new settler affair smells bad."

"The dirtiest piece of work I ever seen, Red," growled Blue Pete. "Yuh shuda seen that woman." It was as if something inside had given way and let him talk. "The skunks shot her from behind fust an' she fell ag'in the stove. Then they—struck her. Ugh! Mighty near made me sick." He dropped his knife and rested his chin on his closed fists.

Red looked him over with puzzled eyes. "Musta been pretty bad to make *you* feel that way—after what you've seen."

"I ain't seen women smashed up like that, never before, an' I do' wanta ag'in." He dropped his hands, and the clenched fists lay on the tablecloth. "If I cud find out who done it I'd—I'd—oh, I wudn' shoot him; that's far too easy fer that skunk. I'd stick a knife in his ribs an'—an' twist it . . . slow . . . givin' him time to 'member wot he done." He had picked up a knife from the table and was slowly turning it about.

Red touched his hand and looked nervously about the almost empty dining-room. "For the love of Mike put that knife down." He tried to laugh. "I didn't do it; honest I didn't." He leaned forward and eyed Blue Pete gravely. "You know, I suppose, there's some in town think the Mounties have got you mixed up in it."

"Shure," said Blue Pete calmly. "I am." Then his teeth closed tightly. "I'm mixed up in it—till they find who done it. Yuh ain't heerd any talk that 'ud help, hev yuh, Red?"

"Them that did a thing like that ain't likely to talk."

"But when tha're drunk they might let it out . . . I wanta git thar 'fore the Mounties."

The bar-tender looked puzzled. "What's the big idea? If you want so bad to find out—"

"I ain't got the patience to wait till the law gits workin'. Thar's too many chances of a slip-up . . . an' it might be too hard to prove in court. The skunk shudn' hev a chance."

"But how could you be sure if it couldn't be proved?"

Blue Pete made a scornful sound. "Gor-swizzle, I'd know. I gotta git that woman outa my head, an' I can't till we git the one wot done it. Ef the Mounties got to the skunk fust—" He stopped and crammed his mouth full of potato.

"You're in for trouble along that line, Pete," Red warned. "You can't buck the Mounties for long." He leaned nearer and whispered: "Do you think it's one of the neighbouring ranchers?"

"Thar ain't nobody else to do it, as I see."

"No, I suppose not, but it's too awful to think of . . . I've heard the boys at the bar talking about what was going to happen to that fence if he ever tried to put it up."

"Did they say wot 'ud happen to Dunlop?"

Red did not reply for a few moments, and when he did he picked his words with care: "I don't remember that. But it doesn't call for much imagination, does it? If Dunlop persisted, what do you think the punchers would do? Sneak away and let him do it? Not likely, and you know it."

They fell to eating, and for a time neither spoke.

Suddenly Red looked up. "Have you seen any more of that Biff Collins? I've been going to warn you about him. He's mean. He'd shoot you in the back as quick as wink. . . . Too bad the Sergeant butted in that night. You'd have done a bit of dustin' with him before you were through. You were sure mad. He asked for it."

"I shudn 'a' done nothin'—not like that, leastwise. But I jes' cudn' stand that grin o' his. I fly off half-cocked. That's me . . . I seen him at the Inverted T, an' thar was no shootin'." He smiled. "Thar mighta bin, but it blew over. I reckon he ain' got no reason fer likin' me no better sence. We jes' seem to butt heads when we git together. He's that kind." After a pause he added: "So 'm I. But I ain't botherin' none 'bout him. It's—that woman."

"Well, take my advice and don't turn your back on him if he has a gun."

Blue Pete grinned. "Ain't nobody told yuh, Red, I got eyes so crossed I kin see around my head?"

"Don't try to laugh it off," Red persisted. "I heard him tell his friend that he doesn't take from anyone what you did to him."

"He took it."

"He's left the hotel, and we're glad."

"Makes it safer fer everybody," laughed the half-breed. Then his face sobered and he returned to eating.

Red regarded him uneasily. "What's on your mind, Pete? Have you made up your mind to go about this thing alone? Have you thought what might happen?"

The half-breed wiped his lips with the back of his hand and rose. "I ain't thinkin' o' nothin' but that woman, the way I seen her."

He left the room, and Red watched him go with shaking head.

Out in the lobby he seated himself before a window from which he could see the Mounted Police barracks across the railway tracks. When he saw the Sergeant emerge and stroll across the railway tracks he retired to a dark corner of the lobby and picked up an illustrated magazine. A few moments later the Sergeant entered from the street. There were two other guests in the lobby, and Mahon passed through without speaking. He went on down the hall and out through the back door to the stable-yard. He did not return, so that he must have continued through the gate to Main Street.

Blue Pete smiled. He understood. It had been no casual visit.

He returned to his seat before the window and presently saw the Sergeant re-enter the barracks. Ten minutes later he appeared on Jupiter around the corner of the barracks and rode across the railway tracks.

Blue Pete hurried through the hotel into the yard and saw him ride up Main Street and disappear over the cutbank to the south.

For a time he paced about the yard. A couple of cowboys from the Diamond K rode into the yard, stabled their broncos, and disappeared into the hotel without speaking to him. It was evident that the whole district knew of the murders, knew, too, something of his connection with them.

Suddenly he stopped and his eyes lighted up. Hastily he re-entered the hotel, called Red from the bar, paid his bill, and bustled back to the stable. Whiskers greeted him with a welcoming whinny and shifted about restlessly until the saddle was on her back.

"No hurry, ole gal," he murmured. "We gotta give him a good start; we do' wanta let him know we're comin'. It'll be dark in a coupla hours, then we kin make time. . . . Don' rightly know wot I'm goin' to do, but I'm itchin' to git at it. I gotta do suthin'. I jes' can't git that woman outa my head."

He idled for several minutes, his hand on the pinto's back, while she nibbled impatiently at him. He hesitated at setting out while it was still so light. Inspector Barker would still be at his desk before the barracks window and would see him. Perhaps if he waited the Inspector might leave and go home.

In the end he could delay no longer. Darkness would not help him for another two hours, and he could not wait long without pushing Whiskers more than he cared. As a group of cowboys rode into Main Street from South Railway Street, passing the gate, he joined them, hoping to escape notice that way. They eyed him suspiciously but said nothing. Did they suspect him of the murders, or did they blame him for bringing in the Mounted Police?

At Fourth Avenue he turned west; it would cut him off from the barracks windows. At Toronto Street he swung once more to the south. He rode slowly. In the clear Western air he would be visible for many miles up on the prairie level, but if he could reach a point on the trail about a mile from the town he would be out of sight for two miles where the trail followed a depression.

At the crest of the cutbank he stopped. As far as he could see along the trail was no sign of life, and he decided Sergeant Mahon must still be moving along the part of the trail below the prairie level. Much depended on that. If he were there it proved that he was in no hurry, that he planned to spend the night at the Police hut at Turner's Crossing, as the Inspector had suggested.

He waited, growing more and more impatient. Then Mahon rose into view, a mere speck on the horizon. The half-breed sighed with relief. Waiting below the cutbank for another half hour, he resumed his way. There was little likelihood that he would be seen now, and he trusted to his own eyes being keener than the Sergeant's. That the latter was keeping an eye on him was proven by that visit to the Royal Hotel before leaving town.

When it was dark—and darkness falls swiftly in the West almost like a curtain—he sent the pinto into a long lope. The twenty-five miles to Turner's Crossing the Sergeant would cover in something more than three hours, at the speed he had set.

When he reached a point about a mile from the Police hut he left the trail and struck around over the prairie to the west. Riding slowly, he knew the thud of the pinto's hoofs would not carry as far as the hut, in spite of the way sound carries on the prairie at night. At a trail branching to the east he hesitated. To follow it would bring him back to the main trail that led to several of the more important ranches whose herds would be interested in Big Slough. To the west the trail ran back toward the 3-Bar-Y—to lead him out of trouble. The Inspector wished that.

But he had no thought of doing in this case what the Inspector wished—or as Mira would advise. Even delay irritated him now, and he turned towards the main trail.

"Gittin' us into more trouble, ole gal," he told the pinto, "but I reckon you 'n' me can't stop now. We gotta find out a lot o' things, an' do it fast. We ain't got time to go slow like the Mounties."

He reached the main trail and followed it for some time. Another trail branched to the east. The part that led onwards was growing more and more indistinct until finally it would fade into the pitiful marks left by Sam Dunlop's buckboard. Almost with the first glint of daylight the Dunlop trail set off towards the east and slowly he turned into it.

He was in no hurry now. It would be hours before the Sergeant would be along, and he had a little thinking of his own to do. Besides, the picture of those lonely little mud buildings and of the crimes he had stumbled on there made him hesitate to repeat the visit. . . . He remembered the dog. Strange creature—half wolf, he would say. And it seemed to have taken strangely to him and Whiskers. Collins it disliked intensely. Probably it had been raised in the West and hated the tenderfoot, just as the oldtimer did. But it had not been any too friendly towards Don Farren. A smile lit up his face as he remembered the way the animal had clung to him. Another friend.

The pleasure of it faded suddenly before the memory of his cowardice in turning off to the Hat when if he had gone straight to the homestead— It rankled with him, accused him—and even now he was loitering. With a tightening of the reins he sent the pinto into a brisker pace.

Just before reaching the depression where Dunlop had erected his pitiful home something made him draw in and sit and listen. He could not be certain that he had heard anything, yet something had startled him. Whiskers, too, was excited. For a time he heard nothing, then he straightened and gathered up the reins.

"Yep, ole gal, we didn' come none too soon. Somebody's ahead of us. Thar's things doin'. They won't be lookin' fer nobody to butt in—but we're goin' to do it an' do it hard." His eyes flashed angrily.

He swung off to the south across the prairie, keeping away from the slope that he might not be seen from the bottom of the depression. He could hear movement now, odd, furtive movement. There were no voices, and that made it more mysterious.

Dismounting, he crept to the edge of the slope. From behind a sage-bush he looked down.

BIG SLOUGH lay directly below him. Around one end a dozen cowboys worked in silence, swiftly, nervously. They were tearing away the barbed wire Dunlop had strung along the posts, snipping it with wire-cutters, here and there wrenching out a post. Their broncos were almost concealed in the trees at the base of the far slope. The wire they kicked into little heaps. A few posts lay on the ground.

The half-breed's face darkened with anger. Hurrying back to Whiskers, he mounted and tore down the slope, skirting about the end of the slough. He had his rifle in his hand—hands that knew better than anyone else's in the district how to use it.

The cowboys heard him coming and stopped their work. They did not run—it was too late for that—but they looked guilty and several dropped their tools. They crowded together, waiting in sullen silence for him.

He reached the nearest group and stopped. His rifle rested across the saddle, his right hand holding it ready for instant use. His .45 he had eased on his left hip, to be within more convenient reach.

They read the meaning of the two guns, and one or two made a movement as if to draw. Then they remembered that it was Blue Pete and their hands dropped free. He could always beat them to the draw, and now he was prepared.

The pinto slithered to a stop.

Blue Pete pointed towards their broncos. "Git the blazes outa here 'fore I make it so yuh can't, yuh dirty skunks."

One of the cowboys, an old fellow with the bowed legs of a life-time puncher, waddled towards him, raising his hands. Fitchy and Blue Pete were old friends. "What's the matter, Pete?" He spoke in a hurt tone. "You're a rancher yourself."

The half-breed scowled. "Yuh ain't the sorta puncher, Fitchy, to do this sorta thing—not now. 'Tain't decent."

"But we gotta git this fence down, Pete. There ain't no need of it, never was, an' now Dunlop's gone—"

"Yes, he's gone. An' him an' the missus ain't even buried yit. An' you durn skunks come an' tear things to bits 'fore tha're in the ground. Looks like yuh knowed they was goin' to be murdered an' was jus' waitin' fer it."

The cowboys reddened. "Hope yu don't think yu mean we done it, Pete."

"Someun done it, didn' they, an' it looks like yuh knowed it was bein' done, ef yuh didn' do it yerselves. Even ef yuh didn't, it's not much better to be tearin' thur things to bits when tha're in the Hat to be buried. Ef the Mounties ketched yuh yuh'd hev some 'splainin' to do."

The group before him had grown. A cowboy at the back called out: "You're just as much interested in Big Slough as we are, Pete, so watchu blowin' off yer head for? If yu don't know what Big Slough means to the cows, ask Tex." Tex was the 3-Bar-Y foreman.

Blue Pete's teeth came together hard. "I'm tellin' yuh to pack yer freight, an' I'm not waitin' much longer neither I'm blowin' off more'n my head in a minute—"

A shot ran out sharply from the top of the slope beyond, and a bullet whistled near enough to Blue Pete's head to be audible. Almost with the sound he was off the pinto, eyes blazing, his rifle pointing across the saddle.

Up the lope two riders were visible. They sat looking down into the hollow and did not move at the half-breed's threatening movement. Blue Pete watched them for a moment, then vaulted into the saddle and raced across the bottom and up the slope towards them.

They waited for him, unmoved. He pulled up before them. He was puzzled as well as angry. Slim Manson, one of the pair, smiled sardonically, and the half-breed knew the bullet had not been intended to hit him. Slim Manson was too good a shot to miss a sitting target at such an easy range.

"Reckon yuh bes' start talkin', Slim, an' you, Ford Welch. Them as shoots at me gotta be mighty smart at 'splainin'."

Manson shrugged. "You know I didn't shoot at you, Pete. I don't miss what I shoot at. What the hell are you interfering for down there?"

"Wot the blazes yuh interferin' 'th me fer?" countered the half-breed.

"You know that fence must come down—"

"Not while them two lie in the Hat, waitin' to be buried, an' I'll shoot it out 'th anybody says no. Bad 'nuff fer the punchers down thar, but fer you two it's jes'—jes' plumb dirty. Next to the skunks wot murdered them yuh're mighty close right now. Shure the fence'll come down, but 'tain't goin' to till it's decent. Wanta fight fer it?" he demanded, a hand on his .45.

They had no desire to fight. Besides, the hint that they might be suspected as the murderers made them more cautious.

Ford Welch said: "They say you found the bodies, Pete."

There was a suggestion in it and in the smile that went with it, and Blue Pete swallowed hard to keep control of himself. "Shure. An' I ain't likely to fergit it, 'thout you talkin' 'bout it. I—seen the woman. Reckon yuh got more dirt in yuh than I got ef yuh seen her an' kin talk 'bout it."

Ford Welch's face went red, and he reined up before the pinto. "What do you mean by that?"

Blue Pete's lip curled. "I don' say much I don't mean. An' yuh ain't skeerin' nobody, Ford. I'm tellin' yuh both that nex' to shootin' them two yuh're doin' things right now. Shure I'm intrusted in Big Slough, an' the fence is comin' down, but it's goin' to be done decent. The nex' puncher wot touches that wire's goin' to reckon 'th me, an yuh ain't goin' to stop it. Bes' keep that in mind ef yuh want yer punchers whole. Shure the fence is goin'. It's barb-wire, an' that's ag'in' the law, an' Sam Dunlop's dead. He was mean 'n nasty, but thar's a time to do things like this an' this ain't the time to mess up that lonely little coulee." He remembered the Inspector's warning. "An' when yuh stop to think yuh'll say the same. So bes' call 'em off pronto."

It left them silent and not a little ashamed. He saw that he had won and without another word he turned and rode back down the slope to the punchers who had waited for some sign from their two bosses. It came, and reluctantly they set off for their broncos.

Blue Pete watched them go. "Ef yuh're nifty yuh might git 'way 'fore the Mounties come, 'cause tha're on the way. Sergeant Mahon'll be here purty soon. An' when yuh're goin' yuh bes' keep to the coulees so he won't see yuh."

In three minutes not a cowboy was visible.

XII   CLUES

BLUE PETE remembered that he had not much time himself and he hurried back to the hut. There was much to do before the Sergeant came, and there was little time to do it. Before the hut he dismounted and, taking a long breath, opened the door and stepped into the shadowed room.

He had no idea what he was looking for, but Mahon had not had time to make a thorough inspection, and something might turn up, something that would help to direct the search. He felt like a conspirator, and it did not make him comfortable to remember that in a way he was working against his friend the Sergeant. But somehow the solving of the murders, and even the punishment of the guilty ones, seemed to depend on him. The ranchers were much too clever to give the Mounted Police much chance, with legal formalities and technicalities to handicap them.

He knew that the cowboys he had seen had not entered the cabin; they would have no stomach for that and there would be no reason for it. With Dunlop dead all that interested them was the fence.

The room was as he remembered it—and every detail was stamped on his memory. He saw the brown stain on the floor beside the stove and turned from it. He went to the chest of drawers. The Sergeant had gone through it hastily and apparently had found nothing.

He had drawn out the second drawer when a low whinny from Whiskers warned him. Hastily he closed the drawer and went to the door. Four mounted men were coming down the trail. Sergeant Mahon rode ahead, and behind came Don Farren and his two guests of two nights before.

At sight of Biff Collins the half-breed muttered a curse. Standing back in the room, he was not visible to the riders but the Sergeant saw that the door was open and he sent Jupiter swiftly forward. He had not hurried from Turner's Crossing, convinced that no one would dare to enter the hut whose door he had closed. The news of the murders would have spread, of course, and that in itself would keep everyone away. He had turned aside to the Inverted T for no good reason except that he wished to satisfy himself concerning the dog. Besides, Don Farren could be depended upon to help the investigation all he could. To have even one rancher on the side of the law in such a case would be valuable.

Farren had suggested that he ride along with the Sergeant, and Collins and his friend had leaped at the chance to get into the excitement.

Mahon dismounted. Blue Pete had come to the door, and the Sergeant frowned at him.

The half-breed laughed. "Thar ain't nothin' touched, Sergeant. I seen the twig yuh put ag'in' the door. It was still thar. Nobody'd bin in."

"How did you come to be here? I saw you in the Royal Hotel only last night. You must have ridden all night."

"Shure. You didn't. I like ridin'at night; it's when I do most of it. Shure yuh seen me at the Royal; that's wot yuh went thar fer. Then I come on here." He jerked a thumb towards the other three now almost up to them. "I see yuh brought yer friends. Didja need help?"

Mahon let the question pass. "How long have you been here?"

"Jes' a minute er two. Didn' hev time to steal the jools. Yuh come too quick fer that."

The Sergeant turned to the other three. "Wait out here for me."

Bill Collins had already dismounted and approached the door. At the order he turned back with a shrug. "You don't need to tell me to. Is it in there you found them? I wouldn't go in on a bet. Br-r-r! What a place to live! They must have been crazy. A perfect setting for a murder—sort of spooky. Is that the stable? Mind if we look in there?"

"I said to wait here," ordered the Sergeant.

He entered the hut. Blue Pete retreated before him and stood to one side, watching the search. Mahon made a quick survey of the room to satisfy himself that nothing had been touched, than he made straight for the chest of drawers. As he emptied the second drawer on the bed he became conscious of the half-breed's attentive eyes.

"What are you thinking of, Pete?"

The half-breed pointed to the rifle resting on the two pegs. "Can't understand that. Sam Dunlop alius carried it when he was out. He musta knowed wot they thought of him around here. Can't see how they managed to ketch him 'thout it."

The Sergeant came and stood beside him. "I've thought a lot about that. Every time I was here Dunlop had it with him. They must have waited around until they got him without it."

"He was shot from close up," said Blue Pete. "Them bullets went clean through."

72

"If he had no gun with him there was nothing to prevent them from getting close."

"Jes' the same 'tain't like a rancher to let himself be seen when it wasn't necessary."

The Sergeant nodded. "It looks as if they wanted to throw it in his teeth—what he was doing, I mean—to know why he was being shot. Otherwise he could have been picked off a thousand times from cover, and the rifle wouldn't have saved him . . . I don't understand it—when all the ranchers wanted was to stop the fence being built."

He reached up and lifted the rifle from the pegs. "I'll take it into town with me this time. It's a good rifle, too." He broke it and squinted through the barrel, and his head shook disapprovingly. "He wasn't much used to a rifle or he wouldn't leave it so dirty. It hasn't been cleaned since it was fired last . . . I wonder what he used it for."

He laid the rifle on the table and continued the search. As the minutes passed with no apparent results he grew worried and impatient. "There isn't a thing to go on, not a written word, not an address. One would think they didn't wish us to trace the murderers—or themselves." He replaced the last drawer and went to the stove to look inside. "Only wood ashes here, so nothing was burned recently." Then he laughed self-deprecatingly. "Of course not. They wouldn't prepare for their own deaths, and the ranchers would have no reason to clean away clues like that."

He turned to the homemade clothes cupboard. Blue Pete lost interest. He left the room and wandered towards the stable. He looked inside. The two horses had been stabled there, and their mangers were half full of grass. That was all. In the implement shed was nothing he had not already seen. Thinking heavily, he set off towards Big Slough. Don Farren and his guests had watched him at first and had then lost interest; now they lay on the grass before the hut, waiting for the Sergeant to finish.

The half-breed had not been unaware of them. He was glad to get away. The very sight of Biff Collins made him want to strike out. Always the fellow wore a smile when he looked at him, a smile that was a fighting smile to the half-breed. It was a sneer, as if recalling that childish scene on the streets of Medicine Hat that had first brought them together.

Passing around the smaller slough, he reached Big Slough. There he stood for a long time, his eyes bent unseeingly on the ground.

More and more poignantly he was aware of the fact that one or more of his neighbours, his fellow-ranchers, had committed what to him was a particularly brutal crime. Always he thought of the woman. The man was a newcomer who had to take his chances. He had done an inexcusable thing and had paid for it in the only way to stop him. But the woman was an entirely different matter. No matter what her husband had done it did not merit such a fate for her, such an awful death.

He shook himself out of it and wandered off to where they had found the horses. Two rolls of barbed wire still lay where Dunlop must have dumped them from the stone-boat. The cowboys had had no time to destroy them. About that side of Big Slough the single strand of wire had been strung along posts. Now loops of the cut wire were scattered about. A few of the posts had been collected as if to burn them.

He looked about, trying to visualize the attack. The murderers must have dismounted up on the prairie and crept down over there to the cover of the trees while Dunlop was busy about the stone-boat. They had waited until he was near, then they had walked boldly out and had shot him in cold blood from close range.

He set off to try to follow the course of the murderers after the crime. Dunlop had been shot only a few yards from where the horses stood. There were marks there of a struggle, with the ground scuffed about a little, as if the first shot had not incapacitated him and he had fought back. The murderers had then dragged him away to bury him beside the slough where the ground was soft and easy to dig. The cowboys that morning had not been near the spot and had not obliterated the marks.

He bent over the ground, every instinct of the hunter and trailer alert, the instinct of the Indian and something more. Yes, there had plainly been some sort of struggle. It would account for the two shots.

He discovered then that the fight had extended further than he at first thought. . . . And then he stopped and stared. There—before him—was the mark of the toe of a boot in the earth. Heel marks, too, but most heel marks were the same. That toe mark was different. .

He knelt over it for a long time, rivetting its shape in his memory. But there was more he could do and he set about doing it. He knew the mark had not been left by the cowboys. Hastening to the edge of the slough, he gathered up a handful of the mud and returned, to pack it carefully in the mark of the toe. Then he rested back on his heels, letting the heat of the sun dry the mud. In less than ten minutes it was hard and he carefully eased it from the mould. For a few minutes he let it dry further in the heat, then he thrust it guiltily in his pocket. With a foot he blotted out the mark and moved away.

There was no certainty that the cast he had would be of use. For one thing he could not be certain that the odd shape had not been made by a toe that shifted in the making. It was unnaturally wide for the ordinary riding-boot of the cowboy. It might have been made by Dunlop himself, but he did not think so. Even if it was a true record of the murderer's toe, how could he hope to trace it to its owner, and if he did what would it prove? Nevertheless it was a clue Sergeant Mahon had missed, and in that he felt that he had accomplished something.

The body had been dragged to where it was buried, but the weight of the body and the softness of the earth had effectively wiped out the footmarks of those who had dragged it, even if the work of the cowboys only an hour before had not done so. The spade they had used and returned to the stone-boat, of course, in the hope that the body would never be found.

He heard the Sergeant calling him and saw him coming. With a guilty feeling his hand flew to the pocket where he had thrust the cast, and he wondered if Mahon would notice the bulge it made. The Sergeant was coming swiftly, and in his eyes was a light that told of some important discovery during the search of the hut.

"Anything more here?" Mahon was trying hard to appear calm.

"Nothin' more I kin see."

The Sergeant wandered about. Suddenly he stopped and pointed.

"What's been going on here since we were here last."

"I bin walkin' about."

Mahon pointed to the coils of cut wire. "You didn't do that. You didn't rip up those posts in the few minutes you've been here." He picked up a strand of wire. Someone's had pliers here. They've been tearing down the fence. They couldn't wait."

"Didju expec' they wud? They do' want the cows to git tangled up—"

"So they cut it up so they'd get more tangled. Don't tell me that, Pete. They've been here and they've gone in a hurry. Perhaps they had a lookout and saw me coming. But you'd have seen them then."

Blue Pete saw he could conceal it no longer. "The boys 'a' bin here—jes' a while ago."

"You saw them?" Mahon inquired angrily.

"Shure. I seen 'em—an' I got 'em movin' pronto. Didn' seem jes' decent to be in sech a hurry."

"How did they know of the murders so quickly?"

The half-breed clacked his tongue. "This afternoon they'll know you 'n' me was here—the hull prairie'll know. You know how 'tis, Sergeant."

"Yes, and they might be in the best position to know of the murders," Mahon declared under his breath.

Blue Pete heard it. "Ef they killed 'em they wudn' show up here fer a long time. Yuh kin bet yer spurs on that. Thar's nothin' to get all worked up 'bout, Sergeant. They didn' go near the house."

"So you made them move on." The Sergeant shook his head gloomily. "They'll be sore. You know what the Inspector said: He doesn't want you to get into this."

"Thar's wuss things kin happen than that."

"What do you mean?"

"Ef they git 'way an' yuh don' ketch 'em."

"That's our concern."

"Shure . . . an' mine. I seen that woman."

The Sergeant studied his face anxiously for several moments but decided not to say more. After all it was the Inspector's business.

Presently Blue Pete asked: "Find anythin' in the house?"

"What I found is for the Inspector," replied Mahon sharply.

"Shure, shure." . . . After a pause he added to himself: "An' wot I found is fer me."

XIII   PREPARING THE GROUND

WHEN they rode away the Sergeant had Dunlop's rifle with him. He had wrapped it in a cloth he had found in the hut.

Biff Collins pointed to it. "What's that got to do with the murder?"

"I don't know that it has anything to do with it," replied the Sergeant, "but it's much too valuable a gun to leave lying about in an empty house. Besides, it needs cleaning."

Collins laughed; there was a teasing note in it. "I thought the first thing a Westerner in particular would do would be to clean his guns after using them. But of course I come from the East and can't be expected to know."

"There are some things," said Mahon deliberately, "that even an Easterner *can* be expected to know— though that is perhaps asking too much of you."

Collins was not disturbed. "If it could only talk! It must have looked on while those people were being killed. But perhaps the Mounties have ways of making even a rifle talk."

Mahon ignored it; he was angry with himself for yielding so readily to his dislike of the two strangers. He handed the rifle to Blue Pete. "Take a good look at it—as good as you can without handling it too much—and tell me if you're certain it's the one Dunlop always carried about with him. A Winchester .45—there are hundreds of them among the outfits. I never paid much attention to Dunlop's."

Blue Pete did not even take the weapon. "It's his awright."

"You seem to be mighty sure, to know a lot about it,"

Collins remarked. "Was he a friend of yours?"

"I seen him a coupla times. . . . He shure needed friends. . . . Ef I hadn' run away mebbe I'd 'a' bin here to stop—things."

" 'To stop things'? You mean the murders?" Collins edged his mount nearer.

"Shure. I was on my way to warn him, then I got sorta skeered an' run off to the Hat. Musta bin jes' the time when they was shot."

"At any rate it's a pretty good alibi," laughed Collins.

The half-breed looked him over, waiting to get himself under control. "I do' need no alibi. . . . It's the skunk wot done it—he's goin' to need more'n an alibi."

Collins threw up his arms in mock dismay. "Don't look at me. I didn't do it, honest."

No one laughed except his friend.

"Better leave alibis to the Mounted Police," Don Farren advised. "They usually know how much—or how little—they're worth. Out here we leave things like that to them. The best we can do in this case is to help, not joke about it."

"Of course." Collins was apologetic. "I can't help wondering, however, that so much is made of this when killings aren't unusual in the West, according to what I read, and not in the stories either."

"There's a difference between killing and murder," said Farren. "We distinguish, at any rate. This was murder, brutal and cold-blooded; and it isn't wise to suggest, even in fun, that anyone needs an alibi."

"Oh, I was only fooling, of course. Pete isn't any more capable of doing a thing like this than—than I am."

"I dunno nothin' 'bout you," muttered the half-breed.

"I hope you will some day, Pete—as a neighbour."

Don Farren turned his back. "What are you going to do about the dog, Sergeant? Those hounds of Jerry's are all the Inverted T can stand. They're useful for wolves, of course, but why didn't someone invent a barkless dog? That dog of Dunlop's sends them crazy with his howling. They think he's a wolf. Jerry, too. He got up last night, sure the wolves were around looking for his hounds. He had his rifle and he almost shot the dog before he remembered."

"I'll find someone to take it off your hands," promised Mahon.

"I'll take it." Blue Pete heard himself make the offer and was more surprised than anyone else. "He'll be comp'ny fer Mira," he explained in some confusion.

"I might borrow him when I go wolf-hunting in the hills, Pete," Collins laughed. "A dog with a howl like that would be valuable as a decoy."

"He'd eat you up and howl with joy afterwards," declared Farren. "How he does love you!"

"Oh, I'd get around him. He doesn't like Ted here any better than he does me. I suppose we're too new. The dog must be an old-timer." Collins laughed again. "I suppose I must admit I blow off a bit at times, but I'll learn. It's the first time I've been West. But every one of you was a tenderfoot once. . . . To tell you the truth, back East we have the idea that the West is still a little—raw, shall we say?"

"Say anything you like," said Mahon. "It isn't apt to arouse much discussion."

"It's a rawness that's becoming—and, I suppose, necessary," ventured Ted Fraleigh, Collins' friend.

" 'The wide open spaces,' I suppose you mean. It's a bromide that flows from every Easterner's lips, in their speech as in their books. Go on."

"I can see," offered Collins, "that you've habits out here that would never fit into the Eastern way of living, and you need them. In a way that's what attracts me. You can take that as a compliment— and Biff Collins isn't in the habit of paying compliments."

"Biff Collins is consistent, if nothing else," said Mahon shortly. "We always feel relieved when an Easterner shows that he's not entirely blind."

"Huh! I can see through a pail when the bottom's kicked out of it, as my dad used to say." Collins turned to Blue Pete. "I wasn't joking when I spoke of taking the dog on the wolf-hunt. I wish you'd come and bring him. If you're looking for a job I'd be glad to pay you. Farren here tells me you know the hills like a book, the only one who does. I have to confess I'm a bit impressed by that strange forest. I'm told one could get lost and never find his way out. The dog seems to like you; he'd probably do as you told him. I'd even dare to face him again if it promised to get me a wolf or two to brag about to my friends back East—if I have to go back. And you, Farren, you've promised me a bit of antelope hunting. I'm holding you to that."

Farren laughed none too comfortably. "I always keep a promise. Better try the wolves first and get your hand in. Hadn't you better settle with Blue Pete right now when you have him? He can show you more about hunting wolves than you'd ever learn otherwise. You notice he hasn't promised anything."

He winked at the half-breed, knowing what his answer would be.

"How about it then, Pete?" pleaded Collins. "You and I didn't hit it off the first time we met, but you can ascribe that to my tenderfoot inexperience. I'm anxious to learn everything about the West, and you can help me. If I'm staying here we've got to be friends, all of us." His eye fell on the rifle across Mahon's saddle, and he shuddered. "Apparently you all aren't friendly to one another. I got here in time to have a demonstration of that, but I'm not going to let that discolour the picture. Will you come, Pete?"

The half-breed appeared to consider, and Mahon and Farren

watched him with a twinkle in their eyes. As a matter of fact he *was* considering, himself surprised that he should. Every instinct urged him to throw the offer back in Collins' face, for more and more he was hating the fellow. Even the newcomer's attempts to be friendly were clumsy and insincere. But he wanted to keep in touch with him, though he could not imagine why. Something about him was puzzling, as if he was not what he seemed to be.

"Reckon I'm too busy jes' now," he decided. "Got lots to do around the 3-Bar-Y. Beef roundup'll be on soon now—jes' a month er two."

Don Farren pursed his lips but did not smile, and Sergeant Mahon looked steadily ahead. Everyone knew that the half-breed's duties about the 3-Bar-Y were unimportant. Mira and Tex ran the ranch.

"Now that's too bad. I'm disappointed." Collins was sincere at last. "I'd be willing to pay you well, of course."

"How much?" Blue Pete inquired.

"Oh . . . anything up to ten or twelve dollars a day, if you demand it."

Blue Pete nodded. "The 3-Bar-Y'll be sellin' 'bout fifteen hundred steers in two months—fer 'bout twenty dollars each."

Everyone laughed, including—tardily—Collins and Fraleigh.

"Oh, I didn't expect it would be a lure," Collins explained. "But I've no right to ask you to come without pay. Oh, well, if you won't, you won't. I suppose I can hire a couple of Indians. I'm told they sometimes bestir themselves to hunt wolves. By the way, the pair you rounded up that day you found the bodies—weren't they going wolf-hunting? They must know something about it. I'll look them up. I wouldn't like to tackle it alone, with Ted here. We're both—well—startled, to say the least, when that dog howls. Even the coyotes send the blood tingling up into my scalp. Not that I'm really scared, of course—"

"I am," said Mahon dryly.

"Thar's lots o' wolves to be skeered of in the hills," said Blue Pete. "An' thar's other things. It's a lonely place, an' thar's critters we ain't seen yet but on'y heerd. In the night it's mighty skeery. . . . Reckon the wolves is the wust."

"Are you trying to frighten me before I go?" laughed Collins.

"Yuh'll be frightened when yuh do go," declared the half-breed. "Ef yuh ain't yuh shudn' settle down in a sleepy place like the West.

Things in the hills is the wust we kin offer yuh. I'm tellin' yuh a timber-wolf is the skeeriest critter God ever made. It's got a howl like a crowd of devils, an it flits 'bout like a ghost, on'y it's a durn sight more dangerous. . . . Then thar's critters look like men but don't act like the men most of us know; they hide in thar, an' tha're apt to shoot fust a' then find out wot they shot at. Mostly tha're rustlers."

Collins watched him soberly but when he noticed the eyes of the others on him he tried to laugh it off. "It takes a lot to frighten Biff Collins, Pete. . . . Are there—other wild animals?"

"Ain't nobody knows fer shure. But thar's nothin' wilder'n a timber-wolf." He rubbed his chin thoughtfully. "I wudn' say thar ain't other wild critters neither. Thar's funny noises in the dark. I've heerd 'em manys a time. Never found out wot they was. Didn't feel like lookin' too much neither."

Farren and the Sergeant shook their heads in solemn agreement. Collins was not quite sure what to make of it. "Well," he decided, with an exaggerated sigh, "I suppose Ted and I must face them. You haven't said anything about the Indians. They play a prominent role in all the stories I read."

Blue Pete shrugged. "Them stories is done by fellows wot never come West."

"So the Indians are not so bad, not so untrustworthy as they're painted, eh?"

Blue Pete looked at Mahon, then away to Farren, and shook his head gloomily. "Tha're a dang sight wuss. We got 'em sorta calmed down here in the open, but tha're apt to break loose any time. Yuh jes' can't trust no Neche but a dead un."

"The old-timer pulling the leg of the tenderfoot," Collins remarked, but there was a question in the tone.

Mahon admitted that perhaps that was true to a limited extent. "But there's lots in what Blue Pete has said about the Hills. I know them better than anyone but Blue Pete, and I'm telling you my scalp creeps all the time I'm there. I don't like them."

Collins had come to the conclusion that it was safer to appear to believe they were not serious. "That does it," he announced. "I've just got to get into those hills, just to feel my scalp tingle."

When they reached the trail that led to the Inverted T Don Farren and his guests turned into it. A moment later he called back to the Sergeant

"Don't be too long finding a home for that dog, Sergeant, if Blue Pete doesn't take it. I won't be responsible much longer for my guests with him around. Besides, if Jerry's hounds ever get at him they'll make mincemeat of him."

Blue Peter pulled the pinto to a stop. "Reckon I'll pick him up right now, Sergeant. Mebbe Mira'd like him. S'long!"

"Pete!" The Sergeant held him back for a few moments while he studied his face gravely. "Pete, I'm not blind. You're taking this affair too seriously, as if it was your concern. It isn't. Don't get mixed up in it, for God's sake. You heard what the Inspector said. It isn't only the danger—and there'll be a lot of that."

Blue Pete nodded. "Th' Inspector said it all, Sergeant."

"But if you interfere—"

"Can't see whar I wud."

The big black the Sergeant rode circled nearer and Mahon leaned towards his friend. "You can't deceive me, Pete. You found some clue, something to work on. What is it?"

"Yuh found suthin' yerself, an' I ain't astin' yuh wot 'tis. I do' need nothin' more'n seein' that woman. It got me started."

Mahon gathered up the reins. "Well, I hope we don't meet again until the murderer is found—and punished by the law."

"I shure hope he's found," murmured the half-breed. He turned away to rejoin the rancher and his guests. To himself he thought: "I shure hope it's not the Mounties wot find him."

As they neared the Inverted T a nerve-shattering wolf-howl brought Whiskers' head up with a jerk, and she neighed with pleasure.

Collins shuddered. "Br-r-r! That's that damned dog again. It's enough to give a fellow the creeps."

"Whiskers," laughed Blue Pete, "recognizes an ole friend."

"How old?" Collins asked it with a leer that might mean anything. In the strained silence that followed he tried to laugh it off. "I almost feel as if it's an old acquaintance of my own: one could never forget that howl. A dog like that must be dangerous. Funny it didn't go to its master's help when he was shot."

"He was tied up," the half-breed explained hotly. He was ashamed of how he felt and he laughed. "Mebbe some time he'll be loose when the skunk wot shot 'em's around. Dog like that ain't likely to fergit."

"Then he must have taken me for the—what you call the skunk;

he seems to have taken such a dislike to me." Collins made a wry face. "I've tried to make friends with him but it doesn't work. He doesn't appear to think much more of anyone else—except you, Pete, and the Sergeant. I was hoping to use him in the hills if no one took him away. I suppose I'm still the newcomer to him—as I am to the rest of you."

The sincere regret in his tone induced Farren to touch him on the shoulder in a kindly way. "Don't worry. When you're here a year—if you're here a year, I mean—you'll be harder on the newcomer than we are. Time mellows us all. The 'effete East,' as we call it, has sent us some pretty raw specimens, but once they settle down we find they're pretty much like the rest of us."

Ted Fraleigh whistled in mock surprise. "Good Lord, I'd hate to have met up with you ranchers before you got mellowed."

Farren sent his guests into the house and with Blue Pete led their mounts on to the stable. The dog was there and heard them coming, and a howl was interrupted and changed to a welcoming bark.

Farren's head shook. "They're a strange pair, I know, but they're not half bad when you get to know them better. Collins' bark is worse than his bite. He came with a bad attack of Eastern superiority, that's all. He has found it doesn't impress us out here. These Easterners come with the idea that we're wild and woolly, that we're just waiting for them to teach us the finer things of life—that we live on raw meat, chew tobacco between meals, and end all our quarrels with the gun. I know something of how they feel. I came from the Old Country, with the idea that Canada was only a colony, that it was willing to get on its knees to us from over there. It hurt when they laughed at me. I discovered that they thought *we* were half a century behind the times. I had the idea that Canada was inhabited by lumbermen and farmers. . . . Fortunately though, I had some of it knocked out of me in Toronto before I came West or I wouldn't have lasted a week.

"Collins and his friend seemed determined to settle here, so we'd better make the best of it. They'll learn." He looked off over the corrals, and one hand tapped the tooled leather of his expensive saddle. "I'm not so sure I wouldn't let them have the Inverted T if it was ten years from now and they raised their offer a few thousand. I've all the money I can use for the rest of my life." He shook his head and smiled. "But I'm talking. I couldn't give up these buildings I have, most of them built largely by my own hands. There's something about them— Oh, well!"

He dismounted and opened the stable door. The dog could be seen tied inside, lying flat, waiting in silence and watchful. At sight of Blue Pete he leaped up and tugged at the rope that tied him. The half-breed untied it, and it licked his hand, then tore loose and ran outside.

Blue Pete followed. "Wal, I'll be gor-swizzled!" For the dog had gone straight to Whiskers and their noses were together. "Wal, you ole flirt yuh! Whiskers, ole gal, yuh never did that before to nobody but Mira 'n' me. Reckon he musta heerd me say I'd take him home."

Farren's face was wreathed in smiles. "With my blessing, Pete. He certainly has taken to you and the pinto. He was lonesome around here, as if he knew he wasn't wanted. None of us could make friends with him. No use asking you to stop and have a bite, I suppose?"

It wasn't. Blue Pete had never eaten a meal in any ranch house in the district, apart from his own at the 3-Bar-Y, except twice at Cooney Featherstone's. Cooney was different. It was not that he would not have been welcome, for every ranch house was open to any visitor, but it was impossible for the ranchers to conceal the something that marked the difference between themselves and the half-breed. When it came to accepting him as a meal-guest they never could forget his Indian blood or his former reputation as a rustler. He had eaten at the bunk-houses, though even there everyone was uncomfortable. That it was not entirely his Indian blood was proven by the fact that there were several half-breed punchers, even a half-breed foreman, in the district.

As he rode past the ranch house, the dog gamboling joyously about the pinto, the door opened and Collins appeared. The dog saw him and instantly stopped and snarled. Then he looked up at Blue Pete, as if awaiting an order.

Collins laughed but kept the door-knob in his hand. "The only thing that would reconcile me to that dog, Pete, is if you'd bring him along and join Ted and me in that wolf-hunt. Won't you change your mind?"

Blue Pete shook his head. "I ain't thought of it sence, so I can't hev changed my mind. . . . Besides, I ain't jes' shure yit Rollo ain't a cannibal."

Collins' eyes widened. "I see you know its name."

Blue Pete's lips came together tightly for a moment, then he said: "I'm namin' him fresh. Ef he et yuh mebbe I'd hev a nicer name fer him."

"Well, if you change your mind you'll find me at the Alberta Hotel. I've changed over from the Royal. I couldn't stand a hotel like that; it isn't my style."

As he rode out of sight over the edge of the depression Blue Pete spat noisily into the grass. "Ef thar's anythin' out here your style, Biff Collins, I'll give yuh the 3-Bar-Y an' pull out. I'd go back to the Badlan's whar they raise skunks wot don' try to hide thur smell."

XIV   A PUZZLED INSPECTOR

SERGEANT MAHON did not reach Medicine Hat until the following day, and even then he had made but a short stop at Turner's Crossing.

Inspector Barker was waiting for him. "Find anything more?" he inquired eagerly even before he read the expression on the Sergeant's face. "Ah, I see you did. What are you doing with that rifle in here?"

Mahon placed it on the desk. "It's Sam Dunlop's, sir. It was in the house, and I never saw him outdoors without it. Neither did Blue Pete. The murderers must have been waiting for the one time he went without it."

The Inspector frowned. "Doesn't seem as if a rancher would be able to do that. . . . There are so many strange slants in this thing that it looks as if we're going to have to switch things about a little . . . only I can't see how. Is that all?"

He watched with growing excitement the Sergeant extract a small scrap of paper from his pocket and laid it on the desk beside the rifle.

"What's this?"

"I found it on the floor of the clothes cupboard, sir, in a dark corner. I think it must have blown under the door some time and been missed. One would think they took care to destroy everything that would assist in tracing them, for there wasn't another piece of paper in the place with any helpful mark on it."

Inspector Barker had picked up the paper and turned it over. His eyes lighted up. "Say, this is something." It was the corner of a business envelope, and he read the address aloud: "The Static Electrical Company, Buffalo, New York." He examined it on both sides. "If only we had the writing that came in it! But this is next best. It means that Dunlop had some sort of connection with this company, or with someone connected with it. It might give us a lead. If he's known at the Static Electrical Company we'll find out. By the way, we had to bury them yesterday, and we took a few pictures, though photos of dead people are seldom recognizable. I've often found even relatives doubtful. . . . We got a bullet from the woman's head, and we're holding it. It's marked a little from striking a bone, but it might be traced. . . . Only it isn't feasible to test a couple of hundred Winchesters."

He drummed nervously on the blotter for a few moments. "One thing sure, the bullet was not fired by the rifles the Indians carried.

Better keep this to yourself; we don't want the owner of the rifle to suspect that we have the bullet." He picked up the piece of paper once more. "I'll get in touch with the Buffalo police right away . . . or I'll write to the electrical company and send some photos. The prints won't be ready for a day or two, but I won't wait. . . .

"So all we have thus far is the bullet and the scrap of paper. Tell me more about this rifle. You say you found it inside, resting on pegs on the wall. . . . Strange that he should go so far from the house as to Big Slough without it, if he usually carried it. Did you notice it when you went to the house the first time?"

"Yes, sir. Didn't I speak of it? Both Blue Pete and I noticed it. I thought I'd better not leave it there any longer; it's a good rifle."

The Inspector smiled. "No fear of anyone going into that house yet for a long time . . . at least until we catch up with the murderer. To the innocent as to the guilty that place will be something to avoid like the plague until we solve the affair. They know they all had murder in their hearts."

Mahon told of the early morning visit of the cowboys and of the tearing down of the fence. "I rather imagine Blue Pete flew completely off the handle when he saw them at it. He was feeling awfully sore even when he spoke about it to me."

The Inspector chuckled. "Isn't that like him? He can shoot a man without a qualm if he thinks he deserves it, but these murders seem to have got under his skin. By the way, was there any evidence of robbery—anything missing that you could trace?"

Mahon considered. "Blue Pete had gone through a drawer, sir, just before I arrived. I can't imagine a rancher would think of taking anything, as you said before. They'd shoot and run. They were both shot from close range, it seems—"

"That's one of the puzzles. I can't see why Dunlop or his wife would let them get so close if they carried guns. They both knew the danger; that's why he carried the rifle all the time, I'm convinced." He threw out his hands in a helpless movement. "Couldn't Blue Pete throw any light on any part of it? Weren't there some marks he could read—anything that would give us a lead?"

Mahon did not reply for a few moments. "I'm not quite sure what he found. I had a feeling that he was concealing something, but I may have imagined it. One thing, he feels personally responsible in some way, that he might have prevented the murders had he gone straight there instead of coming to town."

"Do you mean he's taking on the job of finding out who the murderer is, in spite of what I said?"

"I don't know, sir. But I do know he won't let things lie. If we don't find the murderer soon he'll do something on his own."

Inspector Barker shifted impatiently in the chair and looked worried. "He's apt to do just that, I know . . . and that makes it the harder for us. It's going to be the devil to get anything from the ranchers, guilty or not, but there's no one else to work on, and most of it is up to you, Mahon."

He picked up the rifle, broke it, and squinted through the barrel towards the window. "Sam Dunlop wasn't used to a rifle, that's plain. It's still dirty. Wouldn't you expect that from a tenderfoot? Damned good gun, too, and new. And I see the range is set for the minimum distance—unless you touched that rear sight."

"I was careful not to, sir. I noticed that, but perhaps he knew too little about a rifle to use the sights properly. But that doesn't seem like him. Last time I saw him he'd just shot two coyotes, and that takes some shooting. It doesn't seem to go with a dirty rifle."

The Inspector set the rifle back on the desk and sat for a time in deep thought. Suddenly he roused himself. "Send Langley in. I'll write that company right away."

Long before Mahon reached the barracks Blue Pete rode down the slope to the 3-Bar-Y ranch house. Mira heard him coming and was standing in the doorway when he rode up. She saw the dog and shook her head.

"Hello, Pete! I see you brought the Dunlop dog. What's the idea? Adopting an orphan or what?" It was plain that she had heard about the murders.

The dog ran to her and raised himself to place his paws gently against her waist, lifting his nose to her face and whining softly. Standing thus he was almost as tall as she.

She let a hand fall on his head and rubbed. "What in the world are you going to do with him, Pete? You know the cows can't stand a dog about. You'll have so many stampedes the boys'll be grumbling."

"Reckoned mebbe he's be comp'ny fer you, Mira."

She smiled down on the eager animal. "Perhaps he will be. But we'll have to keep him about the house." She put the dog down and went out to peer into her husband's face. "Pete, where do you figure in this? Tex says you found the bodies, but that must have been a day after you left here to warn Dunlop what was threatening. Did you get to him before the murders or—"

"I slunk off to town instead," he confessed.

"You mean—you're telling me you didn't go straight there? I've got to know. It would be about the time they were shot. Yet I know very well you couldn't do a thing like that." Tears had come into her eyes.

He looked almost as if she had struck him. "Yuh mean—yuh mean I gotta tell yuh I didn't?"

A smile broke through her tears, and she patted his knee affectionately. "I'm trying to place myself in the position of those who don't know you as I do, Pete dear. Put Whiskers in and come and tell me everything."

She watched him ride on to the stable. Absent-mindedly she continued to fondle the dog, while he stood close to her, trying to lick her hand. Two of the cowboys strolled out from the bunkhouse as Blue Pete dismounted. They were full of questions, but something about the half-breed's manner held them silent and they left without a word. In the house he threw his Stetson at a peg, missed it, elaborately recovered it and hung it on a different peg. Playing for time.

She knew it and crowded him for the story, and he told her most of what he could remember. After he had eaten he made a second cast of the toe-mark he had found, wrapped it in paper and placed it in a corner of a seldom used drawer. The original he kept in his pocket; he would go nowhere now without it until he found the one who wore the boot that had made the mark.

She saw how worried he was and she tried to comfort him: "If the Mounties don't know you couldn't do a thing like that they would have reason to suspect you. But you've no need to worry."

"I cuda stopped it," he groaned. . . . "I was skeered to go straight thar, jes' plain skeered. . . . Skeered I was buttin' in, like you said. I cuda stopped it. . . . An' I seen that woman."

Mira, across the table from him, stood with her hands on her hips, watching him narrowly. "And so you've taken on your own shoulders the finding of the murderer. . . . And you won't wait for the law to punish him when you do find him. You're butting in on the Mounties now—"

"That's wot th' Inspector said. He doesn' want me to do nothin'."

"I can see why. He wants you to remain friendly with the other ranchers. He wants—"

"Durn the ranchers—ef they done this."

Mira sighed and returned to her work. But she talked as she worked. "What do you propose to do about it? Are you going to examine every foot in the West to see if it fits that shape you have?"

"Dunno wot I'm goin' to do—'ceptin' to find who done it."

Nothing more was said for a long time. The dog had settled down beside the stove as if it had been raised there. Mira regarded it with shaking head.

"So I'm to keep the dog around here, while you trapez the country. It's to be my care, not yours. By the way, what's his name?"

"Dunno. . . . Sorta like Rollo, an' he's sorta 'dopted it. See?"

The dog had risen at the name and had come to him, to rest his chin on the half-breed's knee and stare into his face.

Blue Pete grinned delightedly. "Ain't that suthin' now, Mira? See how he knows his name an' comes. . . . Wonder ef he'd be any good huntin' coyotes an' wolves. The wolves is gittin' too thick. Boys is grouchin' all 'bout the hills. . . . Like to give him a run in the hills an' see how he carries on. Jerry the Pole's gittin' too old an' lazy to do much huntin' now."

A slow smile spread over his face. She noticed it and asked what he was thinking of.

"Had a chance to make some money. Thar's a coupla tenderfeet want some wolf-huntin' in the hills, an' they ast me to go 'th 'em an' take Rollo. Good money, too."

She slacked her lips with disgust. "And you refused the money and said you'd be glad to go for nothing and take the dog and anything else they wanted. I know you by this time. All anyone need do is—"

"But I ain't goin'. I turned it down."

"Dear me! What a surprise! Must be some good reason."

"Shure is. I don't like the chaps. Biff Collins is the biggest tenderfoot I ever seen—an' a lot other things I don't like 'bout him."

"What are tenderfeet doing here? They haven't come just to hunt wolves surely."

"Tha're tryin' to buy a ranch." He grinned slyly at her. "Yuh'll mebbe meet up 'th 'em 'fore long, 'cause they seem bound to git one."

"I'd like to meet this tenderfoot you hate so much," she laughed. "It won't take long to convince him the 3-Bar-Y isn't for sale. Shall I kick him out—or sic Rollo on him?"

Blue Pete regarded the dog with shaking head. "No need to do that. You'll hev to watch he don't git at this Biff Collins 'thout no sicin'. But jes' do like yuh feel. I'd like to know wot yuh feel 'bout him. Mebbe I got a bad start."

"Perhaps you'd like me to sell," she suggested. "But what would you do with yourself if we hadn't the 3-Bar-Y?"

"Wal-ll cud alius go back to rustlin'."

She made a scornful sound. "After these years in Canada you couldn't go back to rustling, not if there wasn' another job in the world—not here where you've worked with the Mounties."

Later there was excitement about the Mounted Police barracks in Medicine Hat. Sergeant Mahon had just come in from a three days' visit to the Triangle H, the Double X, and the T-Inverted R, and he had discovered nothing to justify the time it had taken. He was depressed. Every mouth in the district seemed to seal up before him so tightly that they would not even discuss the murders it seemed that every cowman in the district was willing to let the murderer escape. The ranchers made no attempt to conceal their satisfaction that Big Slough was free again, no matter what the cost—though they would not go so far as to condone the murders. There were other crimes in the West that ranked with murder, because conditions demanded it.

As Mahon rode dejectedly into the barracks corral, Langley met him.

"The Inspector wants to see you right away, Sergeant."

Mahon dismounted slowly. He was dead-tired, for he had driven himself with little rest all the time he was away. A couple of minutes he spent in his own small office at the back of the building, brushing off some of the brown dust of the trail and wondering what he would say to the Inspector to explain his failure.

The Inspector heard him coming and shouted impatiently to him. "Sit down, Mahon." His voice was sharp, weighted with important news. "Oh, don't look so disgusted with life. I know you've had no success, but I scarcely expected it. I've been more fortunate." His excitement waned suddenly, and he frowned down on the blotter. "Come to think of it, it only adds to the mystery . . . but it gives us something to work on—puts another glint on the mystery."

He leaned across the desk and looked into the Sergeant's face. "We know the rifle that killed those two poor people."

Mahon started. "Then you know who shot them?"

The Inspector shook his head. "Far from it . . . further from it, I should say, than ever. They were shot with that rifle of Dunlop's that you brought in. The bullet we found in the woman's head came from that rifle, and there's every reason to believe all the bullets were fired from it. . . . And how damned clever that is! There's no possible way now of tracing the bullet back to the one who fired it." He flung his hands out despairingly. "And that's that."

XV   A TENDERFOOT BALKED

THE visit of Biff Collins to the 3-Bar-Y in search of a ranch was not long delayed. Blue Pete was not there when the two tenderfeet called. The murders haunted him, so that he could not remain idle; and the certainty that the Mounted Police would lose no time in pushing the search for the murderer goaded him to action that often threatened to be dangerously hasty. He had the feeling that he might learn more from the gossip of the cowboys if he reached them and the ranchers before they were put on guard by the Mounted Police inquiries.

Mira's first intimation of the visit of the two strangers came from Rollo. The dog had taken to his new home from the first minute. His loyalty was divided between Mira and Blue Pete, with embarrassing uncertainty. When the half-breed left the house the dog always hesitated whether to follow or not, looking from one to the other. He knew Blue Pete best, of course, realized that he owed most to him, but underneath appeared to lie the thought that Mira needed him most. At least that was how Mira described it—and she loved him.

When Blue Pete saddled Whiskers, however, there was no hesitation: Rollo wanted to go along. And Mira was forced to close him in the bedroom to keep him from following. When his master was out of hearing he could be released with safety. He would then go to his usual place beside the stove, where he would lie by the hour, watching Mira at her work, now and then raising his head and whining a little for attention. He seemed to fear that somehow she would disappear and leave him, as had happened at his last home.

A couple of the cowboys tried to make friends with him, but he merely accepted their attentions and when they became too familiar a low growl would end proceedings. Don Farren had described him as "the knowingest dog I ever knew. He knows he was left in my care because there was nothing else to do with him at the time. As long as he's here he won't bite me: when he gets away I know enough to steer clear of him."

At the time of Biff Collins' visit Mira had gone to the pantry. She heard Rollo growl and returned to the living-room to find the dog standing half-way to the open door, crouched as if to spring, the hair upright on his neck. She ordered him back and went to the door.

Up the trail two riders were making towards the house. She stood and watched them, unusually excited, for she saw they were strangers.

Some distance from the house they stopped and looked down over the buildings and corrals. One pointed here and there as he talked to his companion. They both nodded and came on.

Mira stood well back in the open doorway, so that she did not think they could see her. Then she became aware that Rollo had crept to her side and now stood quivering with excitement. Menacing snarls broke through his bared teeth. She knew who the visitors were, and she remembered what Blue Pete had said about the dog and them. Rollo plainly agreed with his master. She let her hand drop to his collar, partly to try to calm him, partly to make certain she had him under control.

She was aware then that she agreed with both her husband and the dog.

The pair rode up before the house. Collins saw her and dismounted, sweeping off his hat with a smile and a flourish that made it a form of irony. Then he saw the dog.

"That damned dog again! I seem to meet him everywhere."

"Rollo has been only three places that I know of," said Mira.

He laughed. "That's three too many for me. It's taken a dislike to me—like all the rest of the old-timers around here. I can't help being a newcomer, a tenderfoot, if you like. But it seems to dislike everyone but a half-breed—and you, madam, of course. I don't blame him for that—you, I mean." He bowed low, another touch of mockery that made Mira stiffen.

"He belonged to a man and a woman who were murdered," she told him. "There's plenty of reason for him to be on edge. He must have seen the murders committed."

"Yes, he belonged to that new settler, didn't he? I'd recognize him anywhere. The Mounted Police left him at the Inverted T while I was there. Have you heard him howl—or have you been able to break him of that habit? He'd raise your hair."

"The half-breed you speak of is Blue Pete, my husband," she said, and waited.

"Then this is the 3-Bar-Y. I met him several times. The 3-Bar-Y, eh? They tell me you're the real owner of the ranch. Then it's you I want to see."

"What they tell you," she informed him coldly, "doesn't alter the fact that the 3-Bar-Y belongs to Blue Pete and me. I know who you are. You're the two who are said to be trying to buy a ranch. My husband has spoken of you."

Collins made a w'ry face. "That's not the best introduction we could have. He and I had a silly bit of a run-in the first time we met, but that's blown over. I was pretty raw then. I'm learning. May we come in?"

"Certainly. Just a minute till I put Rollo in another room." She led the dog to the bedroom and closed the door. He protested all the way but did not actively resist. When she returned, both men were already in the living-room, looking about them.

"Won't you sit down?" The invitation came involuntarily to her lips, for she disliked them both intensely.

Collins pointed to the bedroom door. "A strange dog, that. Part wolf, I should say. Part of the part that is wolf, at any rate, is its howl. Whenever I heard it I could feel the blood trickling up to my scalp. I confess I don't like dogs since an experience I had with one as a small child, but a wolf makes me shudder even to think of." He ended it with a smile, as if one could not take him seriously. "That's why I'm going to kill a wolf before I leave, no matter what."

"I hope you'll succeed," she said. "Rollo hasn't howled since he came here, so I can't say anything about that. He has his likes and dislikes, I suppose, like the rest of us."

"Of course. Every dog has his day—and other things. Hm-m! So Rollo's his name. Did you know the new settler well? Perhaps you were a friend of his wife's—though the ranchers around here appear to have been anything but friendly to them, which is only natural."

He tossed his hat on the table. Fraleigh had remained on his feet inside the door, and Mira did not ask him to sit down. It was Collins did that: "Can't you find a chair, Ted?" He turned to Mira. "This is Ted Fraleigh, a friend of mine. We're going into a deal together. . . . You know, I can't understand that husband of yours. I offered him almost anything to come with us to hunt wolves in the hills, and he turned me down. He knows the wolves need cleaning out, but he refuses to help."

"Pete," Mira informed him, "needs no help to hunt wolves."

"But he could help us. They tell me he has lots of time, too, that—"

"If you've learned, as you say you have, you'll have noticed that none of the ranchers do much themselves among the herds. They pay foremen and cowboys to do that."

"One could read that," Collins laughed, "from the big houses on the Esplanade in Medicine Hat. One can't live there and work on a ranch."

"Then you haven't learned quite enough. Those houses are occupied only in winter. The 3-Bar-Y has no house on the Esplanade. Pete and I live here all the year round."

"But—but your husband can't be too busy. I've met him everywhere."

Mira's lips tightened. "The 3-Bar-Y has a good foreman. . . . One thing Pete has done that would not have been done did he not have free time—he has captured more rustlers than all the other ranchers put together." Collins listened with flattering interest. "It makes him all the more interesting. . . . Don Farren has told me something of his past life." He did not look at her as he spoke.

"And if you succeed in buying a ranch, Mr. Collins, (that's what Pete called you) you'll know much about his *present* life—and be grateful that he has free time that can be turned to use. But," coldly, "you didn't come to discuss my husband."

"No-o. He probably told you we're looking for a ranch. We're willing to pay any reasonable price—"

"No reasonable price would buy the 3-Bar-Y, and I wouldn't ask an unreasonable one—or accept it."

"But surely everything has a price."

"Perhaps—with some people. The price for the 3-Bar-Y is more than you could pay."

"But I'm willing—"

"The 3-Bar-Y is not for sale, Mr. Collins, not at any price. Is that answer enough?"

A limp smile appeared on his face. "It's part of the conspiracy, I see. All the old-timers are determined to keep the newcomers out. I face it everywhere."

"You don't surprise me." She turned her back on them and dropped a stick of wood in the stove with an unnecessary clatter.

He eyed her back for a few moments. Then: "I try to be friendly."

"We have our friends already."

"Do you mean if I succeed in getting a ranch that you would refuse to be friends? Is it such a closed corporation—" He stopped, and a significant smile creased his face. "I can see the hazards that new settler faced."

"You should tell the Mounties what you see," she told him. "They're looking for the murderer." She left the stove and stood in the centre of the floor, looking down on him as he sat. "It would help you a lot to make friends if you left to the Mounties the suspicions you appear to have."

" 'They always get their man,'" he sneered.

"They usually do."

"Then there must be some uncomfortable ranchers in these parts." He rose and started for the door. "I'm running into tough luck everywhere I turn, and I'm being misunderstood. I'd like to be one of you, and I haven't given up hope. I've met your husband so often that I almost feel I can call him a friend. Don't you think you could induce him to come along and help in the wolf-hunt?"

"Would *you* be any help? Anyway, Pete decides those things for himself."

Collins sighed. "Then I'll have to hire some Indians, and I don't like them, I don't trust them. I've read too many blood-and-thunder Indian stories as a lad. Well, thank you for an interesting talk." Again with that touch of irony.

She watched them leave the house. Outside they stopped and looked about. They even walked to the corner of the house and looked back towards the stables and the bunkhouse. There was a possessiveness about it that angered her, and she went to the door where they could see her. Laughing uncomfortably then, they returned to their horses and mounted. Collins turned in the saddle and swept his hat off with another flourish. Then he laughed and rode away.

She was there in the door long after they disappeared over the rise. After a time she shook herself and turned back. "I wonder," she muttered, "I wonder." She wondered several times when Rollo, released, rushed out and sniffed at the floor, growling, the hair upright on his neck. She wondered throughout the day as she went about her work.

XVI   A SHOT THAT MISSED

THE field of investigation was wide, so wide that when Blue Pete stopped to lay plans he was almost discouraged. It included every rancher within half a hundred miles and more, and the scores of cowboys in the outfits. Forced to make a choice, he decided on the Diamond K. It was not without reason. It was Slim Manson who had personally protested with his rifle that day as he stopped the cowboys in their destruction of the fence about Big Slough. It was Slim Manson Inspector Barker had mentioned first as a likely suspect. Slim's cowboys had been among those engaged in cutting the wire and tearing up the posts. And Slim had a nasty streak in him—a brooder to whom every wrong, fancied or real, demanded a correcting crusade. He had, too, a rough lot of punchers in his outfit. No other kind would work for him because of his biting tongue and unfriendly habits.

From Slim himself Blue Pete knew there was no chance of learning anything of value. For one thing, he seldom met the ranchers on familiar enough terms to discuss anything not connected with a roundup or rustling. They never trusted him—or he them. The cattle he had saved them in his pursuit of rustlers had earned him little open gratitude. They knew him well enough to be aware of how much the excitement of the chase overtopped the good he did, and it robbed him of the credit he deserved. They could never forget how often he had defied them, how careful they had to be about brands and branding when he was around. For another thing, they would never tell anyone what they knew about the murders.

He did not, therefore, go directly to the Diamond K. Though he did not think the ranchers would hold it seriously against him that he had interfered with the destruction of the fence at that time, they might be more reticent when they remembered it. At least they would not yet have reason to think that he had taken on himself the responsibility of finding the murderer. He hoped they never would.

His memory of the incident about Big Slough that day when Slim Manson had sent a bullet near him was incomplete. He was not quite certain how far he had gone or what he had said. He never could remember what happened when he was really angry. It worried him as he rode along. He hoped the cowboys would not hold it against him, for he saw that he must depend on them now. Fortunately Manson and Welch had intervened before the affair had developed into a fight, for he saw now that a score of cowboys were little likely to be cowed into yielding. It was the two ranchers who had called them off at the last.

He had a pretty good idea where the main herd of the Diamond K was feeding, and he rode in that direction. He tried to develop some plan, to formulate an excuse for visiting it. He was not good at that, and at last he gave up, turning aside instead to Big Slough. It was a ride of a dozen miles after he thought of it, but there was no immediate hurry. Almost involuntarily he clung to the coulees. It was a habit that fitted so often into the work in hand that he had come to follow it when there was no reason. In a coulee he dismounted and lay in the shade of a gnarled cottonwood tree to think things over. And it came to him almost at once that again he was side-stepping an issue, that it was evasion, not caution, that made him hesitate, as it had been when he might have saved the Dunlops.

With jaws set he mounted Whiskers.

He had just picked up the reins when the pinto's ears flicked upward and back, and her head lifted. He knew what it meant and he leaped from the saddle and led her into the trees. Ordering her to lie down in a buffalo wallow, he waited. In the shadow her mottled sides would scarcely be noticed even by anyone riding through the coulee.

In a few moments he heard the thud of hoofs, coming from the north-east. Creeping up the slope, dodging from sage bush to sage bush, he wondered why he strove to conceal himself, but he kept on. Long before he saw them he could follow the course of the oncoming riders. If they kept on as they were going they would pass within a hundred yards of where Whiskers lay.

At last, concealed by a large cactus, he saw them. He had removed his Stetson, for the plant was not large enough to conceal it. Usually the dirty grey Stetson helped to conceal his jet black hair, for it sank into the dead colour of the grass.

He had long read two riders in the sounds. Then he saw them— Biff Collins and his friend! A tingle of excitement raced through him, though he could not explain it. They were riding westward. If they turned to the south they would be making for the hills if they kept on towards the south-west—

The thought sent him racing back to the pinto. To the south-west lay the 3-Bar-Y. And Mira was there alone. Even the bunkhouse was likely to be empty. He had a foot in the stirrup when he stopped, and a low chuckle broke from him. Mira alone? Mira alone was able to look after herself under any condition; it wouldn't take her long to size up the visitors. Besides, there was Rollo. Rollo would have something to say if Mira needed protection; and Collins was afraid of the dog.

He ordered Whiskers down again and himself hid behind a tree. Only for a moment or two were the two men in sight, and they did not look in his direction. He waited until they were well away, then he mounted and went his way. He kept on towards Big Slough.

Presently he was surprised to see a large herd before him, then off a little to his left another herd. Both appeared to pour over into the depression in which was the slough. Three cowboys rode between the herds keeping them separate. Big Slough had never been so popular.

At first it angered him, as it had done the last time he was there. In a way it was defiance, and still a sort of sacrilege. But it would do no good—and it was not his business—to interefere. He rode on, however, and drew up at the top of the slope.

The cows were drinking at the south end of the slough, the cowboys keeping the herds apart. Other cowboys were about the far side, talking together. They looked up and saw him.

He recognized the danger of remaining there, for he was very angry, and he turned the pinto about to ride away.

A shot rang out from below, and a bullet struck the saddle-horn and glanced off.

He did nothing hastily. Instead, he swung the pinto back and sat for a moment, silhouetted against the sky, glowering down at the rip made in the leather. He realized how murderous he felt, realized too that he must control himself. But he had no thought of letting it pass. This bullet was intended for him; it was not merely a warning, such as Slim Manson had sent towards him. And he reacted to it as he always did.

He raised his eyes and looked down on the cowboys below. The cows had been too far away and too absorbed in drinking to be disturbed by the shot. Besides, feed was good there, and the sun was very hot.

He picked out the spot from which the shot had come and rode slowly down the slope towards it. Some cattle before him parted to let him through, and he circled the water, still riding slowly.

The cowboys, except those busy with the cattle, crowded together as he approached, silent and watchful. He recognized some of them as the punchers he had disturbed while tearing down the fence, and he knew the shot had come from one of them.

There was a way to pick out the one who had fired the shot, and his first thought was to make an issue of it. But in the minutes it took to reach the cowboys he had time to remember that the more important thing was not to ruin his chances of learning what these cowboys might know about the murders.

Accordingly he appeared calm enough when he spoke though his lip curled. "Purty rotten shootin', I'd call it." He looked back up the slope to where he had been. "Not more'n four hunderd yards, an' a sittin' mark, an' yuh was inches off." He picked at the torn leather. "Not much better'n an outer, that."

He might have been discussing the weather, and they shifted about in shame-faced silence, waiting for more.

Suddenly he scowled. "I cud find out who done it, but I ain't lookin' at yer guns. The skunk wot missed 's feeling mean 'nuff, I reckon. But nachully I don't like bein' shot at. Yuh're mebbe mad, some o' yuh, 'cause I butted in when yuh was at the fence. But I seen that woman. I hope you didn't. Ef yuh did yuh'd feel like I do 'bout it. Yuh ain't woman-killers. I hope you ain't. Jes' the same ef yuh'd bin a better shot jes' now thar'd 'a' bin a lot o' questions from the Mounties, an' that 'ud 'a' bin too bad fer the skunk what tried to shoot me. 'Tain't practice I need er I'd do a bit o' shootin' myself."

He rode straight through them. They separated to let him pass, and he continued around the other end of the slough and through the cattle there, not once looking back. He heard the cowboys at his back talking; they had things to say to the one who had shot at him, and they were not friendly things. Cowboys did not favour shooting without warning.

THE incident seemed to have cleared his mind, and he decided to do nothing further until dark. He had always known that the ranchers would resent any investigation he might make; now he knew the cowboys felt the same. What information he obtained must come in indirect ways. If only he could hear them talking among themselves!

The Diamond K herd was feeding some ten miles away, he had seen it twice during the week. In the daytime it would stick to what shade it could find in the coulees, moving up to the warmer heights at night to sleep. So that he was able to approach within a mile or so by daylight without being seen. There he waited for the night. On the wind he could smell the herd. It was late afternoon, and he had chosen a coulee where the change of herders at nightfall was unlikely to uncover him.

When it was dark he mounted and rode in the direction he thought would bring him to the herd. On the night air the odour was more distinct, and soon he discovered that the herd had moved a little to the east.

On a height he pulled up and listened. A faint lowing far off to the south-east did not interest him. There were cattle nearer that that; he could smell them, though they were silent.

Whiskers seemed to know what he wanted, and she discovered the exact location of the herd first, pushing out her chin towards the east. She did not whinny. Nighttime had long since become for her a time of silence, of secrecy, of avoiding others. And Blue Pete trusted her as he would never have trusted a human. He dismounted and lay with his ear close to the ground, on the chance that he might hear the pound of hoofs made by the bronchos of the night-herders.

He could hear nothing, but he took his rifle from the saddle holster and set out on foot towards the east.

In a couple of hundred yards he knew that Whiskers had not been mistaken. The odour was unmistakable now, and with the herd definitely located he returned to the pinto and left the rifle in the saddle-holster. For a hurried escape in the dark it would only impede him, as he had often discovered. Besides, any bullet fired from a distance beyond the reach of his .45 would be without aim in such darkness.

Slowly he moved ahead. The cattle had settled down for the first half of the night, but he could hear a cowboy now, humming as he circled the herd. The sound passed off to the right and faded away. But a few minutes later another cowboy passed, going in the opposite direction, humming like his companion. It was a way night-herders had of soothing the cattle. It seemed to denote that the animals were restless or that the night-herders were nervous.

Presently to his left he heard voices. The cowboys were circling the herd in opposite directions, stopping to talk as they passed one another. Not a sound came from the cattle, so that it appeared that the nervousness was a monopoly of the herders.

To the right now another pair could be heard talking. He crept nearer and waited. Sooner or later the circling herders were certain to meet within hearing.

It was almost an hour before it happened, then a pair met almost before him. There was little danger that they would see him, but one could not be sure of their broncos. The latter always responded to their rider's nervousness, and they could see fairly well in the dark.

As the two cowboys met one of them laughed. "Jim's edgy as a coyote to-night," he scoffed. "He wanted to turn around and ride with me."

The other was more sympathetic. "Well, yu can't blame him, can yu? It's a damned dark night, an' I ain't feelin' any too chirpy myself. Besides, I'm mad enough to bite my name in Slim's neck."

"Why, what's the matter, Joe?"

"You weren't along at Big Slough when we tore down the fence. Slim promised to let us off a couple of nights for that job. It wasn't our fault we didn't finish it right then."

His companion swore. "Yes, I heard Blue Pete butted in. Slim was mighty sore about it." He laughed sneeringly. "A bit scared, too, I bet. He thought the Mounties might ask some nasty questions if the breed told on him. If you ask me it was sorta lookin' for trouble anyways."

It was Joe's turn to be contemptuous. "That's what Blue Pete said. That didn' scare me, but it wasn't jus' the wisest thing to do so soon after the pair was croaked off. We shoulda kep' away for a few days. It wasn't as if Big Slough was all fenced in neither; the cows could get to the water from the other side. Kind of a haunted place it was, too, and I didn't like it a bit."

The tone of the other changed. "Yep, that's right. It's all right to shoot a chap when it means both blazin' away, an' things about equal.

But Dunlop was shot when he hadn' his gun, they say. Then shootin' women ain't like us."

"But we had to have Big Slough," Joe contended, "an' the Mounties wouldn' help. We had to take things into our own hands. . . . Whoever done it, I mean. The law said it was Dunlop's place, an' what the cows needed didn' matter. But stop talkin' about it. I ain't heard nothin' else since it happened, an'"—with a sheepish grin—"it ain't no time to talk bout it in the dark. It's enough to make a night-herder trigger-sharp. So cut it out, Shorty."

Shorty laughed uneasily. "You'll have to get used to it. There ain't much else to talk about."

"D'yu think the Mounties'll find who done it?" Joe inquired in a low voice.

"Not if everybody keeps their traps shut."

"Yu mean yu—yu know who done it? "

"I ain't sayin' I know or I don't know. I don't want anybody to get into trouble through me. It's goin' to be damned nasty for the one the Mounties catch . . . an' somebody's sure to talk an'— What the hell!"

His bronco had snorted nervously and sidled away from where Blue Pete lay. Shorty swung towards the spot and peered into the darkness.

The half-breed had heard the warning, and for a breathless moment or two he lay with his hands pressed to the ground, prepared to jump and run. Before he lay down he had planned the route he would follow if he were forced to run; following it he would not be visible against the sky if he kept low.

"Didju—didju hear somethin'?" inquired Joe, in a frightened voice.

"Frisky musta," returned the other. "Somethin' over in that direction."

"Maybe a coyote."

"Don't be silly. Coyotes don't come so close. I'm goin' look-see. Come along."

They started away, moving slowly. Both bronchos were frightened now, but that was not unusual in the dark.

The half-breed had not waited for them to move. Silently he had eased himself down a slope. Long experience, and perhaps his Indian blood, enabled him to move with the minimum of sound, an accomplishment on which his life had depended so often that he was inclined to trust to it too much. The one thing that was certain was that the cowboys would not shoot until they had to. At that hour on such a dark night a shot was almost certain to send the herd into a stampede. Even a bronco's snort had done that many a time.

He was still in danger, for he knew he could not deceive the bronco until he was much further away. That the animal knew he was still there was plain from its continued snorting.

He had almost made up his mind to run for it, when a movement among the cattle saved him. It was close to midnight, a time when a herd is apt to rise from its sleep, walk a few steps and settle down again on the other side. Either it was the time for the movement, or the bronco's snorting had wakened them. The cowboys heard it and stopped, glad to have an excuse for it and waiting until they were certain that the cattle would settle down again.

It was all Blue Pete needed. Quickly he rolled away and ran around a bend in the coulee.

When he reached the pinto he stopped to think over the conversation he had overheard. Had it told him anything? Did Shorty really know anything about the murders? He did not think so, did not think Joe thought so. If only the bronco had not been so restless he might have made sure. Since both rode for the same outfit it did not seem reasonable that one knew much that the other didn't.

If Slim Manson, their boss, was the murderer or one of the murderers they were not likely to know. Slim would be too smart for that. It was significant, of course, that he had sent them to tear down the fence so soon after the murders, but it would not be safe to make too many deductions from that. With the strange speed of lonely places the whole district knew of the murders. Then, too, Slim was an exceptional shot. . . . But it had required no straight shooting to kill Dunlop, since the shots had come from close up, and the settler had not been armed.

The oddness of that remained with him. If the rifle had been found near the stone-boat it would have been simple enough to have inferred that Dunlop had dropped it while he worked and had been shot before he could reach it. But the rifle was in the hut. . . . It was something more than peculiar.

He stood for a time, his hand on the saddle-horn, wondering what more he could do that night. He knew there was another herd a few miles away to the south-east, nearer the hills, but he did not know to whom it belonged. Not that that mattered; there was still time to visit it before daylight.

He had climbed into the saddle and had started out from the cottonwood trees where he had left the pinto, when a tremor of Whiskers' body warned him, and he returned to the deeper shadows and waited." In a few seconds he could hear two broncos approaching from the south-west, and he knew by their gait that they were under control.

He did not dare try to escape towards the north. That would take him towards the herd. And so he waited, turning Whiskers' head away that he might be ready to run for it if they were discovered. He had his .45 in his hand.

The pair came on. To his surprise he recognized from their voices that Joe and Shorty must have circled away towards the south-west in search of the thing that had startled Shorty's bronco and were now on their way back to the herd. They dropped into the coulee. Forty yards from the half-breed both broncos snorted and instantly they were pulled in, while their riders listened.

After a few breathless moments Joe whispered: "There's somethin' funny goin' on to-night. I don't like it." Low as it was, Blue Pete heard every word.

Shorty tried to laugh it off, but the attempt failed; "Oh, the broncs have heard the boys back with the cows. They're narvus. Jus' like we are," he added, with another short laugh. "Let's get back or they'll be wonderin' what's happened to us." There was urgency in his tone, and they sent their mounts along.

Joe said: "I don't like it. It's sorta creepy—after that Big Slough affair. Yu'd think—"

"For heaven's sake," Shorty broke in angrily, "cut it out till we're back at the bunkhouse. It's bad as if we done it ourselves. Come on. Yu make me feel like I *did* do it."

They passed out of hearing.

Blue Pete grinned as the hoofbeats faded away over the ridge. "Thar'll be suthin' else to talk 'bout now to make 'em skeered. They'll tell the hull outfit thar's things in the dark these nights."

He leaned over the pinto's neck as they moved out from the shadows. "I'm goin' to see they ain't goin' to hev no chance to fergit wot they done, whoever done it. . . . But you 'n' me we gotta be keerful, ole gal."

HE worked his way across the prairie in the direction from which had come earlier in the evening the lowing of cattle. Almost three miles to the south-east he came on the herd, and he found a hiding-place for Whiskers and crawled as near as he dare. Now and then he heard voices, but they were too distant to be able to make out what was said. And with the approach of daylight he was forced to return to the pinto and make for the cover of the hills. From there he could ride through towards the west end and the 3-Bar-Y. The hills were half a dozen miles to the south, and he dare not ride fast for fear of being heard. He managed, however, to reach the trees before daylight.

There he rested for a time. In the fastnesses of the hills he knew he was alone, and that was when he felt most comfortable. He had not been long in the forest before he became aware of the wolves that had been attacking the herds. They had returned to the hills with daylight, and they knew he was there and howled their resentment—or their scorn. Yet they seldom howled in the daylight. They were surely getting bolder. Now they might be almost a mile away, yet they knew he was there.

Early in the morning he broke from the hills to the west and made for the 3-Bar-Y. Mira told him of the visit paid the ranch by Collins and his friend. At first he was angry; he had the impression that Collins had called at a time when he knew he would not be at home.

"He thought mebbe yuh'd take his offer 'thout talkin' it over 'th me. He's that kind of a cuss."

She smiled indulgently. "You know I wouldn't do that."

"D'yuh mean yuh'd mebbe consider *any* offer?"

"Not from him. I couldn't think of the 3-Bar-Y under him."

He drew off one of his riding boots and waggled his toes comfortable. "Wonder wot he'd offer fer it."

It was her turn to be shocked. "Do you mean you'd be willing to sell?"

"Same's you—not to that skunk, not ef he offered a million . . . but I'm intrusted in the amount he offers. Don't seem to be much, wot I've heard."

"How you do hate him! Has he done anything to you?"

"Not yit he ain't . . . I wish he had. I'd like the chance—"

She stopped him with a clacking of her tongue. "What does it all mean?"

"I've a sorta feelin' 'bout Biff Collins. Him 'n' me ain't through 'th one 'nother. He rubs me the wrong way jes' to see him. Why didn' yuh tell him to go jump in Elk Lake?"

Mira laughed. "Our cows drink that water. After all, he has a right to ask our price, to offer to buy." She pinched his ear in passing. "You don't like him, but he seems to have taken a shine to you. He wanted me to get you to act as guide on a wolf-hunt in the hills."

He did not so much as smile, and she peered questioningly into his face. "Do you mean you would?"

"I dunna . . . I might."

"You mean you'd take money from him? He wanted to pay you."

"I ain't takin' no money from Biff Collins. . . . I might do a bit o' wolf-huntin' myself, though." He threw a swift glance at her and looked away, knowing she would read his thoughts in his eyes. "Them wolves is gittin' too sassy. Jerry the Pole ain't doin' much 'th his dogs now. Somebody's gotta do some killin'."

"Tex tells me they had Jerry in jail for a week in town for being drunk and shooting out a light or two." He sighed. "Thar ain't no fun fer the boys in town no more. . . . But tha're gittin' mighty sore 'bout the wolves. It makes night-herdin' durn nasty, 'cause the cows stampede jes' smellin' a wolf. Looks like it's up to me to git them wolves, Mira,"—he stopped to drag off the other boot—"Biff Collins er no Biff Collins."

He trotted to the bedroom in his stocking feet and returned with his feet encased in moccasins. "Yuh know, I'd sorta like to be thur when that skunk gits wolf-huntin'. He's skeered stiff o' them—even when Rollo howled like one. He never seen a wolf in all his life. He started talkin' 'bout huntin' 'em, an' now he can't git outa it. A coyote howlin' jes' fer fun makes his hair stand on end."

"If he's so frightened of them he's a braver man than I thought if he insists on going."

"Shucks! 'Tain't that. He ain't brave 'nuff to show he's skeered."

"He says he'll get Indians to go with him."

He nodded. "That's wot he said. . . . Anyways I'll be thar to see who he takes. Sorta think thar'll be things happen."

He learned without delay that Sergeant Mahon was making the rounds of the ranches. There was nothing new in that, but the half-breed had no delusions about the special purpose now of the visits. He encountered the Sergeant under conditions embarrassing to both.

It was late afternoon, and Blue Pete had set out with the intention of visiting the Double X. It belonged to Ford Welch, Slim Manson's companion that day at Big Slough. The Double X was several miles further east, near the border of Saskatchewan. Welch was a skinflint with a reputation that obtained for him a calibre of cowboy much the same as Slim Manson's. Welch, as Blue Pete saw it, would have few compunctions when it came to protecting his herds. The two major crimes in the West were stealing a man's horse, leaving him on foot in an isolated part of the country, and endangering the lives of the cows. These crimes were personal and therefore worse than rustling.

He had set out from the 3-Bar-Y immediately after noon, intending to follow the coulees to the east, keeping out of sight as much as possible. By the time it was dark he would be near where the Double X herds usually ranged. As he rode along, absorbed in his own thoughts and uncomfortably conscious that as yet he had accomplished nothing, had, indeed, no plan that promised anything, he became aware of the hills, a black border to the glare of dead grass to the south. He pulled in and sat looking them over.

They had always attracted him. In some respects they reminded him of the surroundings of the Indian encampment where he was born. He did not know what nostalgia meant, and if it had been explained he would have insisted that there was nothing pleasant, except his mother, in his memories of that camp, nothing he could describe. What he did know and feel was that the hills gave him what he wanted—isolation, a nature to which he could get close and which he need not share with others, a refuge where no one was apt to interrupt. He knew retreats that no other had found, and when he thought of them it revived memories that sent the blood tingling through him. So much had happened in the hills, so many dangers he had faced there and had overcome, so many thrills had made life glamorous and exciting. In the hills he had been gravely wounded— and he had shot to kill. Even the scars he bore—that left shoulder slightly lower than his right, the remains of a bullet wound that had so nearly cost him his life—were thrilling memories that brought a flash to his crooked eyes. The hills were his.

Whiskers was not so impressed; she nibbled at the grass while she waited for the order to move along.

Suddenly a call from behind brought pinto and rider about, Blue Pete's hand flying automatically to the rifle behind him.

From a coulee only a couple of hundred yards away Sergeant Mahon rode into view. Jupiter, his big black mount, whinnied greeting to the pinto and was answered in kind.

Blue Pete would have preferred to meet almost anyone else. He had tried to avoid the Mounted Police, especially his special friend, the Sergeant. It hurt him to remember that in a way they were antagonists now, or rivals.

"Hello, Pete! I've been looking for you. I saw you coming and waited." That was why neither the half-breed nor the pinto had known he was near. "What are you doing here? What are you doing with yourself these days, anyway—since the Big Slough affair?"

Blue Pete smiled wearily. Of course the Sergeant knew all the answers. "Jes' ridin'," he said. "I was lookin' at the hills, wonderin' how nice an' cool it mus' be up thar. Reckoned mebbe I'd do a bit o' wolf-huntin' some o' these days."

"Only wolf-hunting?" Mahon chuckled. "You could have let those two Indians get away to the hills; then you could have had company."

"Them Neches 'ud be harder to ketch 'n the wolves. Tha're mighty cunnin', them lads. Shure, I'd 'a' followed 'em till I did ketch 'em, but when. They cud 'a' give me the slip in thar mebbe, an' that 'ud 'a' hurt."

"It's even harder to catch whites, isn't it?"

"Whachu mean?"

"It's the very devil to get ranchers to talk, isn't it?"

"I don' talk to 'em much no time. So long's they leave the 3-Bar-Y cows alone I ain' got no reason—"

"Not even if they commit murder—if they brutally shoot a woman from behind and then smash her up?"

Blue Pete shuddered. "Can't yuh let me try to fergit that, Sergeant? . . . 'Sides, nobody knows it was ranchers."

"Would you suggest someone else we might suspect?"

"I dunno who done it," sullenly.

"But you're going to find out . . . and you want to find out before we do. The Inspector knows what you're up to."

"I seen that woman," muttered the half-breed.

Mahon shook his head gloomily. "Pete, you shouldn't interfere. You're apt to get yourself into a mess—and it might make it more difficult for us. The Inspector asked you to keep out of it."

"I was in it long 'fore th' Inspector knowed anythin' had happened. . . . an' he didn' see that woman when I did. It's my business. I ain' tellin' him not to interfere."

"But it's the business of the law, Pete, to find the murderers."

"It's anybody's business to find the skunk wot done that."

Mahon sighed. "I'm warning you, Pete, you'll get into trouble. Someone is going to shoot you if they see you're getting close. They know it wouldn't do any good to shoot us. Besides, they know it's our business; they'd think of you only as an interloper. Don't forget, this is probably not a one-man murder."

"I ain't so bad 'th a six-shooter muhself," replied Blue Pete.

"But you could legally shoot only in self-defence. You wouldn't have a chance to draw. Everyone knows how you can shoot."

Blue Pete said with unusual earnestness: "Ef I git that close to the skunk I'll know he—he's jes' a skunk wot 'ud do it. I'll be ready to draw, jes' feelin' that way."

"Why can't you leave it to us, Pete?"

" 'Cause thar's ways fer me an' tha're not your ways . . . an' sometimes my ways is the on'y ones to find things out. You 'n' th' Inspector know that, too."

Sergeant Mahon did know it. "Well, don't look for any help from us when you get yourself into trouble. We couldn't help you."

"Did I ever ast yuh to?" He sent a searching glance about over the prairie. "An' 'tain't goin' to help us none fer us to be seen talkin' like this. Thar ain't nothin' more to talk about, anyways. S'long!" He turned away.

"Where are you going now?" Mahon called after him.

"Goin' to find who done it."

"Then we're sure to meet again."

They did, and within a few hours, under conditions that belied the Sergeant's warning that he could not come to his friend's help in a crisis.

XIX   A NARROW ESCAPE

THE Double X herd was not where he expected to find it, and he did not care to ride about searching for it for fear of arousing suspicion. Already he had been seen by a group of cowboys of the Double Bar-Y, and he could not help noticing that they regarded him with more than casual interest. He was certainly being talked about.

The Double Bar-Y belonged to Cooney Featherstone, and Cooney he had left to the last. Cooney, fat, merry, indolent, liked by everyone even while the other ranchers were slightly afraid of his bantering tongue, would scarcely be a leader at least in such a crime, though he might be induced to join the group that did it.

He kept his eyes about him as he rode, hoping to come on the herd before dark without appearing to search for it. He did not find it, however, and he dismounted in a coulee and lay down to plan the next step. The Double X was in his mind, and he decided to stick to it for the time being.

Sergeant Mahon's warning had remained in the back of his mind, troubling him. The danger the Sergeant had foreseen did not frighten him, but what he had set out to do ranged him against the only real friends he had, the Mounted Police. Nevertheless he could not understand why the police should take it so personally. They were working towards the same end, and they should be thankful— He stopped there, ashamed of the casuistry. He knew well that the foundation of his own zeal in running down the murder was something more than the punishment of the murderer. He himself had made it a personal affair, much more so than the Mounted Police. The image of the dead woman called to him for revenge, yet retribution would not be complete, so far as he was concerned, if the Mounted Police forestalled him. In a way it was the Mounted Police who intruded.

It was natural enough to feel as he did, for he could not wipe from his mind the conviction that had he gone straight to the lonely homestead he could have prevented the murders, since they must have been committed during the hours wasted on the ride to the Hat.

In a way, too, he recognized the fact—though he would not dwell on it—that the affair had developed into a contest between him and the Mounted Police, a contest that might even become serious, though he could not see how it should affect their friendship. Mahon was devoting his entire time to the search, and it was his job. It was unlikely that he would permit the rivalry to disrupt their friendship, though neither would their friendship interfere with their rivalry. Nor was he likely to condone methods not according to the rules and regulations of the Mounted Police.

And Blue Pete knew that his methods were not in line with those rules.

He found himself within a few miles of the Double X, and as it was not yet dark he pulled in to wait. It did not add to his peace of mind to be discovered by a cowboy he failed to recognize. The cowboy appeared at the top of the opposite slope and stared at him for a moment before dashing out of sight.

He decided to visit the ranch buildings when it was dark enough to move about. He would pry about the bunkhouse and perhaps overhear the punchers talking. There would be several there, and they were almost certain to discuss the murders, since nothing else had happened for weeks to talk about.

He knew the plan of the buildings, could find his way to any of them however dark it might be. And so he set out in the darkness, working around to the south of the buildings. One defect in the plan was that, since it was then nearly eleven o'clock—only then was it dark enough to expose himself—the cowboys were apt to be asleep.

Lights burned in the ranch house, however, and when he had made certain that the cowboys were asleep he made for the lighted building beyond. On such a warm night the windows were sure to be open, and if Ford Welch and his wife were up they might tell him even more than the cowboys could.

He had left the pinto about half a mile away, and he crept through the night with little fear of being seen. The sudden cry of a pack of coyotes to the south, however, brought him to a stop. The coyotes knew he was there. If anyone about the ranch understood their howling as he did they would have some idea what it meant. The pack had probably been following him and were now giving him the laugh. He swore under his breath, for coyotes had often interfered with his plans.

Passing the bunkhouse, he moved on to the ranch house. The blinds were not down; there was no need for drawn blinds on the prairie. Creeping around the corner, he found the living-room window wide open. On hands and knees he drew nearer, avoiding tufts of dead grass, feeling his way with his hands.

He could hear voices, and crouched beneath the window he listened. Welch's wife was speaking. She was a peevish little woman with a sharp tongue, probably driven to it by such a husband. Too strong and stubborn to be cowed to silence, she had become irritating and complaining.

"We have our lives to live out here," she was saying, "and nobody has a right to come along and try to spoil them. Heaven knows it's a hard enough life without that. You can't blame us for not feeling much distressed about it. Sam Dunlop got what was coming to him. He'd been warned often enough. I don't know how he got it and I don't much care."

"That's the way I feel, too," declared her husband.

Blue Pete knew they were not talking to themselves, and he waited to know who the other was.

"What about the woman?"

It was Sergeant's Mahon's voice, and Blue Pete's lips puckered to a soundless whistle of surprise. Cautiously he raised his head to look into the room. The Sergeant was seated beside a table, the upper half of his face in shadow from a shaded lamp near by. In the set of his lips was a grimness that told something of the cold anger and disgust he was with difficulty holding in check.

Sarah Welch jabbed a needle into the coat she was mending and tossed her hair back with a petulant movement. "What did she have to come away out here for? A woman couldn't be happy there; she couldn't even be comfortable. She had to take the bad with the good, and the bad was so obvious. I'm not saying she deserved what she got, but she had to face it with such a man. I'm not supporting murder, mind you, Sergeant. No more am I supporting the murder of hundreds of good steers who had done nothing to deserve it—and that's what would have happened if Big Slough had been fenced off. You've got to—yes, even the Mounted Police should—look on both sides. Sam Dunlop was taking the lives from our herds, taking the living from our mouths, deliberately and unnecessarily doing just that, and the law wasn't going to do anything to protect us. We shoot rustlers if they take a single cow, and the law backs us. Then what's wrong with punishing a man who was going to take hundreds of cows? I have no patience with a law like that."

The Sergeant did not speak for several long moments. If her husband had been so blunt he knew what he would have said and without mincing words. When he did speak it was in a quiet voice:

"For many years, Mrs. Welch, the ranchers in these parts have made that living you claim as a right from land that did not belong to them. It hasn't cost them a cent for the grass, and most of them have made a fortune from it. The land belongs to everyone, to all Canada, but the ranchers alone profited from it. There are homestead laws, and they are reasonable laws. A man can take land in these open ranges if he promises to cultivate them, not just leave them lying there to make a comfortable fortune for him without a moment's labour on the land. We want people out here by the thousands, not just a score of ranchers. No matter how you feel about it, that's what the country wants and what in time it is going to get in spite of you."

"Don't forget the scores of punchers we employ," protested Welch, "and the meat we raise for all the world."

The Sergeant frowned impatiently. "Oh, I know all the arguments, Ford. But all your outfits put together are a mere fraction of the people who would make a living out of farming in this ranching country. I'm not contending that it's good farming land—we haven't had a chance to prove that it is or it isn't—but the chances are that it would turn out the same as in other parts where farms supplanted herds. Sixty years ago the land about Winnipeg was almost as barren, and look at it now.

"The ranges are not yours to dictate about. They will belong to the farmer who fulfils the regulations and brings them to cultivation. It was Sam Dunlop's business to find out if he could make farming pay where he was—"

"But why come so far from town, when there's better land nearer?" demanded the woman.

"That's his business, Mrs. Welch, and we've no right to ask why. One might ask why some men chose their wives. There are men who prefer isolation, as there are men who prefer women no one else wants."

"Did it ever strike you there might be other reasons?" asked Welch.

"As I see it the only ones interested in those reasons, whatever they are, apart from Dunlop and his wife, are the Mounted Police. No, Ford, there isn't an argument for the murderer, and you know it. And you know we're going to find out who he is, or who they are, and when we do the law will take its course. There'll be no argument in court about cutting the cattle from that water. If we permitted such a form of lawlessness—"

From far up the trail a shot cut through the still night air, and a bullet thudded into the wall of the house close to the window.

It was close, too, to Blue Pete's head.

At the same moment came the sound of racing hoofs down the trail towards the ranch house.

The Sergeant jerked forward and blew out the light. Then in the darkness he leaped for the open window and dived through.

So swiftly had he moved that Blue Pete had had no time to get out of the way, and Mahon's shoulder struck him as he drew back. The conversation he had heard had held him so spellbound that he had heard nothing behind him until the shot came. At the moment he had his head above the window-sill, and he ducked and whirled on his knees. Drawing his gun had delayed him a fraction of a second. Then the Sergeant had fallen on him.

Like a cat Mahon turned and siezed him.

"Sh-sh! Lemme go, Sergeant." Blue Pete wriggled to release himself, while nearer and nearer came the racing broncos.

Ford Welch had leaped to his rifle and hurried to the door. At his side stood his wife, holding a rifle of her own.

Mahon's arms unwound. "What the—what are you doing here?" he whispered.

"Jes' listenin'. I gotta vamoose. They seen me ag'in' the light an' shot at me. Hold 'em off fer a minute."

Sergeant Mahon thought quickly. Already running feet could be heard on the way from the bunkhouse. "Don't go back that way. They'll head you off. Go through the house. I'll keep them at the front."

He gathered himself up and hurried around the corner to the front door. "Who is it, Ford? What in the world were they shooting at?"

Before Welch could reply two riders pulled in before them, and Biff Collins leaped from the saddle. He pointed around the corner. "There's someone peeking through your window. I shot at him."

Mahon laughed. "We might have known it was a tenderfoot. Collins, in this country we don't go shooting at every shadow, particularly if it's about someone else's house."

Three cowboys came running around the corner, followed by two from the other side of the house. There was no sign of the half-breed.

"Aren't you going to see who it is?" demanded Collins.

The cowboys insisted no one was there.

"But I saw someone, I tell you. Didn't we see someone, Ted?" He appealed to his friend.

"We sure did."

Ford Welch walked around the corner and returned. "Who is this?" he demanded of the Sergeant.

The latter laughed. "Haven't you heard of Biff Collins and his friend Ted Fraleigh? I thought they'd visited every ranch. They claim to want to purchase a ranch—at a price, of course."

Welch grunted. "Huh! So this is the fellow. Yes, I've heard of him. He seems to be a bit excitable."

Collins commenced to sputter. "But we *did* see a head against the light. I knew it must be someone who had no right to be there."

Welch called to his wife standing in the doorway: "Light a lamp, Sarah." Disgust coloured his tone.

They heard her pick her way about in the darkness of the living-room, searching for matches, then one was struck, and the light steadied as it touched the wick.

The Sergeant waited, holding his breath. He could not be certain that Blue Pete had succeeded in getting away, for the cowboys had come around both sides of the house. If his friend were caught there was little he could do for him, and it would surely end his usefulness to the Mounted Police.

Sarah Welch picked up the lamp and brought it to the door, and her husband took it and carried it around the corner. He examined the ground beneath the window. There were fresh marks there, of course, but Mahon explained them as made by himself when he dived through. No one would have had time to escape before he landed outside, he maintained, even if the cowboys had missed him.

Ford Welch's face creased to a sneering smile.

Collins saw it. "Is this the thanks I get for warning you?"

"Thanks," said the rancher dryly.

The Sergeant had something to say: "You say you fired as a warning."

"That's what I said."

Mahon placed his finger against the fresh mark of the bullet in the wall. "Do you call that merely a warning shot? If anyone had been there it would have been—very serious . . . very serious for you,

Collins."

"Have I no right to shoot at a peeker?"

"Certainly not—even at your own house. This isn't your house. If you'd hit anyone I'd have had to arrest you. In fact, if I was certain anyone was there—"

Collins face reddened with anger. He touched the Sergeant on the shoulder. "Are you telling me I'm lying, Sergeant?"

They had come back around the corner to the front door and stood now in the light from a second lamp Sarah Welch had lit. Mahon turned and looked Collins over slowly from head to foot and back. "When I want to tell you you're lying, Collins, I'll say it plainly, with no hesitation whatever. Now I'll complete what I was about to say: If I was convinced that anyone was there I'd have to charge you with shooting with intent to kill. It would be easy to prove that you shot *at* someone, not just as a warning." He returned the touch on the shoulder. "And let me warn you of something more immediate and pressing: Don't be impertinent with me. I don't like it, especially from a stranger."

Collins's anger had evaporated as the Sergeant spoke. "Well, this is the damndest country. I come out here to—"

"To 'the wild and woolly West,' I suppose," interrupted the Sergeant. "I know the reputation the writers give us. But there's a police force out here, and it's very active—and apt to be resentful against strangers who try to teach us what Easterns think we should do. You know, we learn a lot about strangers—we have to. We like to know all about them—and we don't know much about you—yet. When we get scum from the East—"

"Do you—are you—do you mean me?" sputtered Collins.

"We don't yet know enough about you to answer that," replied the Sergeant.

Fraleigh relieved the situation by laughing. "That's one on you, Biff. He's going to look up our records."

Mahon had regained control of himself. "We have a job to do out here, and sometimes it's difficult, but we've managed to get away with a fairly satisfactory piece of work up to the present. And that's not patting my own back. Anyone who joins the Mounted Police is guided by the reputation it has."

They had entered the room. Mahon's eyes flew swiftly about. He laughed. He felt he could afford to laugh. Blue Pete was not there.

And across the room, on the other side of the house, a window was open that had not been open before.

Escape had not been difficult. The half-breed had merely waited inside until the cowboys had run around to the front, then he had noiselessly raised the window on the other side of the room and had climbed through.

"Gor-swizzle," he whispered to Whiskers when he reached her, "it shure pays to hev a Mountie fer a friend. . . . But that skunk kin shure shoot, an' in the dark . . . at long range . . . and from the saddle. Gotta 'member that. I ain't goin' to take no chances 'th him."

He was to forget that later.

XX   A DOG INTERVENES

TEN days passed, ten days of busy nights for Blue Pete—busy without results. And stories spread of a prowler about the herds, of ghosts whose shadow alone anyone had seen. Every puncher in the district, already on edge through the murders and the Mounted Police search was ready to believe the worst. No one attempted to explain why, but it all seemed to be connected somehow with the tragedies at Big Slough. There was even an occasion when a night-herder had shot at one of his own companions. He had missed, but before the mad flight was stopped the resulting stampede had been the death of eight steers ready for the beef roundup in September. It all added to taut nerves.

There were the wolves also. Even when no cattle were lost the wolves could be heard. They seemed to jeer at night-herders.

With the shooting Blue Pete had no connection; he had been nowhere near. But the general nervousness was his fault, for he visited herd after herd to listen to the talk of the punchers. He was encouraged by the fact that nothing had happened in the district to introduce another topic of conversation, and in the darkness of the night the affair was always in the minds of the night-herders.

It was the Triangle H boys who came nearest to solving the mystery of the night prowler, though they did not know it.

Blue Pete had crept up to one of the herds in the darkness and had settled himself near the borders of the sleeping herd to listen. It was that moment the cows chose to change position. He thought he had provided for that by noting the direction they faced as they lay. For some reason, however, this time several of the cattle turned about and advanced towards him. They almost stepped on him.

By night there was little danger in that, so long as he was careful. By day it was sheer lunacy to be on foot in the midst of a herd. So seldom did they see a man unmounted close at hand that their curiosity drove them to investigate; so that when those behind pressed forward to see what this strange creature was, those in front would be forced over the man, trampling him to death. In the darkness, however, they showed little curiosity as long as the man made no sudden move.

Blue Pete knew their ways too well to feel concern in that respect as they surrounded him. It happened, however, that two of the cowboys were close by, and they hurried to round the straying steers back, and Blue Pete found himself surrounded.

He rose boldly to his feet. The movement stopped the cattle instantly. A wave of the hand would have sent them into a stampede, clearing the way for escape if he could get safely through the dozen that had advanced beyond him. But the rancher in him could not face an unnecessary stampede. Instead he made himself known to the cowboys:

"It's awright, boys. I bin doin' a bit o' ridin' to find wot's bin hangin' 'bout the herds at night." Slowly he worked his way through to them. "Thought I seen suthin' over this way, then the cows got around me. Hev yuh seen anythin' to-night? Sorta skeery night, ain't it?"

They were familiar with some of his strange habits, they knew, too, something of his courage and success in capturing rustlers, and they laughed with relief. One of the cowboys called to him: "Jus' you, Pete? Didja find anythin'?"

"Found muhself near in a mess," the half-breed laughed. "But thar shure was suthin' here, an' I don' think it was a coyote."

"Maybe the ghost of Sam Dunlop," suggested a cowboy, with a nervous laugh.

"Aw, shut up!'' It came as a chorus from his companions.

"The ghost 'ud only bother them that killed Sam," said one, hopefully.

One of the cowboys spurred up to the half-breed. "Perhaps the ghost is hangin' about you, Pete. You were the one they say found the bodies."

Blue Pete laid a hand on the bronco's mane. "Meanin yuh think I done it?"

"No, no, certainly not." The bronco was jerked back. "I was jus' foolin'."

"Yuh bes' laugh when yuh fool like that, Buster. . . . I got ghost 'nuff follerin' me around, 'cause I seen that woman. I can't fergit her. I'm tryin to. That's why I'm ridin' at night to git her outa my mind. Mebbe rustlers 'bout, an' the 3-Bar-Y ain't any safer'n you fellows. . . . Er mebbe it's the wolves, an' that ain't nice. Coyotes wudn' dast come so near. Wal, I'll be packin' my freight. Pinto's jes' over thar." He stood for a brief moment facing them. "An, boys, ef yuh find out who done it—that over at Big Slough, I mean—jus let the Mounties know."

He slouched off into the darkness, grinning to himself. "Tha're ready to shoot, ole gal," he told Whiskers. "You 'n' me we gotta be keerful."

The Lazy M he had opportunity to inspect more thoroughly. The ranch buildings were situated in a series of rolls and shallow coulees. That day he had gone off towards the Cypress Hills but had without good reason changed direction towards the east. Mile after mile he rode through the heat of the afternoon, scarcely ever exposing himself on the heights. Each time he neared one he investigated before crossing it to make certain no one was in sight.

Late in the afternoon he had reached a coulee not far from the Lazy M, and there he stopped. Leaving Whiskers in the long grass where her mottled sides were almost invisible, he climbed the height and lay down to watch the buildings. He saw the night-herders leave the bunk-house, and it was still not quite dark when those they relieved returned. They corralled their mounts and went inside. He could follow the course of events then. Half undressing, they would clamour for their night meal, eat it almost in silence, and then would sit and smoke, perhaps play a game of cards, before climbing into their bunks.

A growing despondency had been gathering over him. It had made him impatient, incautious, reckless. This night he could not wait. And so while he was still not quite dark he crept down towards the bunkhouse, keeping it between him and the ranch house, since he might be seen from the windows of the latter building. Of the cookhouse, too, he had to be careful, since it was a separate building, with the cook running back and forth with food and dishes.

He reached the bunkhouse and lay against the wall where the cook could not see him. Just around the corner was the open front door, and the voices of the cowboys reached him.

They talked little, however, for the meal was just commencing. After a time their chairs scraped back from the table. The cook collected the dishes, and a cowboy commenced to play a mouth-organ.

It was dark by the time he had finished. No one had spoken during the little concert. Movement then told of the cowboys preparing for bed. Bunks creaked, there were several sighs, then silence for a time.

But they did not sleep. The bunks continued to creak; there were more sighs; someone swore. The lamps had been extinguished, but the door was left open.

Someone complained of the draught.

A cowboy laughed. "Limpy's skeered the ghost'll get him." The ghost had become general conversation among the punchers.

It would be Limpy who protested: " 'Tain't the ghost. It's the draught from that damned door. . . . Anyways you chaps ain't seen it. I did."

"Did it wear a white sheet an' breath fire?" teased a cowboy.

"Aw, shut up!" A bunk creaked, bare feet padded over the floor.

There would have been no danger to Blue Pete, though he had crept around near the door, had not Limpy decided to look at the night. As he stepped outside he saw the shadow slip around the corner of the bunkhouse, and he cried out to his companions.

They came running, on the way jerking their guns from their belts hanging on the wall.

Only one of them had the courage, however, to advance around the corner. Charging past Limpy, almost knocking him down, he was within twenty feet of Blue Pete, who was moving away, before he saw the shadow. He whipped up his gun.

At such close range it was a sure hit, but before he could take aim a dark form leaped over the half-breed and launched itself directly at the cowboy. The shot came wildly, and the cowboy tumbled back and scrambled away, all his courage gone.

Blue Pete had seen what happened, and he sat back to watch, forgetting even to draw his own gun. For a moment he almost thought he must be dreaming, then a low chuckle broke from him and he rose to his feet and ran.

Close behind came Rollo, his job done. From first to last the dog had not so much as growled.

It was the foundation of more lurid tales of midnight ghosts and werewolves, "unearthly critters." And cowboys went about their duties at night with two revolvers, one always in their hands. Nerves threatened to crack. Stampedes increased because of it, for the cattle could feel how their herders felt. A few punchers resigned.

Rollo had escaped from the bedroom where he was always closed until Blue Pete was well away from the 3-Bar-Y. But Mira had not thought to close the window, and for some reason the dog decided that that was his chance. Whether he had followed his master's trail by scent or by sight none ever knew. After all it didn't matter. What did matter was that he had almost certainly saved the half-breed's life. It would not have been easy to convince Blue Pete of that, though he had no thought of robbing Rollo of the credit he deserved.

THE incident was interpreted, even by the less easily alarmed, as the prowling of rustlers planning some great coup. It carried to the Mounted Police who were accustomed to the fancies of frightened cowboys and could make little of the stories.

Blue Pete's reaction to Rollo's role in the incident was characteristic. All his life he had trusted to his own resources to get him out of trouble—now and then with the assistance of Mira—and he could not admit that rescue was necessary. It meant even more than that—a new friend.

"Yuh're a right smart bit o' dogflesh, Rollo, ole boy, he applauded, as the dog leaped about him and the pinto in the darkness, "an' yuh're not goin to be locked up no more 'less I got lots o' reason fer it. On'y yuh gotta know right now thar's bound to be shootin' ef yuh hang round me, an' a dog ain' got no gun. 'Sides, yuh mightn't be as lucky as I am." He chuckled as the pinto and the dog nosed together. "Th' ole gal backs me in that, too, eh, Whiskers?"

By daylight he was well on his way back to the 3-Bar-Y. Mira had been alarmed at first when she discovered that Rollo had escaped, and she was up at daylight riding about the nearby heights, searching for him. She was back at the ranch house when she heard them coming. When she saw Rollo she pointed to him in disapproving silence.

Blue Pete only grinned and rode on to the stable.

When he was back in the ranch house she said, "I thought he might have gone to you, but I didn't see how he could find you. I didn't notice he was gone until an hour after you left."

"Rollo's a durn good dog," said Blue Pete, and he stooped to fondle the dog's ears.

She saw there was a story to tell, and she drew it from him. Well, she said at the end, "I'm glad someone can keep track of you. I can't."

Rollo laid his nose on the half-breed's knee and stared into his face.

"He's a durn good dog," he repeated. "I'd like to hev him with me, but offen I dassent, 'cause sometimes I dunno wot's goin' to happen, an' most alius I don' wanta be so easy seen. Whiskers 'n' me we got used to keepin' outa sight, but I dunno bout Rollo." He laughed suddenly. "Gor-swizzle, that puncher musta wondered wot hit him. Ef the punchers ever found out they'd shoot him fust time they seen him, an' I didn't bring him to the 3-Bar-Y to be shot."

"Are you going out again to-day?" she asked.

"Gotta hev a bit o' sleep fust—Mebbe do a bit o' ridin' this afternoon." He thrust a hand into his pants pocket and felt the cast of the toe he always carried. Then he rose and compared it with the original he had stored on a shelf.

Mira watched. "It's a funny boot, that one. You haven't told me what it has to do with the murders."

"Wot makes yuh think it has anythin' to do—"

"Don't waste time denying it, Pete. What does it mean?"

"Mebbe nothin'—Mebbe it'll tell who done it. Thar ain't no ridin' boot 'bout these parts like that. I'm thinkin' it mebbe don' mean nothin'. The foot mebbe moved. That 'ud give it that shape."

Mira took the original from the shelf and examined it. "No, it hasn't moved. That's the shape of the toe. There's the mark of a nail, and it hasn't moved." She replaced the cast and laughed. "Do you plan to examine every boot in these parts? You'll probably get them in your teeth before you're through."

She saw that it worried him and she desisted. But as they ate she saw by his eyes that some exciting thought had come to him.

He slept for only four hours. "Make shure Rollo don' come this time," he urged, as he rode up to the door from the stable. "He'd be in the way." The dog stood beside Mira in the doorway, wagging his tail for an invitation. Blue Pete shook a finger at him. "Yuh gotta stay here an' look after the missus, Rollo. I cudn' take yuh 'long fer wot I'm goin' to do."

The dog made no move to follow but stood watching, a melancholy droop to his ears, until the pinto disappeared over the crest.

Mira had heard what her husband said, and she wondered what he was up to now. She knew better, however, than to ask. That he had nothing in mind these days but the murders at Big Slough she knew. That did not worry her as much as the thought that in what he did to solve the murders he was not only not working with the Mounted Police but in a way was working against them. What trouble that would bring she could not imagine; she did not wish to. To think of him at loggerheads with Sergeant Mahon and Inspector Barker was something more than disturbing.

Her worry of the moment would have vanished had she known

that he planned nothing more dangerous than a talk with Texas, their own foreman. He had as yet not tried to find out if his own outfit had learned anything, because the 3-Bar-Y herds seldom went so far east as Big Slough. But it struck him that the speed with which the news had travelled might have brought something of value to his own men. The cowboys of other outfits might talk plainly to them.

Texas met him in the early evening as the cattle were wandering upward to the warmer heights. Texas was thoroughly reliable. He had been with the ranch even in the early days when Mira's brothers owned it. Loyal, honest, hard-working, he would have given his life for Mira, and now he would do almost as much for Blue Pete, though that relationship had come slowly. It arose from his respect for the half-breed's skill with rope and gun, as well as from the frank affection between his mistress and her husband. His feelings towards the Mounted Police were different. He had never been able to forget the suicide of the two brothers, his former employers, rather than surrender to the police who had cornered them for rustling.[2]

With Texas Blue Pete lost no time in getting to the point. Everyone knew he had found the bodies, and no one would be surprised at his interest in what had happened. He counted, too, on the repugnance every decent cowboy would feel for the woman's murder. Certainly his own cowboys could have had nothing to do with it. That repugnance would make them curious, and curiosity would lead to questioning. To the questions it might be that they already had the answer, since cowboys would talk frankly to one another.

Texas, however, had nothing to tell him. But he had something to say, and he said it haltingly, not looking at his employer:

"You—you're going into this rather deep, ain't you, Pete?"

It startled the half-breed. "I seen that woman," he said, "an' I can't fergit. She was awful to look at." He saw the foreman watching him and he went directly to the point: "Wotchu ast that fer, Tex?"

"Well, some of 'em's saying you're sticking yer nose in too much. They say you should leave it to the Mounties."

"Mebbe tha're more 'fraid o' me findin' out than they are the Mounties. Yuh've heerd some talkin, eh?"

Texas rubbed his chin uneasily. "Wel-l, there was a note stuck in a wheel o' the chuckwagon the other morning. It said to tell you to keep yer nose out of it."

---

[2] *Blue Pete: Half-Breed.*

Blue Pete nodded. There was no need to be surprised, he knew now. "I'm not keepin' my nose outa it, Tex, an' yuh wudn' want me to ef yuh'd seen that woman. But wot tha're mad at is I come on some o' the punchers tearin' down the fence about Big Slough jes' the second day after we took the bodies in to town. They wasn't buried yit. . . . I stopped 'em. They was so mad one of 'em shot at me a few days later, right there at Big Slough."

Texas nodded. "We heard about that. . . an' you didn't do anything about it. . . . Next time they won't miss."

"So they think they'll warn me off through you, Tex." His anger flared. "Tell 'em back that when I'm shot at next it's goin' to mean sudden death to somebody. Yep, I let 'em go that time. I won't do it ag'in. Tell 'em they shud otta know they can't skeer me off anythin' I want to do. An' that ain't sayin' I'm buttin' in on the Mounties."

His anger passed, and he sat for a few moments staring at the hills. Suddenly Texas exclaimed and pointed. A rider was coming towards them from the north-east at a fast lope. It was Cooney Featherstone, of the Double Bar-Y. Cooney was easily recognized at any distance. He was a big man, almost a mountainous man, and special broncos were kept to carry him. Not in himself a good rancher, no one made ranching pay better. That was because of his merry ways, his friendliness, his consideration of others. Every puncher in his outfit had his interests at heart and knew Cooney appreciated it. He was the last man in the district one would suspect of murder; he had never been known to do anything strenuous, had never commended violence.

And yet the moment Blue Pete recognized him a sudden light flashed into his crooked eyes, a brightness he instantly masked. Texas noticed it, though the half-breed turned his back quickly.

"Bes' not let him know wot we was talkin' 'bout, Tex. He might think we was blamin' him."

Texas laughed scornfully. "No danger. Cooney Featherstone couldn't hit a bar door for laughing. And from what they tell me the one that shot Sam Dunlop shot mighty straight and had to do it quick. Sam never went out without his rifle."

Blue Pete started to speak but controlled himself. "So it wasn't known that Dunlop had that day been out without his gun. Well, whoever did it wouldn't tell—"

He stopped that line of thought. Come to think of it, that rifle called for some sort of explanation that was not yet evident. Not only did Dunlop always carry his rifle when outdoors, but even when inside it stood against the wall near the door. Twice he had visited the little hut and had found him at home. That rifle was always where it could be seized in a hurry. What was Sam Dunlop afraid of? Would they ever have the answer?

XXII   A RANCHER INQUIRES

COONEY was with them then. He puffed a little. He could ride, none better, but he seldom rode at such a pace; he had too much consideration for his mounts for that, for one thing. With a grin he removed his Stetson and drew a handkerchief to wipe his forehead.

"Whew! Damned hot day, isn't it? But then all days are hot in the sun this time of the year in this country. Just the same two hundred and forty pounds never gets used to it. Take my advice, boys, and diet if you see it coming. I didn't start in time—so I never started at all. I wish I had the backbone of a woman. It isn't decent for a rancher to be so fat."

Cooney was just filling in the time, and both Blue Pete and Texas knew it.

The rancher knew they saw it, and he raised himself in the stirrups and looked about. "Seen any Double Bar-Y cows around this way? The boys tell me there must be strays somewhere."

It was difficult not to smile. Cooney Featherstone was about as likely to hunt strays as to turn a somersault.

"There ain't any over this way, Cooney," Texas assured him. "We handed over a couple of Lazy M's a couple of days ago, and I saw some Inverted T's off towards the hills, but they were being rounded up. A timber wolf started a small stampede the other night in one of their herds."

Cooney saw that his audience was not deceived and he laughed. "I saw you over here, Pete. I wanted to talk to you. You're sort of mixed up in this Dunlop affair, aren't you? I'll bet I'm the only rancher in these parts who hasn't had the story from your own lips."

Blue Pete removed his Stetson and looked into it, as if to find there what he had to say. "I ain' talked it over 'th nobody—not 'ceptin' a bit mebbe 'th Don Farren."

"You don't tell me! That's strange, because they're all talking about the part you played in finding the bodies. You did find them first, didn't you?"

Blue Pete shook his head. " 'Twas a coupla Injuns found 'em fust."

"That's interesting, too. Coming my way?" Cooney turned his bronco towards home.

Blue Pete was surely going his way; he was just as anxious to talk to Cooney Featherstone as Cooney appeared to be to talk to him.

For the half-breed's mind had flown to the little cast of hard clay in his pocket. It reminded him with disturbing abruptness of a peculiarity in Cooney's feet. The rancher wore a peculiar riding-boot that he always had made to order in Winnipeg. Not only were his feet abnormally large, but the shape of the toes demanded a special last. Blue Pete looked down towards those toes, but they were concealed in wide wooden stirrups with stiff leather guards at the end to prevent the feet slipping through.

It seemed to the half-breed at that moment that he had reached the end of the search, and there was no comfort or satisfaction in it, no sense of attainment. He would have preferred to find anyone else guilty before Cooney Featherstone. Cooney alone of all the ranchers in the district treated him as a friend and equal. More than once he had eaten with Cooney and his wife and had felt the better for it each time. Cooney had no sense of class about him.

The half-breed's mind was torn from these unpleasant reflections by what Cooney was saying:

"I suppose the Sergeant—and that means Inspector Barker— asked you all sorts of questions about what you found at Dunlop's place, eh, Pete?"

"The Sergeant come up when I was thar. He seen wot I seen. Thar wasn' nothin' I cud tell him he didn't see himself."

"But he took you into town with the bodies. The Inspector must have talked it over with you."

"Shure. The Sergeant hadta hev help to town. He cudn' go 'long 'th them two Neches."

"Yes, but the Inspector? What did he have to say? What did he think of the Indians being there? I mean, did he think they could have had anything to do with it?"

Blue Pete shrugged. "Th' Inspector ain' tellin' nobody, leastwise not me, wot he thinks."

"But he must have had his suspicions."

"Mebbe. I dunno."

He saw what was happening: Cooney, as his friend, had been sent to worm out of him what the Mounties had in mind, whom they suspected, what they planned to do. Cooney had not set out to look for strays. That was ridiculous. Nor had he gone for a ride, for Cooney never rode unless he simply *had* to get somewhere. He had come to find Blue Pete and to make him talk. Then the ranchers must be getting nervous. The Mounties must be getting dangerously near the murderer.

"Them Neches they cudn' 'a' did it," he said. "They wudn' 'a' bin 'thin fifty miles o' the place two days after they done it. No, sir. An' yuh shuda seen how skeered they was."

Featherstone laughed incredulously. "I can't imagine an Indian being scared of a dead body."

"They'd be skeered o' the Mounties blamin' them."

"Yes . . . perhaps. Perhaps they returned to steal. Then they saw you coming and fled. They say a murderer always returns to the scene of his crime."

"They didn' see me till long after they'd started to run fer the hills."

Cooney said nothing for some time. It was evident that he had not finished the subject, that he was feeling about for what to say next. "Of course," he ventured, "the Mounties would suspect us ranchers, some of us, if they didn't blame the Indians. No one else would have any interest in getting rid of Dunlop." Suddenly he faced his companion. "Did they mention anyone in particular?"

Blue Pete appeared to be trying to remember. "Th' Inspector don' talk none to anybody but his own men, I reckon. . . . Are you thinkin' it was a rancher? . . . Er mebbe a rancher got some of his boys to do it. I dunno. Ef anybody knows who done it it ain't bin talked 'bout that I know of. Didju hear anythin' like that?"

It failed; he should have known it would. Cooney Featherstone rode for a long time in silence, now and then shooting a sidelong glance at his companion. They passed two herds in the distance, and the cowboys on guard watched them.

The rancher laughed. "They'll be talking about us now, Pete. They know about you and Big Slough, and they're wondering where I come in."

"I dunno 'bout you, but all I done was find the bodies . . . an' I wisht I hadn't."

"I suppose they're wondering how much you really know. They're wondering if you found any clues, or if the Mounties did."

The sudden silence that followed made of it a question.

"I ain' got no idee who done it," said Blue Pete.

Cooney laughed slyly. "But you'd like to know. . . . Some of the punchers appear to be sore at you for interfering. They say it was none of your buisness when they were tearing down that fence. All they wanted was to clear Big Slough, and that had to be done soon so the cows wouldn't get tangled in the barbed wire. . . . You know when the boys get sore on anyone it's apt to make trouble. I wouldn't like you to get a bullet in you, Pete."

The half-breed felt cold anger raging through him. "Are yuh warnin' me? Are yuh tellin' me I shudn' otta wonder who done it? Are yuh tellin' me to fergit that woman, the way I seen her? Wal, ef that's it it ain't no go. I don't skeer easy, an' yuh kin tell 'em I'm goin' to keep on wonderin' till somebody finds out. . . an' ef thar's shootin' I'll be doin' some of it muhself. An' yuh know I don' miss offen."

Several times Cooney had tried to stop the flow but had failed. Now he said: "Naturally you're curious. No one can blame you for that. But I'm your friend, Pete, and I'm warning you not to give the boys any more reason to be angry at you. Now let's drop it. One thing I really wanted to talk about with you is the wolves. Something must be done about them. They're getting out of hand, and you're the only one can do much about it. Jerry the Pole's too old and lazy." He laughed. "You can keep your shooting hand in on the wolves. They're playing hell with the herds."

"Jerry's got the dogs, an' he likes huntin' wolves."

"But besides being old and lazy, it's only sport to him, something to keep his dogs in shape. We want wolves killed and quickly, no matter how it's done, and not just a wolf to-day and not another for a couple of weeks. We think you're the man to do it. I'll tell you what I've in mind: Come to the house with me and to-morrow I'll take you to a herd that's had most trouble with the wolves. Every night they hear them about. You've got night eyes, they say."

He scowled at his bronco's ears. "That reminds me—the boys are badly upset about someone or something that keeps creeping about the herds in the dark. At the Lazy M they say some sort of animal attacked one of the punchers when he was about to shoot someone he saw prowling about the bunkhouse. All sorts of stories have started about it, and the boys are badly frightened. We must work out something to straighten things out. I don't know how much there is in the story, but if we could kill off a few of the wolves it would help. Even when no cows are killed stampedes play hell with them." He thudded his heels into the bronco's ribs. "Come on. We'll be in time to get something to eat. You can't get back to the 3-Bar-Y to-night anyway."

Blue Pete followed. There was a chance that he might have a chance to be able to see those boot toes; he would never have a better opportunity. Besides, he might be able to learn the origin of the warnings Cooney had delivered.

"Mira'll be wonderin'," he protested feebly.

"Tut, tut! Don't give me that one, Pete. You're away from home more than you're there. . . . Now there's what I call a perfect setting for ranch buildings—and nearly perfect buildings."

He had pulled in at the crest of a long slope. Down in the bottom they could make out in the twilight a cluster of buildings, better buildings than most of the Medicine Hat district. For Cooney Featherstone might be indolent but he wanted comfort and he knew what paid in the long run. The lamps in the ranch house were alight, the glow beaming warmly from half a dozen windows in the two stories. Cattle bawled lazily from a corral, and in another corral broncos had heard them and were watching over the rails. A bow-legged cowboy swaggered from the stable to the bunkhouse and disappeared. But he must have seen them, for he reappeared and stared up at them. He recognized Cooney and set off towards the ranch house to take the horses.

They rode down the slope. The lowing of the cattle had ceased, only the rattle of a windmill was audible. Then the ranch house door opened and a woman stood in the opening.

"You're late, Tom. Good evening, Pete!" Carrie Featherstone showed no surprise at recognizing her husband's companion. Her prejudices were no more extensive than his.

"I brought Pete along, my dear. I hope you've got something for us to eat. We're going to do something to-morrow about the wolves."

A man came to the door behind the woman. "Did I hear someone mention the wolves? If there's to be a hunt count me in."

It was Biff Collins.

COONEY was half way out of the saddle. At sight of Collins he settled back. "Who the devil is that?" he whispered to his companion.

"That's the tenderfoot wot's tryin' to buy a ranch an' live 'th us in these parts," Blue Pete replied. It expressed something of his dislike. "He's takin' a durn long time to find out thar ain't nobody'll sell to him."

Cooney laughed. Then he addressed himself to the man in the doorway; "If we get up a real hunt we might be glad to take along anyone who can carry a rifle . . . who knows how to use it, of course."

"Well, I certainly won't shoot myself," Collins assured him. "I've done a bit of shooting in my time—deer and moose and bear. They're pretty hard to bring down sometimes. I don't think we've met." He came out to the rancher and held out his hand.

"My name is Biff Collins, and this," pointing to his friend who had followed him out, "is Ted Fraleigh. You may have heard of us."

"There isn't much in these parts we don't hear about pretty quickly," replied the rancher dryly. "Someone told me you were trying to buy a ranch."

"Trying's as far as it's gone to date—but someone told you the truth, which is refreshing."

"Don't they use much of it where you come from?" Fraleigh laughed. "That's one on you, Charlie."

Collins frowned at his friend, then said quickly: "They don't use much of it anywhere in my experience."

"You're a stranger here, I see."

"We've been here long enough to realize how difficult it is to buy a ranch. Someone told me you might consider an offer."

"Of course. Anything and everything is considered out here. We have time to do considering. But go inside. We'll be back in a few minutes."

He waved the cowboy away and rode on to the stable. Blue Pete followed.

As he dismounted Cooney made a scoffing sound. "The damned idiot! Does he really think the Double Bar-Y is for sale? He's trying something—and it won't work. Yes, I've heard a lot about Biff Collins, and a lot of us are wondering."

"Wonderin' wot?"

"Well, the offers he makes would never close a deal, yet he keeps on making them at about the same level. We're wondering what else he has in mind." He laughed. "Yes, I told Slim Manson to tell him that I might consider an offer. I wanted to meet him. We've all been leading him on. We wouldn't foul the West by selling him anything. Did he call at the 3-Bar-Y?"

"Shure. He's tried 'em all now, I reckon. Mira set him back on his heels in short order. Didn' even listen long 'nuff to hear his offer. She didn' like him."

"Nobody does. I don't. Do you?"

"Reckon I've had more run-ins 'th him than all the rest o' yuh put together," laughed Blue Pete. "Thar's sparks when we meet."

"Well, keep your flint wet in my house. It would frighten Carrie. Funny how everyone hates him and his friend." He shook his head thoughtfully, led the bronco into the stable, and slid the saddle from its back. "I wonder why."

Blue Pete shrugged. It made no difference to him what others thought of Collins. "Jes' nachully mean, I reckon. . . . Reckon mebbe I bes' eat at the bunkhouse. Biff Collins jes'—"

Cooney took hold of his arm. "You're coming to eat in the ranch house. Carrie would be disappointed, and we've got to have a talk about those wolves. Besides, I might need support. I'm not accustomed to entertaining tenderfeet; I'm apt to do something against the rules," he chuckled.

When they entered the ranch house Collins and Fraleigh rose to shake hands again. Even for Blue Pete they had a nod and a smile. It was plain that they wished to make a good impression.

"I was just telling your wife that I seem to have landed in the right place at long last," said Collins. "With a ranch in prospect, and now a wolf-hunt—that just about makes the world look bright."

Cooney Featherstone seated himself in a huge chair beside the table. Blue Pete chose a chair and edged it nearer; he remembered the cast in his pocket, but Cooney's feet were concealed beneath the table.

The rancher loosened the kerchief about his neck and threw it on a small table. "There always was the prospect of a ranch, wasn't there?"

An apparently casual remark, but Collins glanced at him swiftly. "What prospect there was has dimmed as our efforts continued. I'd almost given up hope, and I'd like nothing better than to settle here.

I'd like to be a Hatter. That's what they call you about Medicine Hat, I suppose."

"What they call us and what we are may not agree, as you've probably discovered." He reached under the table and removed his riding-boots.

His wife hurried to the bedroom and returned with his slippers. The riding-boots she bore back to the bedroom—and the half-breed's opportunity was gone.

Cooney sighed comfortably. "Sometimes we deserve what they call us." He laughed. "And that's philosophy that isn't suited to the occasion. I'm always glad to meet strangers."

Collins made a wry face. "I can't say we've met many who seem to feel the same. At any rate if we fail to get a ranch, don't rob us of a wolf-hunt. I want a skin or two to take back to show my friends."

"You sound as if it was scalps," Carrie laughed. "The Mounted Police would be curious if they heard you talk like that."

Collins glanced at his friend. "They're curious now. But with so many Indians you probably know more about scalps than we do."

"Times have changed," sighed Cooney. "A scalp or two now and then was a pastime here in the West. Ah, me, the colour has gone out of life." He shifted his position. "But about this wolf-hunt: Blue Pete and I were merely speaking of it. You know, if you two are free you might take the job on yourselves. This is getting to a busy time on the ranges; the beef-roundup will be on in a few weeks, and we're trying to keep the cows contented and quiet, to fatten. Besides, the wolves would never catch your scent as they do ours. They know an oldtimer a mile off—smell him. They might be nothing more than curious about the new scent you and your friend would throw off. . . . They know, too, that we shoot them on sight."

He nodded at Blue Pete. "Here's the best shot, the best hunter, in the West. He's so good that the wolves have a school in the hills to train their cubs to steer clear of him. He's shot more wolves than we ever thought existed in the hills. Why don't you get him to join you and put on a real hunt that would get those scalps you want?" He glanced sideways at the squirming half-breed.

"I've tried that every way I know," said Collins. "For some reason he doesn't take to the idea."

"Perhaps you offered to pay him."

"Well, yes, I did at first. That was one of the things I didn't know about the West. In fact I didn't even know he was a rancher. I wanted him as a guide, and we pay our guides in the East. Out here—"

"Oh, our prices are very high out here." Cooney winked about the room. "They're so high that we never speak of them. The only paid job on the ranges is punching. Of course, if you should suggest that he go along as a companion—"

"I did that, too. Didn't I, Ted?"

Fraleigh nodded. "And when Charlie Musson says he'll do a thing it's as good as done."

Collins laughed awkwardly. " 'Charlie Musson's' my first two names."

"Biff's a funny name," said Carrie Featherstone. "Where did you get it?"

Collins spread his hands self-deprecatingly. "As a kid I lived—on the tough side of the railway tracks in Detroit. It made me pretty nifty with my dukes—my fists, I mean. I think that's where it started. Biff!—and someone hit the ground . . . and it was seldom me." He laughed. "You know how those schoolboy nicknames stick."

Blue Pete had said nothing; he watched and listened. He had heard the "Charlie Musson" and something clicked in his mind when it was evident that Collins was disturbed by it. But it was only one more puzzle about the pair. He dismissed it when Collins continued to talk:

"If I'm lucky enough to get a ranch I can promise that I'll spend much of my time after those wolves. It would mean a lot more then than mere sport."

Cooney had commenced to eat. He laid down his fork and regarded his guest with frank surprise. "We ranchers manage to keep ourselves busy during the summer months without that. Of course you might introduce some new and improved methods, coming fresh from the East. I suppose you have ideas about running a ranch. We're always open to learn."

Collins did not know how to take it. "Oh, I'm not above work, but I must admit that I like hunting better."

"Better start on antelope," suggested Cooney. "They run in the open, and they would give you some hard riding."

Collins seemed to leap at it. "Nothing would suit me better. Those wolves give me the creeps. Just to hear a coyote howl—br-r-r!" He shuddered. "But coming back to the ranch, Featherstone, would you consider selling?"

The rancher looked about the familiar room, as if hesitating—perhaps valuing what he had to sell. In the survey he managed to wink at his wife. "I suppose there's nothing binding in listening to an offer."

Collins was silent for several moments. Suddenly, as if awakening, he laughed and rubbed his hands together.

"Now that's what I call talking turkey, as we say back East."

"Better stick to cow-talk out here; we don't raise turkeys."

"I'd have to know how many cattle you run, of course."

Cooney tilted his head, closed one eye, and squinted at the ceiling. "Hm-m! I suppose that's right. . . . But I can't give you an answer right away; I'll have to consult my foreman."

"But you must have some idea—in round numbers, I mean."

"Yes . . . of course. There must be more than ten thousand . . . and less than twenty."

Collins looked at his friend to see how he was taking it, but Fraleigh appeared uninterested; he was toying with a pair of spurs that hung near him on the wall, large, engraved silver spurs. Nevertheless his eyes were free to follow Carrie Featherstone as she moved about the room.

"Of course," said Collins, "I'd have to know something nearer the number than that. I'd have to know where you stand—"

Cooney scraped his chair back but leaned forward over the table, resting on his forearms. "I can tell you where I stand: I still own the Double Bar-Y."

A flush spread over Collins' face. "I'm in no hurry, though I'd like to get the thing settled. I'll fill in the time on that wolf-hunt."

Suddenly he laughed, a short, unpleasant laugh. "Or I might get a commission from the Mounted Police to find out for them who killed those two settlers at Big Slough. The Mounties don't seem to be getting anywhere, and I'm more or less interested, as the half-breed here knows. The bodies were brought to the Inverted T while I was there, and Don Farren and Fraleigh and I rode over with Sergeant Mahon when he went to make a search of the hut. I used to do a bit of under-cover work back East. Private detective for a time. Made a success of it, too." He grinned at his host. "But I shouldn't even hint at running the murderer down—not before a rancher, should I?"

The rancher's face was expressionless. "Why not?"

"Well . . . surely the Mounties must blame it on a cowman. Of course I don't say it was a rancher but somebody concerned with the cows."

Cooney nodded as if in casual agreement. "Seems like that, doesn't it." He turned to Blue Pete. "You found the bodies. What's your opinion?"

Blue Pete shifted uneasily. "I'd bet it wasn't no cowman—ef I cud think o' anybody else. I ain' got no opinion."

"Oh, you can speak plainly here," said Cooney.

Collins added his word: "Yes, nothing would go beyond the walls of this room. What did the Sergeant find? Were there any clues? He appeared a little excited that day, I noticed, as if he had something. Did he tell you what it was?"

The half-breed shook his head. "He didn' tell me nothin'."

"If I could be of any assistance I wish they'd call on me." Collins winked at his friend. "Just the same I've a bet with Ted that they won't find who did it."

Cooney nodded reflectively. Suddenly he fixed his eyes on his guest. "Would you like to expand that bet a little—or is it private? I'd like to get in on it—and give you odds."

"Any amount?"

"Any amount."

A slow smile gathered on Collins' face. "Is your ranch too high a bet?"

The rancher's teeth snapped together, but he did not hesitate. "What have you got to bet that would approximate the value of the ranch? Have you enough money?"

"Not in my pocket, of course. But I'll bet half the value of the ranch as appraised by—say—the Mounted Police Inspector."

"Get the money," snapped Cooney.

Collins was evidently not happy about it. "I didn't plan to bet with anyone but Ted. I don't think it would make you ranchers more friendly if I won such a bet, and I want them to be friends. I'll withdraw the bet if you'll let me."

"Frightened?"

"Cha—Biff Collins doesn't know what fright is. The bet stands. I'll get the money. . . . Fact is, I'd hate to see one of you ranchers convicted."

"And in the interests of the bet—and of that desire—as a private detective you'd do your utmost to see that the Mounted Police failed. Is that it?"

"The bet stands." There was an angry grimness about it, but almost immediately he laughed. "I can't imagine any rancher I've met doing a thing like that—and I think I've met them all now. No matter who did it the Mounted Police will have an unusual murderer to deal with. Besides, everyone thinks the settler deserved what he got."

"Was there ever a murder where the murderer at least didn't think his victim deserved it?" asked Cooney. "It was a brutal affair, and I still don't think any rancher in these parts capable of it. That's my opinion."

"Then where does that lead you?"

"That's for the Mounties to say, and I've faith in them. . . . It doesn't seem possible that the scoundrel who did such a thing would escape his just punishment. It's the woman I'm thinking most of."

"I seen the woman," muttered Blue Pete.

Collins shook his head solemnly. "Yes, that must have been pretty bad. It does seem a bit—a bit Western, if I may say so."

"You may. . . . Also I read the papers. Things happen back East. We may look at things differently out here, but we aren't brutal to women."

Collins said nothing for a time; his attention was fixed on his finger-nails. "How in the world did we get on such a gruesome subject? I'd like to forget it all. It'll always be a nasty spot in my memory, whether I get a ranch or not. I'd like to get started on that wolf-hunt, just to help me forget, if for nothing else." He turned pleadingly to Blue Pete. "Won't you reconsider and come with us, Pete, just for the sport?"

Blue Pete had not been listening. He was still trying to catch a glimpse of Cooney Featherstone's feet.

Collins was forced to repeat the request: "Come along, Pete, and help us help you. Every wolf we get means something to the herds."

The half-breed rubbed his chin and hesitated. He was curious about the two strangers, doubly curious during the past hour in Featherstone's house. There was something about the name Fraleigh had called his friend that tumbled about in his mind. If he could be with them on the wolf-hunt he might learn something about the things that puzzled him. But he could not see himself associated with them in any way for any purpose.

"I ain't changed my mind," he grunted. "I got lots o' things to do. . . . But I'd shure liketa know wot sorta luck yuh hev. Yuh offered to pay me. I'll tell yuh wot I'll do: I'll go in with any o' th' other ranchers an' pay yuh five dollars fer every wolf yuh shoot. On'y thing—don' go in them hills alone. Tha're no place fer a tenderfoot."

Collins laughed contemptuously, yet it did not sound spontaneous. "I've heard a lot about that, and I suppose I'll do the sensible thing and take someone with me who knows the hills. As a matter of fact I don't like the sound of the howling I hear every night, even when I know it's only coyotes. That dog of yours, Pete—its howl resembles a wolf's, they tell me. That's enough for me. If a wolf howls any worse than that I can see myself ducking under the bed. Should I take one with me for that purpose?" He saw that no one so much as smiled, except his friend, and he changed his manner. "No, I'm going to get some Indians. There are a couple of them in the camp in town who might go. I confess that I'd like company on a hunt like that."

"Yuh shure done right ef yuh're gittin' Indians," Blue Pete approved. " 'Twudn' be safe 'thout 'em. Them wolves is big 'n fierce, an' when they git real mad er cornered it takes a bullet smack in the heart to stop 'em. Tha're p'ison. I know them hills better'n anybody else, an' I go keerful in thar."

"Are you trying to frighten me?" asked Collins.

"Ef that frightens yuh yuh'd bes' not go near the hills, 'cause that ain't half the truth. The hills ain't no place fer anybody wot's skeered."

Biff Collins squared his shoulders. "That's enough. I'm going into the hills to hunt wolves."

"The boys'll shure be shouting fer yuh. Yuh shure got spunk."

Collins expanded under the approbation. He seemed to sit straighter in his chair. "Over at the Lazy M they were telling me of a ghost or something that haunts the herds at night. There was some sort of animal that attacked one of the boys and gave the ghost a chance to escape. A fanciful story. One wouldn't think these chaps would be so nervous."

Cooney shook his head. "There's no telling what comes out of the hills in the dark of night . . . less telling what never comes out. I've got a foreman who never had a nerve in his life, and he's carrying two six-shooters right now and never goes out at night without a companion. Three of my outfit saw that ghost." He winked at Blue Pete from the shadow of his hand.

"Why didn't they shoot it?" Collins inquired.

"What? Shoot and start a stampede? You've got a lot to learn before you'll be a rancher, Collins."

"Perhaps," said Collins, "I could fill in the time by taking a job as a cowboy, until some rancher decides to sell. I'd like to catch a ghost."

"Go and make a name for yourself first by killing wolves," said Cooney sharply.

"I'm going. Ted and I are going, and we're going this very next Monday. I've already hired those two Indians as guides. We're going into the hills, and we won't come out without a hide or two. And no one will need to pay me. . . . But I'd still like to have you along, Pete."

"I kin git into 'nuff trouble right out here on the ranges," said the half-breed.

He would not stop for the night; he had never slept in a ranch house, other than the 3-Bar-Y, since coming to Canada.

Cooney went to the stable with him, chuckling all the way. "What in the world are you up to, Pete? You've got him shaking in his boots. He'd like to cave in on that wolf-hunt, but you sure fixed it so he daren't. I saw what you were after, and I helped you along as best I could."

"I want him to go on that wolf-hunt."

"Why?"

"I don't rightly know . . . but mebbe I'll be thar in the hills to do a bit o' huntin' muhself 'bout nex' Monday."

XXIV   AN IMPORTANT DISCOVERY

THE Mounted Police had not been idle. For two weeks Sergeant Mahon had moved among the ranches. There was nothing in that to arouse suspicion of any special purpose, since that was his job, but never for a moment were eyes or ears closed to a clue to the murderer. He did not deceive the ranchers; none knew better than they that the Mounted Police would never rest until the murderer was found.

At no time did any of them attempt to conceal his satisfaction that Big Slough was open again. They even talked openly of Western justice, though they carefully avoided speaking of the woman. A few talked more bluntly than they need, and Mahon decided that they knew nothing of the identity of the murderer. It helped to cut down the suspects.

Among the cowboys he had no better luck, with the difference that he soon convinced himself that not one of them knew as much about the murders as he himself did.

He seemed to have run up against a stone wall, and it irritated and worried him. Inspector Barker, too, worried and was sometimes sharp-tongued, so that Mahon was tempted to resign.

Nevertheless on one of his visits to the barracks he found the Inspector an absent-minded listener; he seemed to have other things on his mind.

Suddenly the old swivel chair swayed and creaked as the Inspector swung around. "Yes, it's a difficult case, Mahon. I know how you feel. Those ranchers will stand together to make as little of the murders as they can. . . . I'm beginning to think no cowboys were concerned in it. They'd be too likely to let the cat out of the bag, and I don't think the ranchers would trust them. You're tired out. Better knock off for a couple of days and have a good rest. Get it off your mind. Then you can start out fresh."

He sat for a time, drumming on the tobacco-strewn blotter. "Get a change of scene—something to take your mind off the Dunlops. For instance, I've been thinking a lot about those two tenderfeet. Are they still dickering for a ranch? Haven't they got onto the fact yet that they haven't a chance? I understand the ranchers are playing them for fools. Yet they persist . . . and somehow I don't think they're stupid. Langley tells me they've been out to the Indian camp, hiring guides to take them on a wolf-hunt in the hills. They've been here almost a month, haven't they? . . . There's something about it I don't understand. The offers they make don't appear to be serious, or else they know nothing of the value of cattle. We haven't learned as much about them as we usually take pains to find out about newcomers. This Big Slough business has interfered. I've asked among the banks. They brought some money—or Collins did—and deposited it in the Bank of Commerce—someone saw them in there cashing a cheque—but it must be nearly gone now. Of course it has cost them mighty little, living among the ranches."

He scowled through the fly-blown window. "Perhaps I'm more curious because I don't like the looks of that fellow Collins. I've seen him at the Alberta—he changed over from the Royal—and he's much too mouthy for me. Do you know anything about him?"

"Blue Pete knows more about him, sir, than anyone else," Mahon replied with a laugh. "He had a run-in with him over at the Royal that day he was in town before the murders. I didn't report it because it didn't go far enough to amount to anything . . . and I think perhaps Blue Pete was wearing a chip on his shoulder. But I'll accept Pete's estimate of a man any time, and he sure hates Collins. . . . There seems to be more in it, too, than I know of."

He dropped his eyes.

The Inspector frowned. "What is it? Tell me."

"I know you don't want him to work on these murders, sir, yet that's what he's doing. He doesn't seem to be able to get the woman out of his mind."

He told of the incident at the Double X, of Collins' shot at the peeking half-breed and of the means by which the latter made his escape. "And we've reason to know, sir, what Blue Pete thinks of anyone who dare take a shot at him."

The Inspector had commenced to laugh. "Doesn't he have the devil's own luck? . . . But Collins had no right to shoot like that. You should have brought him in."

"I daren't, sir. I'd have had to tell on Blue Pete."

"Yes, that's right. . . . At the same time it might have done that half-breed good to get him into a little trouble, and it might have put him out of the way till we find more about the murderers. . . . But let's drop that now for a while. It'll give you a chance to poke about and find out more about Collins and his friend. If they aren't in earnest about buying a ranch, what has brought them, what keeps them?" He considered for a few moments. "Take a run to the Indian encampment and make some inquiries about that wolf-hunt."

A mounted policeman passed the window and entered the barracks. A moment later someone knocked on the office door.

"This'll be the mail. Go and have some rest, then skip out to the camp and see what you can unearth."

Constable Langley entered with a handful of letters and dropped them on the desk. Mahon left the office and made his way back to his own small office at the rear of the building. He was free for a few hours, and he knew he should go to his rooming-house and try to make up for lost-sleep, but his mind was too active. And so he threw himself into his chair, raised his feet to the desk, locked his hands behind his head, and closed his eyes while he tried to work out where he had failed.

He had little success, partly because Blue Pete kept crowding into his thoughts. He had an idea that the half-breed was working on clues he himself had missed. That was not surprising, since Blue Pete had been there both times before him. Then, too, he was at liberty to use methods denied the Mounted Police. Besides, being a rancher, he had an approach to the other ranchers impossible to the law.

Following the thought through, he was shocked to picture where it led: Blue Pete, if he found who the murderer was, would probably take punishment into his own hands. That was how serious he was; nothing else would satisfy him. It would force the police to take action against him, a disturbing picture for a friend to have to face, doubly disturbing for the Mounted Police who would surely miss him.

Mahon shifted his position, as if it might change the direction of his thoughts. He remembered the Inspector's orders to the half-breed. It reminded him of the orders to himself, and he roused himself with the thought that he would spend an hour among the Indians—

The frantic ringing of his bell on the wall above the door brought his feet to the floor with a crash. Inspector Barker was shouting for him.

He hurried along the hall, automatically straightening his tunic. Before he could knock the Inspector shouted to enter.

A letter lay open before the Inspector and he tapped it with one finger. "Look here, Mahon. A letter from the East, from Detroit. It gives us some of the low-down on Sam Dunlop. I sent a photograph, you remember. They know him—that electrical company. Dunlop is not his name. His right name is Mason . . . and Mason was not married! That woman wasn't his wife. He'd run off with a woman by the name of Musson."

XXV WAITING

OUT on the prairie the sun beat mercilessly on a yellow world of dead grass, a blinding glare without relief. But where Blue Pete sat within the edge of the trees that crowned the Cypress Hills the air was pleasantly cool. He slouched in the saddle, one leg thrown about the horn, the reins dropped idly across his knee.

It was a silent, lifeless scene, except for the gentle rustle of leaves high up in the trees over his head. Rollo squatted beside the pinto, tongue hanging, now and then looking up at his master as if inquiring what came next. As far as the half-breed could see—and his crooked eyes missed nothing across many miles of prairie below him— nothing moved except the fringes of a solitary herd six or seven miles away. High as he was, he could see against the sky the standtank thirty miles away in Medicine Hat, and he smiled and shook his head at the incongruous modern touch of it. He did not like it, yet he could never get away from it except in the deeper coulees. Always it was there, prophesying things to come that made any rancher uncomfortable. It threatened their existence, yet they could do nothing about it.

Behind him, in the thick fastnesses of the forest, it was almost as still. Just the faintest rustle of leaves, like nature breathing peacefully in her sleep. At long intervals a bird cheeped sleepily. But back there, no one knew so well as he, a vast world lived and moved—and watched. Just now in the heat of the August day it was sleepy and limp.

There was a world there, too, less innocent than the birds, a world of life that crept about on noiseless feet, looking for prey, pursuing and pursued—rabbits, foxes, curious rats like mountain rats, and the enemy of them all, the timber-wolf. Seldom was the wolf heard except at night, especially if humans were about. In the darkness it was more vocal if there were humans; it seemed to know the terror its howl aroused in its inveterate foes, and to glory in it.

Suddenly a bird screamed, a startlingly sharp call that sent the half-breed's mind back to a time when perhaps the very same bird had given the signal that ended a feud between two bitter enemies with bullets.[3] The hills were crammed with memories like that, adventures that made life worth living, escapes whose narrowness made them no

---

[3] *Blue Pete Breaks the Rules.*

more than exciting. He loved the hills. They were more to him than any other place in the world.

So still he sat, with Whiskers dozing and Rollo waiting impatiently, that a bird flew down to a branch close to his head and sat twittering and wondering, turning its head from side to side as if trusting neither eye. Few humans were seen in the Cypress Hills.

Interested as he was in the prairie before him, he missed nothing about him. He saw the bird and raised his dark face to grin at it. He even snapped a finger at it, and the bird flitted to a higher twig and continued to mutter wonderingly.

He had left the 3-Bar-Y while it was still too early for the sun. In early August that meant before three, and he had ridden fast, keeping to the coulees. His route had carried him far to the south of the western end of the Hills, around Elk Lake. There would be no one to see him there. Yet he had avoided approaching the trees until he had passed further south where no herds dare feed because of the danger of rustlers bursting forth from the Montana Badlands. Through the forest he had come to the spot where he now sat waiting and watching. Everything to the north was under his eyes, eyes that scarcely blinked.

The morning had passed. At first he had left the pinto in a ravine and had gone on foot to where he was now. Whiskers had whinnied pleadingly after him, for she knew something important and exciting was in the air and she wanted to be in on it. He had slapped her on the thigh before leaving her.

"Hang 'bout, ole gal. Reckon thar'll be lots o' time fer yuh to see wot's goin' on later." He knew she would not wander far; she would be there when she was needed.

He had picked out this spot and had seated himself on the ground. Rollo had kept with him, and he fondled the hairy ears absent-mindedly. It was getting much warmer even in the shade, and he sidled back out of the sun and leaned against a tree. The sun found him there presently and he was forced to move again. Rollo moved with him always within reach of his hand.

He picked up a stick and commenced to whittle. But only for a few seconds did his eyes leave the prairie. "Dunno why I brought yuh, ole boy," as the dog hugged against his legs. "Mebbe yuh'll jes' be in the way. But yuh begged to come an' I cudn' say no. So yuh gotta look after yerself—like Whiskers . . . an' the wolves won't like yuh bein' around." He twisted the dog's ears playfully. "Reckon yuh kin look after yerself purty well . . . an' mebbe yuh think yuh kin look after me. Never had a dog before; never had anybody to look after me—'ceptin' Mira, o' course. But keep yer eyes skinned fer the wolves. They don' like dogs. . . . 'Taint' no place fer a dog in the hills, an' I shudn' 'a' brought yuh, but mebbe yuh kin find suthin' to do."

A grin spread over his face. "Wonder ef yuh 'member wot I trained yuh to do. All ready?" He raised his hand over the dog's head and snapped his fingers.

And Rollo, raising to his haunches, lifted his face and howled.

"Gor-swizzle, it'll fool the wolves themselves. Beats anythin' how yuh manage it. Mus' be lots o' wolf in yuh. Hope nobody don' shoot yuh fer a wolf. I'll teach yuh more tricks too when I git time. Ef yuh cud—"

His head jerked forward. Never for more than a few seconds at a time had his eyes left the prairie. He rose excitedly now to his knees. Far to the north a rider had come racing into view from a coulee, had cut across to the east and disappeared in another coulee. With a loud breath the half-breed relaxed. Only a cowboy on duty.

But a few minutes later far off towards Medicine Hat something moved against the dead yellow of the grass. For a time it was only a speck, then it spread apart to a pair of riders. He rose to his feet, a fixed smile on his face. He knew this was what he waited for.

He watched. Now and then the pair were lost to view. They were riding slightly towards the south-east but always coming nearer. They were hours away still, but his crooked eyes danced with excitement.

The pair disappeared. So long were they out of sight that he became anxious. Then he remembered that they had disappeared where the trail struck off to the east. Could it be that he was too hopeful, that it was not the ones he expected? If they were coming to the hills they would have left the trail there and come straight south. Besides, there should be four of them.

He gritted his teeth together. "It was them awright. I'd know them was Neches by the way they rode. I kin 'most smell 'em too. They've gone to pick Collins up."

He raised his eyes to the sky, studying the position of the sun. It must be about four o'clock. It would be dusk before they reached the hills. The T-Inverted R was not far from where they had disappeared.

Perhaps Collins and his friend were there, waiting to be called for.

He hoped it was that but he waited so long that he was almost in despair. The strain was intolerable, and he considered getting Whiskers and riding out to make sure. In his anxiety he paced about under the trees. Rollo kept at his heels, silent and distressed.

And then four riders came into view. It was far to the east of where the Indians had last been seen. And it was them again, with two more.

Blue Pete grinned. He rubbed his hands together and whistled.

"Yuh gotta be keerful from now on, Rollo," he warned "Yuh gotta do zackly wot I say. Lemme do the thinkin'. You ain't useta this sorta thing. I am—me 'n' Whiskers."

He made sure that the quartette was making for the hills, then he hurried back to the pinto and brought her to where he could watch the four approaching. They would reach the hills half a mile to the east where a steady and smooth slope led upward. Slowly he rode in that direction.

They were coming rapidly now, eager to make camp before darkness set in. In half an hour they would be in the trees. The Indians had come all the way from Medicine Hat; they would take the slope at a leisurely pace.

"Tha're comin' to git wolves," he said aloud to his animal friends. "Mebbe they'll git more'n that, more'n they reckoned fer. But I gotta watch out fer them Neches. You, too, Rollo. Tha're cunnin'. Whiskers knows 'em."

He was in no hurry. He had lots of time to reach the spot where they would enter the forest. Keeping well within the trees, he moved along. Presently he retired further into the trees and found a thicket where he left the pinto. It suited his purpose admirably, for it was surrounded by a growth of larger trees through which a mounted man would ride with difficulty. Whiskers would be safe there.

He considered the dog. Rollo was as yet an unknown quantity in some respects. But the dog looked appealingly into his face, wagging his tail.

The half-breed wagged a warning finger back. "No, yuh can't come 'th me. Yuh bes' stay here 'th th' ole gal. Ef yuh're goin' to be any good to me 'taint now. I got to be whar I won't hev no cover like this."

He pointed to the pinto, and Rollo dropped his tail, went to

Whiskers, and lay down beside her.

When he reached a spot where he could see the riders again they were less than a mile away, almost at the bottom of the slope. The Indians rode side by side in the lead. Collins and Fraleigh seemed to have dropped behind to talk without being heard.

The half-breed found cover for himself, examined it carefully from every side to make sure he would not be exposed, then returned to watch the riders.

He could see them so plainly now that he thought he could read the expressions on their faces. The two Indians, stolid, silent, their bodies relaxed in a manner that made a day's ride of little physical consequence, rode as if they were part of their ponies. They used saddles, not because they needed them but because they furnished a fixture on which to carry their rifles and supplies. They had come prepared to hunt for several days.

Behind came the two white men. They did not ride like Westerners but stiffly, formally, as the Easterner is trained. Already they appeared tired. Collins' eyes were fixed on the forest before him, and Blue Pete imagined those eyes flashed with excitement and not a little dread of the unknown. He chuckled. He had prepared the fellow for that.

Better and braver men than Biff Collins had been uneasy in the haunting silences of the Cypress Hills, silences everyone knew were packed with watching life. For the first time Collins was impressed with his inexperience, and he made no attempt to conceal it. Fraleigh was less sensitive, a mere hanger-on, leaving everything, even emotion, to his companion. He was talking—laughing about something. Collins did not seem to be listening.

Blue Pete nodded and grinned. "He's thinkin' o' them wolves. Ef I made Rollo howl now he'd like's not turn tail an' scoot back fer town. I'll git him fust whar he can't run. . . . Biff Collins is goin' to hear wolves ef he never meets one."

THE four entered the forest. Blue Pete watched every move from his hiding-place. They had come together now, Collins speeding up to join the Indians. They rode in a tight group, as if for companionship in the shadows.

Collins glanced nervously about. "My God, how dark it gets in here!"

Only then did it strike the half-breed—and it came with a real shock—that the two Indians were He Dog and Wadoo, the pair he had chased from Big Slough.

Then he wondered why it surprised him. Wadoo and He Dog were confirmed wolf-hunters; they would be the pair Collins would naturally have supplied him from the Indian encampment. But the coincidence stuck to him.

So close did they pass to his hiding-place that he could almost have touched one of the Indian ponies. At first they kept straight on into the forest, but after fifty yards the Indians shifted abruptly towards the west. That direction led to where Whiskers and Rollo were concealed, and for a few moments Blue Pete scarcely breathed. He was not sure of Rollo, and if the dog recognized Collins he might do anything. The broncos, too, might sense the proximity of another bronco.

His hand fell on his .45 as he saw the Indians fall into single file and advance through the outer edge of the trees about the thicket. Collins and Fraleigh kept outside. One of the Indian ponies whinnied, and its rider pulled in sharply and peered about. Seeing and hearing nothing, he spurred on to fall in behind his companion. But he was not satisfied, for he muttered something and kept looking back.

Blue Pete found pinto and dog where he had left them. Rollo was lying tight against the ground, trembling, and the half-breed patted him. "Gor-swizzle, but yuh're goin' to be awright. Yuh knowed that was Collins an' yu didn' move, like I told yuh. Good dog."

With his ears he could follow the course of the four. They were working now towards the south-east. Except for Collins' remark about the darkness and the grunt or two of the Indians not a word had been uttered since entering the forest. Then suddenly Collins was talking. The words were inaudible, but the tone was anxious and unsatisfied.

If Collins was asking where they were going, Blue Pete could have told him. There was a good place for a camp not far ahead, and the Indians knew of it, had often used it. There was a cave there, with water and grass. They would reach it in time to make camp before it was too dark. There they would remain until morning.

The half-breed wondered what plan the Indians had in mind for getting the wolves. With two such tenderfeet success was remote, no matter what they tried. Alone the Indians could hunt in a manner denied them now; they were paid to attempt the impossible.

Jerry the Pole had his own way. In his case the whole thing depended on his dogs, Jerry only coming in for the kill. There were three dogs, two of them Russian wolf hounds, the other half Russian, half grey hound. They were all very fast, and in that lay their success. They had been brought up at the age of a year and a half to hunt coyotes. At two and a half they were turned on the wolves. Their diet was strict—one meal a day only, given them in the evening. On one or two days in the week they had nothing to eat but shorts. At all times food was limited. It made them ravenous and untiring in the chase.

The dogs and Jerry were out before daylight, to head the wolves off after their night prowling. At dawn the wolves would make for the hills. Since the herds were purposely kept at night several miles from the hills, the wolves had a long distance to go to gain cover. It was then the speedy dogs got in their work. Faster than the wolves, they would run them down, one wolf at a time, and either attack or hold at bay until Jerry arrived to despatch the animal, not with a rifle as a rule but with a club. Then the dogs were off after another wolf, though a second one was seldom killed in a morning's work.

Jerry had never taken his dogs into the hills. That would have been foolish, for the wolves were at home there and were likely to be attackers instead of attacked. They usually hunted in small packs, and even on the prairie it was not so much that they could not have defended themselves from the three dogs as that they could see Jerry coming, and in the open they never felt brave.

Hunting in the hills was a vastly different matter. There the wolves usually hunted, singly or in pairs, but a howl would attract a pack. Ample cover, too, made them bolder and more dangerous. Sometimes the Indians managed to arouse themselves to the energy required to hunt in force, and the ranchers were prepared to pay them well for the skins. More frequently, however, they were content to hunt in pairs, though with indifferent success. Wadoo and He Dog were the best of them, but even they had to be hungry to spur them to the effort.

Seldom did they have white men to guide.

Blue Pete understood them as Collins and his friend never would. The two Indians were not likely to overexert themselves, so that a wolf was little likely to be killed. Not only were all Indians constitutionally lazy but they lent their special skill to the whites with the greatest reluctance. They would be clever enough in this case to work up excitement and hope, but that would probably be all.

It gave him an idea. He might do something himself to arouse excitement, but of a different kind. The prospect tickled him. . . . The presence of these two Indians lingered with him. Though he had not yet arranged the coincidence in his mind into any definite form, he wondered that once more he would meet the pair he had chased from Big Slough. In some way it seemed to bring the murders into the wolf-hunt, yet what connection could there possibly be?

He set out to follow them. That was simple enough, for they rode steadily south-east, making no effort to conceal their movements. Except when addressed the Indians were silent, but Collins and Fraleigh chattered, plainly not comfortable. The silence and the darkness and the strangeness of their surroundings were working on their nerves.

He was certain he knew where they were going to make camp, and he did not try to keep in close touch with them. Because it was a favourite camping-place he himself usually avoided it. Now he dropped far behind and followed slowly.

His ears told him when they stopped, and he found a hiding-place for the pinto and went on on foot. Rollo was with him, picking his way along with the soundlessness of a wild animal. Blue Pete did not order him back; there was no need of that, for the group ahead would remain where they were all night. At any rate this was as good a time as any to test the dog.

He did not approach directly but rounded off to the south. He knew where he could lie and look down on the camp in safety.

Before long he heard their voices, and he dropped to his knees and advanced more cautiously, keeping Rollo in mind. He need have had no fear: Rollo sensed the need for caution. Crouched low, he kept his eyes on his master, and never a leaf rustled or a twig snapped.

Suddenly the dog's manner changed, and a low growl broke from his throat. Collins' laugh had rung through the forest. A reproving tap on the head reduced him to shivering silence, and even his eyes were apologetic.

They reached a point directly above and looked down on the group.

Collins was just emerging from the cave. He made an exclamation of disgust. "Hell, I'd have rheumatism in an hour in that damn hole. It's horribly damp. I'm all for sleeping out here in the open. We can keep the fire going, and it's going to be a lovely night. It'll be lighter out here. That place is like a dungeon. I'd be imagining weird creatures all night crawling out at me from the darkness back deeper in the cave. Don't you feel the same, Ted?"

Ted was certain to feel the same. "It's like a morgue," he said. Then he laughed abruptly. "I don't want to think of morgues. Do you, Charlie? It's all right for the Indians, I suppose—they can stand anything—but it's not for you and me."

Collins addressed the Indians: "What do you say, He Dog? Can't we keep a fire going out here and sleep beside it?"

The Indian shrugged. "Indians stand anything. Okay here."

"Well, we're not Indians." Collins raised his face towards the sky. "There won't be a storm or anything, will there? I'd hate to be caught asleep in the rain."

"No rain," grunted one of the Indians, without looking at the sky. "Nice night."

Collins laughed nervously. "Do you mean a nice night for the wolves to come and surprise us? I'll keep my gun handy, you can bet."

He Dog swept his arms about. "Wolves everywhere. Never know where. Maybe watching us now up there." He pointed directly to where the half-breed lay. "All over. Hills full of them."

Collins shivered extravagantly, but Blue Pete knew it had started involuntarily. "For God's sake don't make it any creepier than it is. This is a new sort of thing for us." His face sobered. "They—they wouldn't attack us here, would they?"

He Dog replied by pointing to the gun Collins carried on his hip, and his lip seemed to curl. Then he turned away and proceeded to build the fire. Their broncos were hobbled some distance away in the ravine.

Blue Pete crept away, grinning into the darkness. Two hundred yards away he stopped. The dog had kept close to him, and he looked back on him, the grin slowly widening.

"Now yuh got yer chance, Rollo, ole boy, an' do yer dangdest."

He raised his hand and snapped his fingers. Rollo did his dangdest: He pointed his nose to the sky and howled. Never had he made such a dismal, terrifying clamour. Perhaps there in the forest his wolf-blood came more closely to the surface. No wolf had ever done better. The sound of it made even the half-breed wince.

The silence that followed was almost as terrifying. Then from three directions came answering howls, real wolves replying to a comrade. They started on a low note, like a gentle breeze, and rose slowly and clearly to a ringing height where they lingered for several moments. Gradually then they sank back to a lower note that seemed to fade away so gently that one could not be certain when they ceased. Again and again they came, while Rollo listened, trembling.

Blue Pete gathered himself up. "We bes' git outa here, an' pronto." He led back to where he had left the pinto. Rollo kept at his side, nosing at his hand, and the half-breed fondled his ears. Finally he stopped and took the dog's head in his hands. "Easy, ole boy, easy! Yuh're doin' this on'y fer fun—our fun. Mebbe 'tain't fair to git yuh so close to yer grandad's folks, but I'm countin' on yuh not to go wild on me. I do' wanta lose yuh yit." He started on. "Bes' git yuh back to Whiskers; she'll keep yuh straight."

Whiskers filled the role perfectly. She placed her nose against the dog's and the latter's trembling ceased.

Blue Pete watched, a smile broadening his dark face. "You done fine, Rollo. I bet Collins is shakin' in his shoes. I gotta git back an' see wot's happenin'. I hate to leave yuh now but I gotta. Yuh bes' stay 'th Whiskers this time, ole boy."

He gestured to the dog to remain and started back towards the cave. At intervals the wolves continued to howl, and he hesitated, even turning back once. "Hope yuh're awright thar, Rollo, but I can't stay to make shure."

When he looked down on the camp again the Indians had the fire burning brightly. No one of the four spoke. At every howl from the surrounding darkness they listened. The Indians were plainly mystified. Collins and Fraleigh stood close together in the full light of the fire, their backs against the cliff at the side of the entrance to the cave.

The tone of the howling changed. At first clear and ringing, the love song of the wolf, it became more terrifying, more aggressive and clamorous. It was as if the wolves had discovered how they had been deceived and resented it. Blue Pete was uneasy.

Collins' terror increased. "Wadoo," he called, "is the damn woods full of them? What does all the howling mean? Is it for us—do they know we're here? Is there anything we should do—to be safer, I mean?"

In the light of the fire Wadoo faced him, and he made no effort to conceal his scorn. "Wolves everywhere. Wolves know everything."

"But they wouldn't attack us, not here in the light of the fire, would they?" inquired Fraleigh.

Wadoo spat into the fire but made no reply.

The two white men looked at each other. "Perhaps," Collins ventured, "we'd better sleep in the cave, after all. I wouldn't get any sleep with all that noise."

"You come to hunt wolves," Wadoo reminded him. "Warmer out here. You said damp in cave. Still damp."

It was clever. After that Collins dare not insist. With a shrug he made an effort to recover his dignity. "That's right. Anyway, I can't think they'd attack us out here, not with the fire and our guns." He turned to his companion. "It's part of the hunt, I suppose. We'll get used to it." He stepped forward to the fire and held out his hands to it. They trembled. He must have noticed it himself, for he jerked them away and stooped to pick up a burning twig and light a cigarette.

It had a flourish about it that did not deceive Blue Pete, and with a wide grin he set off back to where he had left the pinto and the dog.

He had gone only a few yards when a terrific din broke out before him, the snarling of wild animals in deadly battle. With the blood tingling beneath his scalp he raced ahead, drawing his gun as he ran.

XXVII   DOG AGAINST WOLVES

IT was growing dark quickly within the forest, but his night eyes carried him ahead at full speed. He opened his mouth to call the dog's name but changed his mind in time and ran silently on.

The battle had reached a fury of snarling and yelping. Some animal yelped and was silent, a death call that sent the blood racing once more through the half-breed's veins. But the snarling continued, and he knew that Rollo was still in the fight. He burst into the thicket where he had left the dog. The pinto was not there; it was light enough for him to see that at a glance, but a limp body near by, with a crushed skull, showed where she had left her mark before escaping. Rollo was backed against a tree, crouched, teeth bared, every hair on end, a formidable foe. Before him were three wolves. Another lay dead directly in front of him, its throat torn open. It partly protected him.

So intent were the wolves on the fray that they were unaware of the presence of the half-breed until he burst in on them and landed a kick on the hind quarters of the nearest wolf that sent it flying over Rollo's head against the tree. In a flash the dog was on it, his teeth anchored in its throat. A choking gurgle, and another wolf had paid dearly for the attack. The other two had taken to flight.

Blue Pete had not used his gun; he did not wish his presence to be known. Wrenching Rollo from his latest victim, he ran. The dog kept close at his heels, silent now. A tear in his right shoulder bled a little and he limped. A few yards away Whiskers joined them, and they hurried away into the forest. Blue Pete chuckled as he ran.

He had escaped none too soon. At the clamour of the fight the Indians had seized their rifles and hurried to investigate. Only the fact that the steepness of the cliff delayed them saved the situation for Blue Pete. After the Indians came Collins and Fraleigh, too frightened to have waited even for their rifles. They dare not remain behind.

The Indians located the scene of the fight quickly enough. Wadoo stood over the three dead wolves.

"Hmph!"

That was all, and it told the two white men nothing they could not see with their own eyes. Collins backed away. "Good God! Isn't that a—a wolf—two of them— three?"

The Indians did not appear to have heard. He Dog leaned over and examined the one with the crushed skull.

160

"Hmph!"

Collins crowded up to his side. "What—what happened? Do they—fight among themselves like that?"

"Hmph!" replied the two Indians in unison.

"But it doesn't—it doesn't seem natural."

"Wolves no fight wolves," jerked He Dog, "not like that."

"I've heard," ventured Collins, "that they'll eat one of their mates if it's wounded."

He Dog pointed to the one with the crushed skull. "Hmph!" he grunted. His head shook in a bewildered way.

Collins chattered on: "Some say they won't attack a human being—unless he's wounded or unable to defend himself."

The Indians paid no attention. They looked at each other and shook their heads.

Collins was getting his nerves more under control. He tried to laugh. "Say, this gets more exciting every minute. Three wolves already. That'll almost make a skin for each of us." He looked nervously about into the growing darkness. "That ought to be enough. We don't need to spend more time in this dismal place. It's the weirdest hole I ever got into. Those howls—that fight—I'll never forget them."

Fraleigh made no effort to conceal his fear. He shivered. "That suits me. I could start right out to-night and feel that what I've missed I'd give half my life to miss."

The frankness of his terror stiffened Collins. He threw back his shoulders. "We came to hunt wolves, Ted. If they're this easy to get we'll go out loaded with skins. Just an hour in camp and—three wolves! Some hunting, eh?"

"No hunting, this," grunted He Dog contemptuously.

"Well, it gets the same results. Can you skin them, boys?"

"Too dark. Wait till morning." He Dog picked up one of the wolves, Wadoo the other two, and they draped them over low branches of a nearby tree. Then without another word they led the way back to the campfire.

Blue Pete had crept back to where he could hear their conversation, and when the four were gone he took the wolves and dragged them away. The Indians would find the trail, though nothing would tell them what had really happened. He picked his way cautiously toward their own camp, and when he had gone as far as he dare he raised the wolves to his shoulders and went to find the pinto and Rollo.

Circling around to the east, he hid the carcasses in a thicket and dropped into a tight little ravine. Dark as it was, he could have found his way around there blindfolded. In the ravine was a cave he had often used. Few but himself had discovered it. A tangle of vines hung over the entrance, and a rippling stream ran through the vines. He had always kept it supplied with grass for Whiskers, because he often left her there while he prowled about, hunting for rustlers.

He dismounted before the vines and passed through, Whiskers and Rollo following. Whiskers trotted straight back to where the grass was piled, and Blue Pete turned his attention to Rollo's wound. A pine knot from a store he kept in the cave he set alight and fixed among some rocks, so that he could see what to do.

It relieved him to find that the wound was merely a rip of the skin. Rollo lay down without a sound and submitted. He seemed to know that the half-breed had saved his life, for the wolves would have fought to the end, and the odds were still too great.

The wound was washed and the skin laid back. There it was bound with the kerchief from his neck. Then he sat back and grinned at the dog.

"Rollo," he said, "yuh're fit to keep comp'ny 'th Whiskers, an' that's sayin' suthin'. Yuh kin fight like blazes, an' yuh got the guts fer it as well's the brains an' the teeth. You 'n' me 'n' Whiskers, we're goin' to hev some good times together. . . . Never thought I'd take to a dog. 'Course the on'y dogs I know's the ones in the Neche camps, an' they ain't the same kind o' critters. Now thar's Mira 'n' you 'n' Whiskers 'n me. Sorta big family, eh?"

He drew an old corn-cob pipe from his belt and filled it with tobacco. Before lighting it he went through the vines and listened for a long time. He knew how the smell of tobacco would carry through the forest, particularly to the keen Indians. The wolves were silent now, two of them probably licking their wounds. Since the fight not a howl had been heard. He chuckled as he thought of the Indians' surprise when they discovered the dead wolves were gone in the morning—surprise to add on surprise. The fight had made them wonder. Now they would almost be thrown into a panic when they found that the dead wolves had been dragged so near them and then had disappeared. It was never a long step from bewilderment to panic among Indians.

Inside once more he sat down on a pile of dead grass and smoked, his back against the rock wall. Then he lay down and slept. Only when he nestled back in the grass did he realize how tired he was.

He slept longer than he intended. It was broad daylight when he wakened and went to look through the vines, shocked to find that it was seven o'clock. He led the pinto outside and mounted. At first Rollo was stiff, scarcely able to use the wounded leg, but after hobbling for a few yards he seemed to feel better and followed without effort

The half-breed eyed the dog with shaking head. "Yuh ain't goin' to feel too spry fer a coupla weeks mebbe, but I bet yuh got sweet memories o' that fight. I know how 'tis. That's the wolf in yuh. . . . Wot 'tis in me I ain't sayin'. The wolf an' the dog in yuh fought them critters, the wolf part 'cause wolves'll fight anythin', the dog part 'cause dogs hate wolves like p'ison. Yuh got a dog's brains an' a wolf's teeth." He pursed his lips and frowned. "But I ain't goin' to hev yuh howl no more, 'n' then leave yuh to face the music alone. I didn' think yuh'd fetch 'em so quick."

For almost half an hour he rode, stopping to listen every few minutes. Presently he dismounted and went forward on foot. As he neared the scene of the camp he became anxious. He could hear no sound to tell him that the men were still there. Of course he was late. If they seriously planned to hunt they would have set out hours ago.

The ravine was empty. The remains of the fire were still there but nothing else. By the ashes he knew it had been kept going all night.

Finding a way down into the ravine, he looked about. Perhaps they had moved on to make another camp elsewhere. The horses had been hobbled some distance away along the ravine, and from there he picked up the trail. He followed it up the eastern slope.

Returning to Whiskers, he mounted. The trail was easy to follow. The Indians were leading more deeply into the hills, working towards the south-east. He kept after them, not hurrying. What they did during the daylight hours was of little interest to him. All he wanted was to keep near enough when they were at rest to overhear their conversation. Something they would say was bound to lighten the mystery they were to him. He wondered where they would make camp now. The one they had left suited his purpose admirably, since it was easy to lie within hearing with no chance of discovery and with escape simple. More and more curious he was growing about Biff Collins, and he found himself marvelling that the Mounted Police seemed to ignore him and his friend. There was something about him that he did not understand—and he wanted to understand, wanted it so badly that at times he forgot the murders at Big Slough.

ABOUT noon he heard a shot some distance to the east.

It told him nothing he did not know already. From the trail he knew how far they were ahead of him. The shot might have been fired by the Indians, in which case it was probably at a wolf; or it might be some casual shot Collins had fired at game that crossed his trail. A tenderfoot could not be expected to know the technique of hunting wolves.

He did not think the Indians would go far before making camp. Riding about through the forest was not hunting. Only from a fixed camp could they do what they had come to do, and they had surely not yet made camp.

It was not long after that that he heard Collins laugh, and he left Whiskers and Rollo and went ahead on foot. They had reached the thickest part of the forest, where the wolves were most likely to be. There would be no sense in going further before making camp.

From his knowledge of the hills he could locate in his mind the spot they would select for the camp. It was another ravine, much like the one they had left, with grass and water, and a cave to which to retreat in bad weather. As before they would sleep in the open as long as the weather was fine—and at that time of the year it was always fine. That was as he wished it, since it would enable him to overhear their conversation.

When he came to them the Indians were already preparing the camp. They had cleared away the leaves and fallen branches before the cave and had piled them for a fire, while Collins and Fraleigh pottered unhelpfully about. At last the two white men took their rifles and left. The two Indians looked after them, shaking their heads. In turn they grunted.

He returned to the pinto and waited. When it was almost dark he found his way back, taking Rollo with him. He was afraid now to leave the dog too long alone. It was not late, and out on the prairie it would still be bright, but there among the trees the shadows were deep. The Indians had already prepared the night meal, and the four were squatted about the fire eating. He Dog and Wadoo were off to one side, eating noisily. Collins and his friend had brought camp cutlery and appeared to enjoy the meal almost as much as their guides.

For a time they ate in silence. It was broken by Collins suddenly laughing. "Too busy to talk?" he asked, looking towards the Indians. The latter paid no attention but went on with their meal. "Think the wolves'll visit us to-night again, or did they have such a licking last night that they'll blame it on us?"

Wadoo swept his arm about, even as with the other hand he picked up a strip of sizzling bacon. "Wolves not licked last night. Wolves never licked." He filled his mouth. "Wolves not scared in the hills."

"But with three of them gone to a wolves' hell it must have left them wondering."

Wadoo looked through him blankly. "Wadoo wondering."

"You mean you're wondering why their friends returned and carried them away?"

"Wolves no do that."

"What else could it be?"

Wadoo's reply was a shrug.

"But they do eat one another, don't they?" Fraleigh asked. "What else could have happened? We got to them too quickly for them to finish the job."

Again Wadoo shrugged.

Collins laughed. "Perhaps they put on a special show for the tenderfeet. All I'm sorry for is that we haven't the skins. No one will believe us when we tell them what happened."

"Indians no believe either," muttered He Dog.

Collins glanced nervously about into the growing darkness. "You appear to be none too happy about things yourselves. Do you think they're around us now, listening to what we're saying, watching us eat?"

"Wolves everywhere," declared both Indians.

"If only they'll not make so much noise. I could do without another howl. Much as I want to kill them, I'd rather do it by the silent treatment. They make me feel as if they're jeering at me, and there's nothing I can do about it. I'm ready to bet they're right up there now, looking down on us." Directly where he pointed was the half-breed looking down on them, and involuntarily he slipped backward.

Wadoo spat into the fire. "Howls no hurt nobody."

"It's all right for you to talk like that. You've hunted them. You can stand their howls. I could do without another peep from them—

even without another word about them. That's how I feel right now, because I can feel their eyes boring into me." He had finished his meal, and he rested back on his elbow, facing the Indians. "By the way, you chaps were starting on a hunt like this that day you came on the bodies at Big Slough."

The Indians were silent—and uneasy.

Collins persisted: "You were there when the Mounted Police made a search of the place. Did they discover any clues, did they talk about any suspects?"

He Dog slowly raised his eyes and looked across the fire at him for several silent moments. "Mounties no tell Indians what they find. Mounties tell nobody till they—jump."

" 'Jump?' What do you mean?"

"Jump on the men they want."

Collins turned to his friend and laughed sneeringly. "Some jump, eh, Ted?" He turned back to the Indians. "Then they didn't seem to be interested in anything in particular?"

The Indians looked at each other and away.

"Gun on wall," Wadoo grunted.

Collins sat up in some excitement. "That rifle, you mean? What about it? Did it appear to surprise them?"

"White man always carry gun, Sergeant say—and Blue Pete."

Fraleigh was watching his friend closely, a stiff smile twisting his lips.

Collins gathered up some loose earth and tossed it carelessly in the air. "Yes . . . Blue Pete. That's the breed. He was there, too. He might see things that would escape the Mounted Police. . . . By the way, are you sure he wasn't there before you got there?"

"Breed not there. Chase Indians. Blue Pete look at gun and wonder."

Fraleigh's mirthless laugh broke in on the conversation. "What in the world did you hope to learn, Charlie? He Dog has told you the gun on the wall made them curious. It was a mistake."

Collins turned angrily on him. "Oh, keep quiet! I thought they might have noticed what the Sergeant found to interest him. But of course there was no one they could suspect but a rancher. They had to have that water, and Sam knew it—"

"Indians know nothing," He Dog interrupted. "Mounties work. Mounties find out."

Collins sneered. "Think so? Want to bet on it?"

The Indians shook their heads and were silent.

Blue Pete had heard every word, and a tingle of excitement ran through him. It mystified him more than ever. Collins and Fraleigh not unnaturally were interested in the crimes, since they had been in touch with the affair almost from the first. Somehow, however, it failed to justify their persistent questioning of the Indians. It could not be that they were concerned for the ranchers. . . . Could it be that Collins was in earnest when he said he might help the Mounted Police to find the murderer?

Fraleigh was speaking: "That rifle—did it seem to matter very much with the Sergeant?"

"Mountie stand and look long time. Blue Pete too." Wadoo shook his head solemnly.

"This breed," said Collins, "what in hell has he to do with it? Why wouldn't the Sergeant suspect him? You can't tell me it was merely a coincidence that he should turn up at that moment."

Shocked and furious, Blue Pete half rose to his feet in his anger.

"Breed too smart to be there if he done it," scoffed He Dog.

"A real detective might suspect it as too good an alibi," said Collins.

"It'll take more than that, Charlie," laughed Fraleigh, "to fasten it on the breed."

There it was again—"Charlie"—and Blue Pete almost missed what followed.

Collins whistled a rising and falling note and laughed nastily. "Say, that would be a lark—to get the breed into a mess over it. I'll bet it wouldn't need much proof to get his neck in a noose, not around these parts, from what I can discover. That would about pay what I owe him."

Blue Pete had risen to his feet. His rifle came up. But that would be too easy an end for Biff Collins. What he wanted was to feel his fingers close about the fellow's throat, to hear his gasping struggle for breath, to see his eyes bulge with terror and the approach of death. About him was something vile, like a rattlesnake or a timber-wolf—a nasty animal that had to be killed for the good of everyone.

He caught himself in time and grimly walked away. He knew if he remained there would be trouble, and he was not yet prepared to push things to a crisis; there was much yet to learn. With every word he heard the mystery of the two men increased, a puzzle that would not be solved by shooting them.

When he was back with the pinto and the dog he stood for a time with his hand on the saddle, scowling into the night. Rollo pawed gently at him for attention, and for a moment he considered drawing another wolf-howl from the dog. With the Indians, however, that might be too much. Already puzzled, they might work out the explanation. And so he gently rubbed Rollo's ears.

Through the foliage he could see the sky. In another half hour the stars would be out. Down there in the ravine where the camp was pitched it would be very dark, but he waited for another half hour.

When he walked away Rollo whined softly to go, and he returned and took the dog's head in his hands. "Yuh gotta larn, ole boy, larn from Whiskers. She never makes a sound when she shudn't. I can't bring yuh 'long ef yuh don't larn that."

Rollo licked his hands apologetically and silently watched him depart.

The meal was over when the half-breed looked down on the camp again, and the four men were settled into their blankets. The fire had been freshly piled with wood and the new blaze had caught. In its light Collins face was visible. The Indians lay with their feet to the fire, settled for the night. Collins and Fraleigh had chosen to lie with their heads to the fire, the tenderfoot way.

Collins was restless, constantly changing his position, grunting irritably. Twice he raised on his elbow and stared off into the night, evidently listening—and afraid to hear what he thought he might hear. After a time he settled back, drawing the blanket well over his head.

The fire burned up and sank. Blue Pete waited. Once Collins wakened and sat up abruptly, as if disturbed by a dream. The light from the fire flickered in his eyes and he looked about. There was fear in them.

Presently he lay down. But he did not sleep; instead he appeared to be working at something beneath the blankets. After a time his hand appeared. In it was his revolver. Without a sound he laid it on the ground beside him.

When sleep had fallen over the four of them Blue Pete crept noiselessly down the bank. The fire was almost out; only a few coals remained, and an intermittent flame at the end of a branch not far from where Collins lay.

Slowly he crept nearer. He did not know what he had in mind except that something drew him on, something that promised to lighten the mystery. His eyes were on the gun that lay in the open where Collins could sieze it swiftly if it was needed.

He was angry. So the fellow would like to fasten the crime on him—this man he hated, whom everyone disliked. . . . The fire sank lower and he moved ahead more swiftly.

A yard from Collins' feet he stopped. He was flat on the ground now, only his head raised a little to watch the four sleeping men. Inch by inch he advanced. Collins had pulled the blanket more tightly over his head and in doing so had exposed his feet. Blue Pete raised his head higher.

Suddenly he stopped, his gaze fixed on the feet within inches of him. His lips fell slowly apart. A tremor shot through him.

Then he reached out, picked up the gun and emptied it, muffling the click with his body. He drew the shells and thrust them in his pocket. The gun he replaced. Backwards he crept and disappeared into the darkness.

XXIX   THE INSPECTOR GETS WARM

THE sun found a battered tin that lay beside the railway track. It struck in a dazzling flash that rebounded through the front window of the Mounted Police barracks, straight into Inspector Barker's eyes. The window was fly-specked and dusty, but the reflection scorned such a barrier. It had scorned it at the same hour for several days, but this time he was in no mood to endure it.

He reached for a bell beneath his desk and pushed. Hurrying feet came along the hall and someone knocked.

"Come in, Langley." The Inspector pointed. "Get out there and pick up that tin; it's been battering at my eyes for days in the sun. Someone's been using the railway for a garbage dump."

As Langley started away, the Inspector asked: "Has Sergeant Mahon come back yet?"

"No, sir."

"Send him to me right away when he returns."

Langley hurried out, passed along the hall and out the front door. The Inspector watched him walk along the railway track and pick up the tin, and with a sigh of relief, as if some great task had been accomplished, he sat back and relaxed. His nerves were on edge, and he leaned his elbows on the desk and upbraided himself:

"What's the matter with me?" He growled it into the stillness of the room and immediately laughed shame-facedly at himself. He shifted his position, as if to shift his mood, and the old swivel chair tottered, so that he was forced to grasp the edge of the desk to steady himself. From one of the drawers he drew a pipe and clawed some of the loose tobacco from the scatter on the blotter, packed it carefully in the bowl—and went no further. His mind was not on the act. Langley, he remembered, had not yet returned. In a flash of annoyance he dropped the pipe and did not so much as pick it up.

"What the devil's keeping him? Where did he go?"

He had the answer almost as he asked himself the question, for Langley and Mahon together passed the window.

They entered the barracks, and the Sergeant knocked at the door and entered.

The Inspector did not even turn to him. "Well! Well! What did you find?"

"They got the two Indians to act as guides, sir, He Dog and Wadoo."

Inspector Barker felt a tingle shoot through him. "He Dog and Wadoo, you say? Why, that's the pair Blue Pete caught running from the murders at Big Slough."

"Yes, sir. They're considered the best hunters among the Indians."

"I know it, but—" He frowned at his fingers drumming nervously on the blotter.

"I thought of that, sir. I did some inquiring. The Indians didn't want to talk, but I managed to get He Who Shoots to open up a little. Collins asked for those two particularly. He said he understood they were experienced wolf-hunters—"

"Sounds reasonable," muttered the Inspector. He raised his eyes to the Sergeant's. "But is it as simple as that. . . ? I'm more curious than ever about that pair. I haven't been satisfied about them ever since they came. I've a feeling there's something about them we haven't got to the bottom of. I've been making inquiries, and their attempts to purchase a ranch are part of the mystery, since they surely could not expect their offers to be accepted." He stopped and sank more deeply into the chair. "I've been trying to make up my mind about them, but I don't seem to be able to get my teeth into anything of consequence. . . . I've been thinking . . . I've been thinking I might arrange for one of the ranchers to appear to consider their offer, just to find out if they really have the money to buy. The bank they deal with here could then tell me something. If they hesitate, if they back water, then I'll have some excuse to bring them in here and put them through some questioning. . . . I don't like them around. I've a feeling there's something in the wind, something that should have our attention . . . something not connected with buying a ranch. . . . Then comes this— these two Indians, I mean. By the way, when do they plan to leave for the hunt?"

"They left on Monday, sir."

"Day before yesterday, eh?" He sat thinking for a long time, his forehead lined and his waxed moustache moving grotesquely about.

Suddenly he made up his mind. "Get out there to the hills and find out what they're about. Keep out of sight but don't lose touch with them. They'll talk more freely if there's no one but the Indians about. Perhaps you might hear enough to give us something to work on." He glanced at the office clock. "You can leave in an hour. Spend the night at Turner's Crossing, then to-morrow early make for the hills. . . . You'd better work in from the west end; they're not likely to see you at that end—if they're looking for anyone." He smiled sheepishly. "I can't imagine why they should be."

He was silent then, staring at the ceiling. Mahon knew he had not finished and he waited.

"By the way, it wouldn't be much out of your way to call at the 3-Bar-Y. If Blue Pete is there see if you can't induce him to go with you. He'd be able to help to stalk these fellows. . . . Yes, better get him if you can. For one thing it might help to get his mind off these murders. I've a feeling he's going to get things messed up for us if he keeps on. Besides, I'd like to keep an eye on him."

Mahon hesitated. "You mean, sir, you want me to do this and to forget about the murders? Who's going to follow them up?"

"Don't worry about that, Mahon," said the Inspector soothingly. "This will give you a rest, a change of scene. You'll be all the better for it. Leave the murders to me for the time being. They'll still be around when we want to work on them. It might put the murderer off guard to see us apparently giving up. Anyway, I want to know more about this Collins and his friend, and this seems too good an opportunity to miss. If they're still in the hills you're the only one I have to do this job; you know the hills better than anyone but Blue Pete. If you can get him to go along something is sure to come of it."

WHEN Blue Pete crept from the sleeping group about the fire he did not go far. Throughout the remainder of the night he remained where he could be at hand if any move was made. He saw the Indians waken with the first light and replenish the fire that had died down to a few live coals. Collins and Fraleigh slept on, the former with his head almost covered by the blanket.

He Dog made a gesture to his companion and the pair crept away and disappeared along the ravine. Blue Pete watched with some misgiving, for they acted like conspirators. Still he could not imagine they were deserting; there would be no gain to them in that, for they had not yet been paid. Then he noticed that they had left their blankets on the ground beside the fire.

Not many minutes later Collins awoke with a start. He threw the blanket from his head and raised himself on his elbow. The empty space beyond the fire, where the Indians had slept, startled him at first and he called to Fraleigh. The latter started up with a wild jerk and called out. When, however, he saw Collins laughing at him he grinned back sheepishly.

"Guess I must have been dreaming, Charlie."

Collins' face straightened and he looked about in the early morning light, his fingers pressed to his lips. "For Heavens' sake cut out that 'Charlie'. You've pretty nearly given us away half a dozen times. That time at the Double Bar-Y I thought our goose was cooked. If these ranchers weren't so stupid—and that breed—they'd smell a mouse. I had to do some quick thinking that time, but it won't work forever."

Fraleigh saw that they were alone and it appeared to upset him. "Where have the Indians gone?" he whispered.

Collins shook his head. "That's what I was wondering." Then he noticed the blankets and laughed. "It's all right. They're around somewhere. They'd never go and leave their blankets." He rolled nearer his friend. "I want to do some talking while they're out of hearing." Blue Pete's ears strained as never before, and the tight ravine seemed to catch the sound and send it up to him. "Say, Ted, I'm getting sick of this. You're no more interested in the wolves than I am—and you're just as uneasy about things. I hate this place. I hate the hills most of all. I didn't think we were going to get up against this sort of thing or I'd never have proposed it. Besides, we didn't need to come here. No one suspects us.

"I want to get away, and the sooner the better. They don't like us around here, which doesn't surprise me, because I don't like them any better. But with them disliking us there's always the chance that something will direct suspicion to us. For one thing, I don't feel any too easy about that breed. He seems to have something against us, and I know that sort of fellow. He'll never be content until he's fixed something on us, and we can't stand to be questioned."

"But," Fraleigh protested, "they can't get anything on us. There isn't a thing to connect us with—what happened." His tone betrayed the fact that he felt none too certain of it.

"Yes, that's so—just yet. But I'm frightened. I wakened this morning with the oddest feeling that someone had come to the camp in the night and had looked us over. I wakened once earlier and had the feeling. That's why I got my gun out and put it there to have it handy." He pointed to the gun beside him on the ground. . . . "I'm afraid of the Mounted Police. We've never been up against these fellows before, and they say they're mighty smart—they never give up."

"But if they'd had anything on us," said Fraleigh, "they'd have nabbed us long ago. The trail's too cold now."

Collins shook his head doubtfully. "That's the way I'd reason it out, but I've always found it wise to follow a hunch, and the hunch this time tells me to clear out as fast as we can go."

"What's your plan then?"

Collins looked cautiously about and moved still nearer, so that only with the greatest difficulty could the half-breed hear. "We'll hang on here for a day more, then we'll let on we can't spend any more time on it, that we've had enough. We'll go out and make another offer or two for a ranch, then we'll give up and get the hell out of this."

Fraleigh laughed nervously. "For the love of Mike, Charlie—no, Biff, I mean—don't act this way. I never saw you frightened like this before."

Collins clambered to his feet, thrusting the empty gun into his pocket. "Well, better safe than sorry, I say." He commenced to fold his blanket. "You know, Ted, I'm scared stiff of that breed, and the worst of it is I haven't any idea why I should feel this way. I seem to be running into him everywhere I turn, and he looks at me as if he's watching to leap. . . . I wouldn't be surprised to find him right here in the hills."

"But he refused to come with us. . . . If you're so scared of him why did you try to get him to come?"

"Because I'd feel safer to have him under my eyes. When I can't see him I fancy he sees me. I don't think he's satisfied about us. You know, some of these crossbreeds are—sort of psychic. You'll laugh, but last night in the night I dreamt that he was here, throwing it in our faces that we'd killed June and Sam. I won't feel easy till we're back in Detroit."

"At any rate there's no Sam Mason to bother you now, if that's what you mean. No—June, either." He picked up his own blanket and commenced to fold it.

Collins stood with his blanket over his arm. "I had to kill her too, Ted. It wouldn't have straightened anything out just to kill Sam."

"Of course you had to. She wouldn't have let you get away with killing Sam. Besides, she deserved it as much as he did. Not," with a shrug, "that I liked seeing you do it. Here's the Indians!" he ended, in a frantic whisper. He turned to the fire and poked at it.

Blue Pete had heard almost every word. He scarcely breathed as he listened, afraid to drown the conversation even with a breath. He drew the cast from his pocket and smiled coldly down on it. The smile had a grimness about it that told something of what he had in mind. Almost unconsciously he had drawn his .45, but with a shake of the head he returned it to his belt and walked thoughtfully away.

Back with Whiskers and Rollo he muttered: "So now wot d'I do, ole gal? I know who done it, an' the Mounties don't. I jes' stumbled on it. Ef I tell the Sergeant, then I ain' got not proof wot I heerd . . . an' this mark of his boot that I got to prove he was thar, thar ain't nothin' to prove whar I got it, 'cause I stamped the mark out. Sometimes I ain't got much sense. I cud say wot I heerd an' whar I got this piece o' mud, but no jedge 'ud believe me.

"The Mounties 'ud mebbe believe me—th' Inspector. But he ain't the jedge. So wot then?" He considered the answer for several minutes and sighed. "Reckon I gotta do muhself wot the law won't be able to do. . . . I cud shoot 'em both here an' nobody'd know who done it, not even the Neches. But that ain't 'nuff, no, sir-ee, 'taint. . . . Reckon fust thing is to git rid o' them Neches, git 'em to clear out. . . . But how'd I do that, ole gal? Gor-swizzle!"

Neither Whiskers nor Rollo, though they were plainly interested, had the answer.

"Anyways, tha're not goin' to git 'way 'th it, ef I hev to shoot 'em out o' hand."

He started back towards the camp. When he could look down on it breakfast was over. The fire had been carefully extinguished by the Indians, and everything was ready for the day's hunt. As he watched, the broncos were brought and the four rode away.

On foot Blue Pete followed. He knew the camp they had left was permanent, because they had folded their blankets and placed them in the cave. Their supplies, too, must be there, for they carried nothing with them but their rifles. He knew what the plan would be: the Indians would leave their charges in some good hiding-place while they themselves rode in a wide circle in different directions in the hope of driving a wolf back to the rifles lying in wait for them. The Indians could draw the wolves by imitating their howl. That was their one chance, and a slim one; and the Indians must know it.

He made a note of the hiding-place chosen for Collins and Fraleigh. It was well-chosen. For fifty yards around the forest was thin and what trees there were small. It would furnish little cover for a wolf.

The Indians rode away. Blue Pete followed. When they turned to separate he walked out to them. When they saw him they crowded together, startled, eyeing him with frank alarm.

He walked up to them. "Whar yuh goin', boys?"

They looked at each other, each waiting for the other to speak. He Dog said, "Indians hunt wolves."

Blue Pete nodded. "That's wot yuh said out from Big Slough. Yuh was settin' off to hunt wolves. Yuh didn' hev to hunt fer wot yuh found at Big Slough."

They were silent, their faces a mask. But their eyes betrayed their fear.

"Yuh bes' not do any huntin' this time neither."

"Indians hunt wolves for two white men," declared Wadoo.

"Shure. I know. But them white man do' want no wolves. They do' want no wolves more'n they want a ranch they say tha're tryin' to buy. I bin near yer camps sence yuh come to the Hills an' I heerd them fellows talk. I heerd 'em ast yuh 'bout the murders at Big Slough. They wanted to know ef the Mounties had found anythin'.

They ast ef I had. They was mighty curyus, wasn't they?"

The Indians nodded.

"Shure. An' I heerd 'em talkin' this mornin' when yuh was 'way from the camp. They didn't know I was listenin'. . . . So now I know suthin' you don't. I know why they ast them questions. I know why they wanted to know ef the Mounties had found anythin'." He went and stood between them, his hands thrust in his belt. "I'm goin' to tell yuh why: It was them killed the man 'n' the woman at Big Slough."

It shocked them from their impassivity. They said nothing, but Blue Pete knew they believed him.

He continued, watching them closely: "They got yuh to come here so nobody's know wot they come to the Hat fer. Tha're tryin' to fool the Mounties. Ef the Mounties knowed yuh knowed wot I'm tellin' yuh, an' yuh went on huntin' 'th 'em, yuh'd be in trouble. Yuh know that. I'm tellin' yuh so yuh kin skip out an' keep outa trouble. Ef yuh don't, en yuh stay, the Mounties'll 'member yuh was thar at Big Slough that day when I caught yuh runnin' 'way."

He Dog grunted. "Indians go, quick."

They did. They left no doubt that they would go without loss of time. Whirling their ponies about, they struck back towards the cave. Blue Pete watched them go, a cold smile on his face. When he dare he set off after them; he wanted to be sure. He reached the height overlooking the camp in time to see them take their blankets and some of the food from the cave and ride away north towards the prairie.

Thoughtfully he worked his way back through the forest. He was not sure what to do now, but it was something to feel that he and the two murderers had the Hills to themselves. There would be no witnesses of whatever happened.

As he went along the Inspector and Sergeant Mahon kept forcing their way into his mind. What would they say when they knew? Could he hope to conceal from them what he was about to do? There were lapses in his determination when he asked himself if it would not be better to hand everything over now to the Mounted Police. But no, they would have no proof to convince a court. Straightening his shoulders, he kept on his way.

When he came near to where the two men were concealed he advanced with the utmost caution. He wanted to get near enough to hear them talk once more. The murders were on their minds; they would be sure to continue the conversation of the morning. But the comparatively open space about the thicket in which they were hidden made that almost impossible. Scouting about, he selected the most promising approach and, flat on his stomach, wormed his way nearer.

For a long time the two men were silent. But as the hours passed with no sign of wolves or Indians, they became impatient.

"What in the world's happened now?" Collins demanded irritably.

"Sh-sh! Those wolves are mighty cute. They'll hear you."

"I don't believe there's a wolf within miles. If they're so acute they're not going to let themselves be rounded up like this. . . . You know, I wouldn't put anything past those Indians. They're more apt to run out on us than to do anything that looks like work. I was fool enough to pay them something in advance. They could run off with the supplies, too. We'd have a devil of a time finding our way out of this maze. Everyone warned us it's the worst spot on earth to get lost in."

He was silent for several minutes. Then: "If they did a thing like that I'd run them down, if I had to go right into their camp to do it. No one plays that sort of game on Charlie Musson. I'd drill them like I did Sam Mason. I'd—"

Fraleigh stopped him. "Hold on, Charlie. There's going to be no more shooting while I'm around. We're going to get out of this as fast as we can and forget everything that's happened. I've got to. It haunts me. I'm just as afraid as you are that things aren't right. Everyone seems to look at us as if they suspected us."

Collins swore under his breath. "I wish we'd pulled out long ago."

"Yes," Fraleigh agreed, "we didn't need to stick around so long, just to divert suspicion. It looked like a good alibi, but we needn't have stayed so long. That was your plan. I'm getting more nervous every hour."

Collins walked out from the thicket and looked about. "We should have heard them long before this. . . . I wonder if they've got themselves lost. That would be a joke—a nasty one on us. . . . But they'd fire their rifles if they wanted to find us. . . . I think I'll fire a shot."

Fraleigh had come to stand beside him. He cupped his hands about his mouth and sent a long "haloo!" into the forest.

There was no answer, of course. After listening for a time both shouted together. At last Collins aimed his rifle into the tree-tops and pulled the trigger.

Blue Pete lay close to the ground, but from behind a tree he could see the two men. His eyes lit up as they fixed themselves on the revolver in Collins' belt, and he grinned.

Collins could stand it no longer. "They've gone, damn' them. They've given us the slip. I've been half expecting they'd play some dirty trick on us. I'm going back to the camp. If they're still around they'll look for us there. Our blankets are there, anyway, and the food . . . unless they're run off with them. Come on."

They hurried to their mounts.

Blue Pete made straight for the height overlooking the site of the camp. He was there when the two men rode along the ravine and dismounted before the cave. It had taken them most of the day to find their way. Leaving the bronco with Fraleigh, Collins ran to the cave. In a few moments he reappeared, swearing violently.

"They've gone all right. They've taken their blankets."

"What about the food?"

"They've taken it too—some of it." Collins raised his eyes to the sky. It was still bright overhead but shadows lay deep about them. "We daren't try to make the prairie now, not till daylight. If we tried to-night we'd get ourselves into a tangle. Light the fire, Ted. I don't like the thought of staying here a night alone, but it can't be helped. I'll take another look in the cave to see what they've left."

As he entered the cave he called back: "My God, won't I be glad to get back to good old Detroit!" He turned. "One thing I want to do before I go—get that breed. I owe him too much to be able to sleep till I get even with him." A nasty laugh broke from his thin lips. "That's why I wanted him to guide us into the hills: a bullet would be the end of him. No one would ever find him, or if they did they could prove nothing. When we meet—"

He stopped, his mouth open, staring up the side of the ravine.

Down the bank came Blue Pete. He had left his rifle on the height and appeared unarmed except for the .45 showing in his belt. He came slowly, almost lounging, sliding a little on the steep slope. His thumbs were thrust in the belt, a fixed smile twisted his dark face.

FOR a moment or two the pair in the bottom of the ravine stared, scarcely believing their eyes. Then Collins' hand went to his gun. But he did not draw it.

"What the hell?"

The half-breed grinned. "Sorta knocks yuh cold, don't it, Charlie Musson?"

Collins' face paled a little. "Why do you call me that?"

"I alius like to know a man's real name, even ef he's a skunk an' a murderer."

Collins' gun came out like a flash. It was plain once more that drawing a gun was nothing new to him. He did not raise it but waited, held somehow to inactivity by the half-breed's nonchalance.

The latter came fearlessly on. He shook his head reprovingly, like a parent chiding a naughty child. "Gor-swizzle, Charlie, yuh wudn' shoot 'nother man out here, not so soon, wud yuh? Ain't one man 'n' a woman 'nuff? 'Course yuh cudn' think o' skippin' back to good ole Detroit till yuh'd paid me back, cud yuh? An' now yuh think yuh got the chance at last. Wal, I don' blame yuh none, 'cause yuh know I knowed all the time wot a skunk yuh was. Now yuh know somethin' else that I know 'bout yuh, so yuh jes' gotta kill me like yuh killed Sam Dunlop 'n' his wife."

"She wasn't his wife," Collins snarled. "She was *my* wife. He ran off with her."

Blue Pete whistled. "So that's wot yuh done it fer. Wal, kin yuh blame her fer gittin' 'way from you 'th anybody? How'd yuh bamboozle her into marryin' yuh anyways?" It was too much. Collins jerked the gun up and pulled the trigger. There was an explosion.

Even before the bullet crashed into his right arm and passed down into his thigh incredulity widened the half-breed's eyes. Because only a split second earlier another trigger had snapped off on his left, with no explosion. Fraleigh had tried to shoot him. Even as Blue Pete sank sideways he knew that some time during the day the two men had somehow exchanged guns.

The bullet had been aimed at his stomach, but involuntarily his right hand had shot across his body to his gun on his left hip and had taken the bullet, turning it aside.

Collins had not made another move. The gun was still raised, pointing. On the instant that he had slumped to the ground Blue Pete noticed it and he rolled over on his back and lay as if dead.

Collins laughed brutally. "Go and get his guns, Ted. Look out for one under his left arm. Don't be afraid. If he moves I'll give him something more for good measure, but there's not much chance of that. I think he's done for."

Fraleigh approached hesitantly. He moved as if scarcely knowing what he did. The sudden turn in events had stupified him.

"Hurry up. We've got to get out of this. Someone may have heard the shot."

Fraleigh bent over the half-breed. The latter daren't open his eyes, but if arm and leg had not been so helpless he would have taken a chance and grabbed him, holding him as a shield. But he could hear Collins shift his position in order to keep him covered, and he realized that it would have been a fatal move. He felt his .45 jerked from his belt, and the .38 beneath his shirt went with it. Then the pair ran to their broncos and mounted.

He heard them ride away at a wild gallop, tearing up the slope into the trees towards the north, and he raised himself with difficulty and looked about. A wide stain on his chaps and pants told him, even more than the pain, that he was badly wounded. The wound in his arm was less serious and he found he could move it, though with much pain. The stain widened swiftly. It warned him that certain death was before him unless the blood could be stopped. But how to stop it?

He could not hope for help. No one but the two who had thought to kill him, and the Indians who must be already at the home camp, knew he was in the hills. He had purposely not told Mira, since she would have known what was in his mind. She might guess, but she could not hope to arrive in time when he had been absent long enough to induce her to go in search of him. Often he remained absent from the ranch for days.

He managed to raise himself on his side. The entrance to the cave was only a few feet away. With the greatest difficulty, and aware that movement only made the wound bleed more freely, he dragged himself to the opening and inside.

At the entrance he remembered Whiskers, and he sent two shrill whistles into the growing darkness. He waited there, whistling at intervals. Presently a slight noise reached him, and Rollo came bounding down the slope, whining a little, and tried to lick his face. From the top of the slope Whiskers whinnied, then stumbled and slid down to him.

He dragged himself further into the cave, the pinto and the dog hovering about him, aware that catastrophe had befallen their master.

He was just in time. Into the ravine rode Collins and Fraleigh. They had heard the whistling and, the first panic over, had turned back to finish what they thought they had completed. They had to do that now; then they must bury the body, so that no trace of the shooting would remain.

When they saw that their victim was not in sight they stopped.

Collins pointed. "He's—gone!"

Rollo heard the voice and snarled.

Fraleigh heard it. "That's the dog," he whispered.

Collins dismounted and crept along the side of the ravine. On the way he saw the marks left on the slope by the pinto. "His bronco's gone in to him," he warned his friend. "There'd be his rifle in the saddle holster, so we'll have to be careful. . . . But we must get him now. We can't let him go."

Fraleigh started to protest but Collins cut him short brutally. "Don't be such a fool. We're safe, if we're careful. With that wound he can't last long. All we need do is wait. But we must get him."

"The—the Indians," Fraleigh whined, "what about them?"

"I told you they've sneaked off on us. Good thing, too. There's no one now to interfere. They wouldn't know the breed was in the hills, and if they did they'd have no reason to think we'd shot him. When it's daylight—and safe—we'll have to clear away that blood there, but there's no hurry. We mustn't leave a mark anywhere around the camp. But—we stay here till we know he's dead. He knows we killed Sam and June. If we let him get away he'd tell the Mounted Police."

"There's the bronco, too, and the dog."

"I'll kill that dog, whatever else I do. All we need do with the bronco is get her out of that and scare her away towards the prairie."

Fraleigh glanced fearfully about. "It'll be too dark to see anything in a few minutes. What'll we do then— how'll we keep him there?"

"Wait, that's all. He can't move far or fast with that wound. He can't get away." Collins laughed; he was getting more confident every minute. "We'll keep an eye on the cave all night. You take one side and I'll take the other. He certainly can't walk, and we could hear the bronco coming—and it would be an easy mark even in the dark.

You've loaded your gun, haven't you. That's the strangest thing—what happened to it. I certainly carried it loaded. Just keep away from the front of the cave where he might shoot you. . . . We haven't heard a sound from him. I wouldn't be surprised if he was already dead, but we needn't take a chance."

From inside the cave Blue Pete heard nothing of this, but he knew they were there and why they had returned. He knew, too, that they daren't let him escape now. He surmised also that for the moment they would not dare to enter the cave, and he turned his attention to the wounds. His arm had stopped bleeding and he found no bone had been broken. With difficulty he removed chaps and pants and, taking the kerchief from Rollo's torn shoulder that was already partly healed, he bound it around his thigh. It, too, had stopped bleeding, but the amount of blood he had lost had left him weak.

If only he had left his rifle in the saddle instead of at the top of the slope!

For a time he considered trying to climb into the saddle and making a rush to get away, but he quickly gave the idea up. The effort would be sure to start the bleeding, and he dare not risk that. Besides, he realized that, weak as he was, he would not be able to ride far, even if he succeeded in breaking through.

Rollo crouched just inside the entrance, on guard, trembling with the strain of holding himself back. For he heard the hated voices near by, and his teeth bared. Blue Pete understood now why he hated the men so. He must have seen something of the killing, or have sensed it, though he was tied up at the time. He would at least have seen them burying his master beside the slough.

In the most comfortable position he could find he rested. He wondered why Collins did not enter the cave and finish his work. The dog would have been little protection from their guns.

Rollo came back to him, rustling through some dead leaves that had blown into the cave.

The half-breed heard the sound and an idea flashed into his mind. Collecting a handful of the leaves, he called the dog to him. Beneath the animal's collar he tucked the leaves and tied them there with a string he found in his vest pocket.

"Listen, ole boy," he whispered. "It's upta you now. Go home!"

The dog half rose, whined a little, puzzled and hesitating to leave him. Against the lighter outdoors the half-breed could see the dog's head turned inquiringly towards him.

"Go home!" he ordered.

The dog waited for nothing more. The dark form leaped out of sight around the wall of the cave. . . . A shot rang out, and Blue Pete dragged himself to the entrance and listened. He trembled.

Fraleigh called from the left, asking what had happened, and Collins ordered him to shut up. That was all.

An hour passed. Then from the darkness on the right Collins shouted: "I got the dog, you damned breed. You can't get away. Come out and we'll make a deal. No need for any more blood. You need that wound bound up, or you'll bleed to death—or starve, because you can't get away."

Blue Pete did not reply. He was scarcely conscious of what was said, for a great weakness had come over him. Movement had started the bleeding again. Whiskers came to him and rubbed his shoulder with her nose. His wits returned in part and he tried to rise, but a strange, mind-numbing weakness overcame him and he dropped back. Between sleeping and waking he lay, dreaming a little. He forgot Collins. He was thinking of Mira—calling to her.

XXXII A DOG REPAYS

MIRA was wakened by the dog scratching at the bedroom window and whining to be let in. It was two o'clock in the morning and not yet light, but a rosiness showed in the east. She rose, found her gun, and crept to the window. She made out the dog's outline and quickly raised the window higher and let him in.

He panted heavily, and he raised himself and placed his feet against her. She knew something had happened and he was trying to tell her about it. It meant that Blue Pete needed her. She saw then the torn shoulder, the leaves tied to his collar, and she knew where those leaves had come from; they never grew on the prairie.

But the Cypress Hills were thirty miles to the southeast. She could not know that the dog had come a dozen miles further than that. He whined, following her about the room as she dressed. Now and then he made as if to return through the window.

She understood. "All right, Rollo. I'll go with you . . . But you'll have to lead me. Just give me time to dress." He seemed to understand, for he lay down and slept, his nose on his paws; and gradually the gasping breathing of the long race eased. But every few moments he wakened and watched her inquiringly. To dress for the ride occupied only a few minutes, and she hurried. She knew that only some desperate need had brought the dog, and she collected bandages and iodine, and homemade splints always kept ready for the frequent injuries to the cowboys. Her rifle she loaded. When she ran to the stable for her bronco Rollo galloped at her side, wildly excited.

The moment she was in the saddle he was off. But the pace was too fast for her and she was forced to call him back. Straight to the hills he led.

She rode hard, at the long lope a bronco can maintain for hours. She did not push her mount but let him have his head. For ten miles it paid to follow the trail, then she turned directly towards the dark line of the forest that was by that time plainly visible in the morning light.

Suddenly Rollo, far before her, stopped and looked towards the north-east. She turned and saw a Mounted Policeman racing towards her. It was Sergeant Mahon.

She beckoned to him but did not stop, merely slowing her bronco down.

He quickly overtook her. "What is it, Mira? Why are you out—"

"We must go as fast as we can," she said. "I don't know what's

186

happened, but Rollo has come to me from the hills. Pete must have sent him. It means that something's happened, that he needs me."

He asked no more questions, and they tore along. The forest-clad heights were now less than an hour away.

Presently he said: "It's strange, but I had a funny feeling myself. I planned to spend the night at Turner's Crossing, but I couldn't see myself wasting so much time. I've been riding all night. I was coming to the 3-Bar-Y to get Pete to go to the hills with me. The Inspector asked me to do that."

The questions were in her eyes.

He answered them: "We're interested in those two newcomers. They've been all around the ranches, we understand. We know nothing about them, and the Inspector is curious. We've been told they've gone to the hills now to—"

She stopped him with a startled exclamation. "That's it: They're there—and Pete. And they hate each other."

"Did you know Pete was going to the hills?"

"No, he didn't say where he was going. He seldom does, because he doesn't want me to worry. . . . He hated Collins—as everyone does. He mentioned the fact that Collins was planning to hunt wolves in the hills. Collins wanted to hire him as guide. I remember Pete said once he wouldn't work with him but he'd like to be there to see them hunting. I don't know what he had in mind. I'm—I'm frightened."

"So am I." They rode in silence for a time. "The Inspector has a suspicion that these fellows aren't what they seem to be. He doesn't believe they really want a ranch; he wonders why they're here."

The dog raced ahead, too fast for Mahon's weary mount that had been travelling all night. Now and then Mira called him back.

They tore up the slope and the forest swallowed them. Both Mira and the Sergeant knew the hills fairly well at the western end, and for a time they made good progress. Rollo followed a straight line to the south-east. It was broad daylight long since, though the sun was still too low to clear away all the shadows from the depressions.

At last they lost the dog. It was impossible for them to move through the trees as he did, and they were left behind. Mira called once, but the Sergeant silenced her.

"Wait. He'll come back and find us if we're not within hearing. He's in a hurry, and he thinks he has good reason. We know the direction now, and that's enough."

As in a dream Blue Pete lay within the cave. At intervals of semi-consciousness, he knew something had happened him, that he was in danger, but that he must not move. He could not think clearly. He knew Whiskers was beside him, licking his face and nudging him gently with her nose.

"Yah, ole gal," he muttered. "Time to git up—But I mus'n't. . . . Suthin' wrong, ole gal. . . . I dunno. . . . Whar's—Mira?"

Outside the cave in the daylight Collins walked confidently about. He climbed the height overlooking the cave and there he found Blue Pete's rifle leaning against a tree. With a raucous, triumphant laugh he slithered down the slope. He called to Fraleigh and beckoned.

"Come on. It's all right. He hasn't a gun. His rifle is up there on the bank. We've got him now—if he isn't already dead. We'll get it over with and skip. Things always work out right for Charlie Musson. Hey-ho for Jericho—only it'll be good old Detroit instead."

Rollo could not wait for the pair he had brought to the rescue. He knew his master needed him, knew he needed him more at that moment than ever, and he rushed ahead. He ran silently, like the wolf that was part of him.

Nearing the ravine all his wolfish instincts came to the surface and he slowed down, crawling forward, sniffing as he went. From cover to cover he made his way, but he did not hesitate.

Suddenly his teeth bared. A hated voice had come to his ears. He reached the top of the bank. That hated figure was directly below him, moving forward to the entrance to the cave. He waited, his legs gathered beneath him, as Collins looked into the cave.

Blue Pete lay there, only half a dozen paces away. His eyes were closed. Now and then he moved restlessly; his breath came heavily.

Collins stood and watched for a few moments, a brutal grin twisting his thin lips. He went no further. No need. At five yards he could not miss. He raised his gun.

Rollo leaped. He struck Collins on the shoulder and bore him to the ground. His teeth closed on the man's throat and held. They held in the grip of death, for Collins, in his last gesture, had brought the gun around and pulled the trigger.

Sergeant Mahon and Mira reached the top of the slope as the shot rang out. The Sergeant, gun in hand, leaped down. Fraleigh, gaping and motionless, looked on only twenty yards away. The Sergeant covered him and beckoned to Mira.

"Watch him. Shoot if he makes so much as a move." With only a glance at the dog and the motionless form beneath him, he entered the cave.

Mira slid down the slope, all the time covering Fraleigh with her gun. But Fraleigh did not even see her; he could not take his eyes from his dead friend. Collins lay in a pool of blood, his throat ripped open, but the bullet he had fired with his last convulsive effort had reached Rollo's heart.

Inspector Barker looked up anxiously as Sergeant Mahon entered the office, and for a moment he studied his subordinate's face. He sighed and nodded.

"Of course. Failed again. I knew you would. He'd rather die out at the 3-Bar-Y than live in comfort in here in the hospital."

"Doctor Grange, sir, says the only thing that could kill Blue Pete is comfort," laughed the Sergeant. "It's no use urging. And Mira backs him. She says she knows better than the nurses what's good for him."

Inspector Barker shook his head and scowled at the blotter before him. "Anyone else would have been dead from the blood he lost, but I suppose he's doomed to hang in the end."

"He isn't likely to hang, sir, if you can keep him busy on these jobs we have for him."

The Inspector nodded. "And as long as this old world keeps ticking along we'll have the sort of jobs he hungers for." A sheepish grin spread over his lean face, "You know, damn him, I ought to be furious at him. Here he's gone and beaten us again at our own game—and directly against my orders. I should be grateful, of course, and I am, but it hurts to be shown so often that disobeying orders, breaking all the regulations, gets the rogues behind the bars. By the way, there should be some sort of medal for that dog—only that isn't in the regulations either. Simmons tells me there was quite a funeral. He went as my representative."

"There was. They buried Rollo not far from the house, with Blue Pete sitting up before the window as chief mourner. He insisted on sitting up—said he'd walk to the funeral if they didn't let him. The other mourners were half a dozen ranchers and swarms of cowboys. They felt they owed a lot to Blue Pete and the dog for clearing them of suspicion. Things had almost reached a point where they avoided one another as suspects. Ranchers don't murder; they don't mingle with murderers."

"Good!" The Inspector shuffled absent-mindedly through some papers on his desk. "How long does the doctor say he'll be laid up?"

"Not more than two or three weeks."

"I suppose I'll have to find something more for him to do then to keep him out of mischief, but it doesn't get any easier to thank him for what he does for us—or to be blind to how he does it."

THE END

www.ingramcontent.com/pod-product-compliance
Lightning Source LLC
Chambersburg PA
CBHW031344170626
46807CB00002B/817